Avoiding the
PITY PARTY

MEL A ROWE

Also by Mel A ROWE

Australian Bestselling ELSIE CREEK SERIES:

The ART of DUST

DIAMOND in the DUST

CAKED in DUST

XMAS DUST

MUSTER in the DUST

ROLLED in DUST

WRITTEN in DUST

Standalone Stories:

Avoiding the Pity Party

Unplanned Party

The Football Whisperer

USA Bestseller—Winter's Walk

Run Beautiful Run

The Sister Trip

Receive exclusive insights, and news on upcoming releases by joining: https://melarowe.com/newsletter/

COPYRIGHT

***Caveat: As a courtesy, since there may be some sparse language choices in this story that may represent an obstacle for the reader, I am offering this warning. Please note this language and cultural references are purely for fictional purposes only and not designed to offend any individual persons, culture, or religions implied.*

The Following Is Written in Australian English

"Families are like fudge – mostly sweet, with a few nuts."

Les Dawson

ONE

Her stomach spiralled like a stone sliding off the cliff's edge. 'Can I do this?' Deanne Harrison clenched sweaty palms as she peeked through the door's gap to spy on her seated guests. Light streamed through stained-glass windows that haloed the groom standing beside his groomsmen adjusting their suits.

And they all waited for her.

Piped organ music began, and Deanne scooted to the side of the curtain just as the doors opened. 'You can do this, Lou.' She urged the first bridesmaid, who scowled at her. 'Please?'

'*Fine.*' With a death grip on her delicate floral arrangement that contrasted against her bulging bodybuilder's frame, Lou started down the aisle. Her strapless cocktail gown complimented her bleached hair spiked to near dagger points. In her mannish gait, she hobble-plodded on heels, glaring at the groom, then lurched towards the sidelines to wait the rest of the bridal party's arrival.

'Can't believe we're doing this,' muttered the petite Jane, as the next bridesmaid to walk down the aisle. With each step, Jane choked the stems of her bouquet, while her rogue ringlets sprung-free in their rebellion against the attempted intricate up-do that Deanne knew Jane had tried so hard to achieve. At the end of the aisle, Jane stopped beside Lou, scowled sideways at the groom for all to see, and then forced a smile, as another one of her curls escaped from its clutches.

The matron of honour, the statuesque Clare, made her appearance, with her thin-lipped grimace and red-rimmed eyes, she glared at the groom from the start of the aisle.

'Clare, it'll be fine,' said Deanne, urging her friend on.

'I hope so.' Clare raised her chin, her complexion pale against her midnight hair slicked into an elegant French twist. With her graceful, long-legged stride, Clare made short work of the aisle, to stand beside the other bridesmaids. There she faced the crowd, sniffed back tears, and with pursed lips she waited.

At the doorway, the father of the bride, Reg, tugged at his collar, brushed fingers through his grey receding hairline, pushed his glasses up his nose and puffed out ruddy cheeks. He then held out his bent elbow. 'You ready to do this, luv?'

Deanne nodded beneath the fragile veil. The delicate diamantes detailed within her gown sparkled like tiny rainbows.

She swallowed an oversized lump and tried to shake the tremors in her hands. 'Let's do this.' She wrapped her arm around her father's extended elbow, re-gripped her bouquet of lilies, and counted. 'One, two, and three…' And they stepped in time to the music, hoping her gown's small train would trail perfectly behind them.

Reg nodded to the gathered guests as they headed down the aisle and at the end of the red-carpet, he unveiled the intended bride.

Deanne couldn't fool her father when the worry in his eyes mirrored her own.

'Um?' Reg's brow crinkled. He blinked back tears as his teeth clamped on his quivering bottom lip.

Deanne squeezed his hand. 'It'll be okay, Dad.'

'You sure?'

'I know what I'm doing.' She hoped.

'Well, okay then...' Reg kissed his baby girl on the cheek and replaced her veil. He took his seat in the front row beside his sniffling mother, Nan, where they gripped hands and prepared to watch in teary silence.

The groom, Darren, in his tailored suit, turned on his movie-star smile that spread across his spray-tanned features. He swept a hand through his blond hair, and winked at the crowd where his bright blue contact lenses caught the light. He stepped in alongside his wife-to-be and they stood before the Minister and the ceremony began.

The service was well underway when the Minister called out, 'Should anyone object to this union, speak now or forever hold your peace?'

Darren twitched his shoulders, his palms clasped tightly in front, as beads of sweat trickled down the sides of his face. He licked his lips and stared at the carpet.

Time dragged.

Outside birds twittered. Traffic shuffled. Children's laughter carried across from the park.

Inside, gowns rustled, paper programmes fanned faces, but no one spoke.

The minister's chest rose high as he inhaled to continue.

Darren exhaled as his stature relaxed.

'STOP.' Deanne flung her veil back as her words reverberated off the walls.

'What?' Darren asked.

'Did you sleep with my cousin, Katrina?'

The crowd gasped.

Darren gulped, blinking fast. Raking fingers though his thick hair, he shared a taut smile at the seated audience. 'Everyone's watching,' he said through gritted over-white teeth.

Deanne's skirts swished as she turned to search the gathered guests. 'Katrina, I hear you're pregnant and congratulations are in order?'

Katrina sat in a low-cut, skin-tight, red dress, a few rows behind Deanne's dad. Her smudged lips parted, her wide racoon eyes darted between the bride and groom as she sunk lower into her seat.

'Is it true, Katrina, that you're pregnant to my future husband?' Deanne lifted her gown's hem, kicking out at the train. Her bouquet slapped against her skirts, scattering frosty petals as she stomped down the steps.

Katrina sunk lower into her seat, while those around her shuffled aside to give the incoming bride access.

'Don't. Lie. To. Me. This is the house of God, and you'll go straight to hell if you do.'

Katrina lowered her head, as loud, wet sobs echoed off the cathedral ceiling.

'ANSWER ME.'

'Yes,' Katrina said between whimpers.

Deanne cupped a hand behind her ear. *I can't hear you?'*

'Yes. I'm pregnant.' With makeup smeared and tears flowing, Katrina stood and pointed with a trembling finger. *'And it's Darren's baby.'*

The crowd gasped. Their heads pivoted from Katrina to the groom, to the bride, then back again

'She's lying.' Darren frowned. He tugged at his tight collar, then reached for Deanne's hand. 'What are you doing, Dee? Not in front of everyone, please?'

Deanne peered up at her intended husband who was handsome. Charming. And what every woman desired. Should she surrender?

Instead, she pulled away, clenched her fist, and punched him.

It was a direct hit.

Darren collapsed on the steps below the altar. He covered his eye, moaning in pain, while everyone remained motionless.

Deanne hitched up her many skirts and sprinted down the aisle. She burst through the church doors and into the blinding sunlight. Jumped the front steps, scattering pigeons in her way, as she cut straight across the road. A car horn blared, and a taxi screeched to a halt, as Deanne ran through the park and never looked back.

TWO

Deanne's legs burned, with her skirt's layers hitched up in front, petticoats stuck to her sweaty skin as she ran. Well away from the church, well past the park, unsure where she was. With no more road to run, only the jetty lay ahead of her, and she ran. All she saw was the tall light pole at the end of the jetty where seagulls hovered, and there Deanne collapsed on the bench-seat, ignoring the group of boys packing up their fishing gear onto their bikes.

She tried to catch her breath tasting the salty air, staring at the calm sea spread before her that reflected a warm orange from the autumn setting sun.

Deanne fingered the soft material of her bridal gown. The hems were browned, the veil tattered. She didn't need a mirror to reflect the way she felt—rejected and miserable.

How could she have been so blind to fall in love with the handsome and charming Darren?

She'd played her part as the ugly duckling that never became a swan but remained the goose inside this nightmare. A part she'd excelled at as an obese kid with a frizzy bomb of auburn hair and freckles. Lots of freckles, which was a mystery because Deanne never saw the sun.

Bullied at high school as the easy target because no one could miss her wide waddle down the hallways. Yet here she was, still that fat, frizzy-haired, ostracised geek.

So, when the dazzling Darren asked her out, he wined and dined her, and she changed for him to be part of the perfect romantic dream. After all, Deanne's only experience of all things romantic came from books and movies, where she believed in her own fantasy.

No wonder her perceptions on the real world were beyond warped, now stuck in the final act of her personal teary tragedy. How dare she take on fate, when destined to be single for eternity?

True love didn't exist for her when she couldn't even pass as a normal bride—running away from her own wedding.

Deanne let her tears fall as she sighed like a deflating bleached balloon. Shoulders drooped. Her lower lip trembled. The skirt's material scrunched under her fists.

Her head fell to her chest as waves of nausea washed over from the torturous visions of the two-timing couple passing behind closed eyelids. The shame of their betrayal and her bizarre public humiliation unleashed fresh tears.

Deanne had ignored the signs from the start. The gossip, the words of warning, where hindsight just sucked. How stupid and naïve had she been?

She'd had her doubts, and all those niggling questions. Yet, she'd never questioned Darren. He'd made it clear he didn't like people who pried into his business. So, she never dared to voice her fears.

Instead, she'd trusted Darren, to never ask and upset Darren, but to please him, always. Especially in the beginning, when in awe of the demigod who wanted to be with her—in public.

But all those late-night meetings, the regular weekend trips away, his phone switched off and unreachable, the hint of another's perfume, and the condoms he carried…

Condoms! *Ha.*

'Bastard. Bitch.' Her voice sounded foreign as it cut through the evening air.

Katrina was a blossoming, unrestrained, nineteen-year-old. Her notorious nocturnal activities fed the rumour treadmill, which included her alleged attempts to entrap a man by becoming pregnant.

Hearsay was now publicly proven.

Deanne's guesstimated time of the affair's conception—since her engagement party. A memory she'd once adored. Not anymore.

Today definitely topped the top ten most tortured moments of her life. *Did Hallmark make cards for this crap?*

And what dark part of her brain her forced her to tell all in front of everyone?!

She'd never had the courage to deny Darren anything, when she'd been nothing more than a glorified slave to him.

Yes, a slave.

Darren's slave.

She'd slaved on her body-image, the wedding planning, and all his day-to-day domestic duties. She'd done it all for Darren. For what?

Everything was dashed to dust now. She had nothing else going for her. But her job.

Would Katrina have the guts to return to work on Monday?

Was it a sackable offence to be pregnant to the

supervisor's future-husband?

Could she dare face her friends and family after what had happened?

Could she face herself?

Identical to the shift of an incoming tide, the waves of shame enveloped her hunched stature as salt laden tears tracked through her makeup. They fell from her chin to create grey blotches that spread across her gown. Helpless and hopeless to stop their spread, she cried.

And cried…

Deanne sat up and licked her dry lips. Under the light of the wharf's tall lamp, she gazed out at the darkened ocean.

How long had she been sitting here?

A slight autumn chill carried on the sea breeze that brought a shiver across her exposed skin. With vicious swipes to rid the last of her tears, she straightened up her gown, and headed towards the esplanade's lights.

Ignoring the other people's stares, Deanne didn't care where she went, she wanted a drink. She wanted to get lost in the city and avoid facing her own pity-party.

Tomorrow didn't matter anymore, because today she had nothing left to lose.

THREE

Sean Bryst blinked at the mirrored wall's reflection of a bride entering through the double doors of the bar.

'This is new,' he said to Mickey, the barman standing nearby, where they both watched the bride glance at the assorted historic newspaper headlines decorating the walls.

The other few customers gawked at her. Even the kissing couple stopped to stare from one of the booths that ran along the stained-glass frontage.

It wasn't every day you saw a woman, in a bar, in a wedding dress.

So where was the groom?

Sean rested his elbow against the bar to watch the tough barman, Mickey, suss out the bride to see if it was a scam. Or was it real? Because those tear stains across her shiny cheeks, accompanied by a quivering bottom lip looked real.

From behind the bar, Mickey cocked a grey eyebrow at the female in a white wedding gown. 'You've gotta be the saddest thing I've seen today. You all right, luv?'

'I'd love a drink. Sadly, I've got no money, but I do have this.' The bride yanked off her engagement ring and dumped it on the counter.

'Dunno, luv,' said Mickey. 'But you look like you need

one, so my shout. Name ya poison.'

She grimaced a smile. 'Scotch shot and a beer chaser. Please?'

Mickey poured scotch into the glass that rested on the counter before the bride.

As if thirsting from a year in a desert, she swallowed her nip. Eyelids closed; she sighed as her shoulders drooped. 'Are you sure I can't sell you the ring?'

'For a drink, luv, no,' replied Mickey.

'I don't want it for one drink. I intend to buy bucket-loads. And this,' she said, drawing a circle around her face, '… is me, putting on my best pity look to feed me more booze, good sir.'

Sean chuckled. Sure, she was upset, but he had to give her credit, the lady had style. 'Give the lady what she needs, Mickey.' Sean placed his empty glass on the bar top beside hers. 'Put the drinks on my tab.'

The bride glanced sideways at Sean for approval, and he gave a nod. How could he refuse? Not when she held out her nip-glass as if a small child about to receive her spoonful of sugar-flavoured medicine.

'Thanks, Mickey,' she said. 'Wow, I know the barman's name—that's a first for me.'

Both men grinned as Mickey topped up her glass. She was cute because few women Sean knew could claim that first-time-fame.

'Do you want to buy a ring? Going cheap.' With the back of her hand, the bride pushed the diamond trinket across the bar.

Sean flicked his hair free from his eyes, picked up the diamond and examined its cut and quality. His primal instinct was to give her fifty and quadruple it in one easy sale. He had the cash to turn a quick profit, and she seemed desperate enough to sell it at any price.

Instead, Sean placed the jewellery piece in front of her. 'No, I won't buy it. Put it away for safe keeping.'

'Maybe I'll hock it later.' The bride shoved it onto her right hand's index finger, leaving her ring finger naked.

Scorned bride — this might be dangerous. 'Are you okay?' Sean asked, flicking open his silver lighter and relit his cigar. She seemed miserable enough to sprout waterworks any second now.

'D-do you have any cigarettes?'

'Do you want one?'

'I quit a while ago. But right now, I could handle a smoke.'

Tears formed in her eyes, exposing her raw emotion like a sea changing its aquamarine colours on sunrise after a storm. He'd never seen anything so gorgeous. 'Mickey, packet of cigs for the lady, please. And my name's Sean.'

The barman passed a packet to the sad bride, who ripped it open. She pinched a cigarette with trembling fingers like an addict desperate for their fix. Sean ignited his silver lighter and lit her cancer stick, to watch her inhale the nicotine deep, then exhale stress in a stream of smoke. Her eyelids closed then re-opened to reveal eyes altered to a cool aquarium blue, scattered with teal crystals of magnificence.

'Deanne. But people call me Dee.'

'Which do you prefer, Deanne or Dee?' Sean watched her irises react to her inner sea of emotion. She was like an optical illusion of a mystical mermaid. But was she for real?

In her strapless gown, Deanne shrugged her bare, freckle-flecked, creamy shoulders. The tight bodice emphasised her delicious curves. The veil profiled her perfect posture and her tiara shimmered in the dim light to emphasise her auburn hair. Sean had to admit the bride's complete package was exquisite.

'Deanne.'

'Nice to meet you, Deanne.' Sean cleared his throat, blinking fast as if to awaken from this glamour spell. Mermaids? What the hell was in his bourbon? *The woman's a jilted bride—damaged, dude. Do not go there.*

Sean stepped back, slipping into his normal stance on life with the cool stand-offish approach. He had no emotional attachment to anything, especially women—which cost him too much in the hip pocket. Not when he'd only just freed himself of all things female.

But he had to take one more look. To inspect her from afar, like a high-end car in a showroom he'd never test drive. Yeah, he could do that.

So, with tilted head, Sean conducted a re-scan of the bride. Not too skinny. Not too tall. Fit, healthy physique. The cleavage view from the bodice—*down boy*—and wiped his watering mouth. Not good.

Sean massaged his temples, then refocused. She appeared to be wholesome. Clean. Obviously overdressed. Yet, tastefully conservative. She wore minimal jewellery, except for the delicate tiara that twinkled in the bar's overhead lights. The slight makeup smudged around the eyes should've been a flaw, but it only accentuated those amazing eyes of hers. As a whole, Deanne was beautiful. Truly beautiful.

Which sucked.

He should leave, but his feet refused to shuffle for the exit.

Instead, Sean wanted to help the fallen angel with copper curls, reading the abyss of sorrow in her eyes. It just lured him in with a look he recognised from his own past—it was the face of disbelieving isolated grief.

One he knew so well.

He had to leave—fast. Right now.

'Thanks for the drink, Sean.' She shared a slight smile.

Sean leaned against the bar and loosened his silk tie, he couldn't leave her, not now she'd smiled at him.

'Do you normally dress-up to scam free drinks?' *Idiot.* Why did he say that for?

'No. I don't normally dress like this.' Deanne choked out a laugh, her hands smoothing down the top layer of her soiled skirt. 'Do I resemble a white puffy marshmallow in this? My friend, Lou, called me that the first time I tried on this dress.'

'Don't make me answer that obvious female trip-up question? It's like a woman asking if she looked fat in a dress.' When she looked divine.

Deanne's lips pursed, as her eyelids narrowed at him with her eyes flashing a stormy Caribbean green. Sean had never been there and had no idea where the inspirational colour came from. Was he due for a tropical holiday?

But the way Deanne stared at him, Sean had to respond. Yet knew he was tempting fate if he answered that question and should save his sanity and walk away.

Now… Soon?

Dammit.

'No,' he said. 'You'd never be mistaken for a white puffy marshmallow.'

'I feel like one.' Deanne blew cigarette smoke at her gown. 'I got talked into lots of things, like I got talked into buying this dress.'

'You don't strike me as the type who'd get pressured into anything.'

She glared at him. It was ferociously beautiful. 'Don't you dare pretend to know me.'

'Sorry.' Sean should leave and forget her. But his sanity had surrendered to the quicksand from the flash of fire he'd seen in her eyes that broadcasted a streak of passion that was so unbelievably pure. 'You look angry with the world.'

He also wanted to tell her in a million ways she was beautiful.

But how could he compliment her without it sounding creepy? The woman couldn't be expected to listen to flattery while in such a delicate mood, even if it was true.

'No, just one person should be sorry. No, make that two people, plus my pathetic self. So that's three of us, not a threesome. Ugh, not that...' Deanne puffed out flushed cheeks as her shoulders tightened with tension. 'Can I get another scotch, please?'

'Sure.' Sean signalled towards the barman. 'Dare I ask?' Fascinated by her internal strength and courage to maintain calm.

'Ask what? Why am I standing here in a bridal gown, in a strange bar, allowing a stranger to buy me drinks and smokes because I'd left my purse at home?' Deanne blurted it out in one breath, blinked a few times, and then laughed.

'It's ridiculous.' She pulled the tattered veil over her shoulder to assess the damage.

Sean tried to stop smiling with her. His resistance was futile against the way her smile lit up her face. Her expressions hid nothing, except captivate him more.

But as fast as the sun shone from her smile, it set, and once again she wore the face of abandonment. The same expression from a past Sean wanted to forget.

Yet, Deanne was sinking without a life-raft in her despair, and his shielded heart began to thaw. Again, he had to ask, 'Are you okay?'

Sean wasn't. Her presence was making him reel deeper into an unknown emotional turbulent tide.

Deanne turned away from him.

Without thought, Sean reached out and touched her upper bare arm. 'Hey, are you okay?' Her skin was so soft and warm, and his arctic soul—liquefied.

'No.' Deanne pulled her arm free.

'Sorry.' *Idiot!* How dare he touch her. He stepped back, slipping back into his cool, detached persona. That's who he was. A man who cared for no one.

So why did this woman affect him so much?

'Fine, if you must know.' Deanne inhaled deeply on the cigarette then exhaled heavily. 'Ten minutes before I was about to get married, I overheard my sweet slut of a cousin telling her friend she's six weeks pregnant to the man she slept with last night, which was the groom I nearly married.' She grabbed Sean's wrist, checked his watch, and raised her eyebrows. 'I didn't realise it was this late.' Deanne took a deep swill from her glass and blinked away tears.

Sean wanted to do or say something to help her, yet he'd learned from his sisters to never interrupt the female rant. But what words could he possibly offer to heal someone so emotionally wounded?

'This time of night I'd planned to be a *wife*. The professional photos would've finished. The fabulous five-course dinner, the embarrassing speeches, and that first dance would've been done and dusted by now.' Her chest heaved as her lower lip quivered. 'The reception would've been in full swing, with everyone performing their drunken dancing-diva routines. But not now...' Deanne lowered her head and puffed on her cigarette. 'Can we talk about something else?'

'Have you eaten lately?' Pleased with her surprised expression, he wanted to keep this conversation going. Most of all he wanted to make her happy.

But did he need to bother?

Yes. He did.

'It must've been a while if you're standing there trying to remember your last meal. The chef's good, not your flash five-course restaurant kind, but he cooks a decent feed. Mickey,' Sean called to the bartender already reaching for the menus.

Deanne seemed unsure, and Sean couldn't explain his reasons, but went with it and passed Deanne a menu.

Her seductive perfume trailed into his lungs, he craved to wrap his body around hers, skin to skin. He swallowed hard at her plump chest. 'Um... steaks the best dish they have here.'

He stepped back, jamming his fists into his pockets to not touch her.

What was the matter with him? The woman was an emotional shipwreck and he wanted to weigh-in alongside her like an anchor begging to be chained.

Sean stopped short of smacking his own skull to empty his rampant thoughts. Now he was thinking in maritime terminologies, shipwrecks, mermaids, and anchors? And why the sudden need to buy a boat to find his sea legs?

Not real. Something's wrong with this bourbon!

'I didn't realise I was hungry. But I am,' said Deanne. 'In fact, I'm starving! I've been suffering for months on this ridiculous diet designed for mung-bean-munching-mice. Not to mention the torture from this gruelling marathon man's fitness regime suited for Navy seals. To prepare for what? Sacrifice for what?' Deanne bit her bottom lip as tears formed. 'Sorry.'

'Don't be.' Sean's stone heart cracked at the sight of her tears and couldn't help but admire her strength in keeping it together.

'I'm not picky, and being a regular, you'd know what's best on the menu. I'm used to men ordering.' Deanne dropped the menu onto bar. Frowning at her glass as she sniffed back those tears.

'Please, choose whatever you like. I'm only aware of what's best for me.' Shame he couldn't listen to himself now and leave.

Instead, Sean smiled, which wasn't like him because his facial expressions were normally limited to smirks. But he was so glad Deanne smiled back at him, which made it okay.

Sean ordered their steak dinner with a bottle of wine, there'll be no more mind-altering bourbon tonight. 'Come on, let's get a table and Mickey will deliver the rest.' He offered his elbow to Deanne.

Though hesitant at first, Deanne let Sean guide her to a booth by the stained-glass windows. There they sat, a man in suit and tie, the woman in bridal couture, where they appeared every part the bride and groom.

FOUR

'I think those three women belong to you. Or they're from an all-girl band wearing the same dresses.' Sean pointed his unlit cigar towards the bar's front doors.

Deanne swivelled in the booth's seat only for her heart and smile to grow. 'It's my bridesmaids. Hey girls, I'm over here.'

Jane rushed over and flung her arms around Deanne. 'Thank goodness we found you. Are you okay? We've been so worried about you.'

'I'm fine. Girl's, meet Sean, he's in security.' Deanne pointed to Sean seated opposite. 'Sean, meet the Greatest-Girls-of-the-Galaxy. It sounds geeky, but it's true. Wow, I think I've had a re-birth of my inner geek.' Deanne again laughed; her hot cheeks ached.

Lou hobbled over in shoes like a bandy-legged cowgirl who'd been trapped in the desert for one very long summer. 'We were expecting you to be fu —'

'We,' said Clare, pressing her hands on Lou's shoulders, 'thought you'd be miserable.'

'I feel fantastic, thanks to Sean.' Deanne smiled wider at the man who'd been her champion. *Wow — a true champion.* 'Sean, meet the cutesy, loveable, solid-as-a-pretty-pet-rock, Jane.' She playfully pinched Jane's petite cheeks. 'She's pregnant. I can't wait for the sesame seed to become a full-grown baby in, oh, another thirty-something weeks.' Her hand rested on Jane's belly and both women smiled, sharing a moment.

Then Deanne pointed to Clare. 'This is Clare. She's the sassy, artistic, fantabulous woman, who could've been a model, but prefers to be a self-proclaimed man-eater.'

On cue, Clare winked at Sean.

Deanne laughed and flicked her thumb towards Lou, in her typical solid-wall-of-steel pose. 'And this is the muscle-building, personal trainer, and part-time bodyguard who won't take crap from no-one, whom I respect and adore, Lou.'

Lou scowled at Sean, in-between winces of pain while wobbling unsteadily in her heels.

'I'm so proud of you, Lou, you're still in that dress,' said Deanne. 'But you can stop your death glare because Sean's been a thorough gentleman, looking after me.' Deanne stared at the grains that made up the table top. 'Why is it that no one looks after me? Not even Darren. Since when did I win the part as saviour of the puniverse to look after everyone—but me? And will I remember this epiphany in the morning?' She hoped so. Still trying to remember how she ended up behaving like Doormat-Dee for Darren in the first place. She'd never said no to Darren, not once.

But she'd done it today—and had yet to face the consequences.

'Have you forgotten you're a non-smoker and how hard it was for you to quit?' Jane's face screwed up as she fanned the cigarette smoke away.

'Don't you give me that practising-mother look. If you hadn't noticed, I've had a rough day and Sean's been kind enough to buy my smokes, drinks, and dinner.' The man even put up with her unleashed mouth that ran free, which wasn't like her.

But then again, she had nothing left to lose. Besides, she'd probably forget all about tonight because she wanted to forget all about today.

Too bad Sean was going to be a part of her wishful amnesia too. She grinned at Sean with his loosened silk tie and his well-rehearsed casual hair flick that revealed his sexy shadowy eyes. He was so handsome.

Yet, handsome men were nothing but cheating trouble.

But Sean had been polite and that friend she'd needed who didn't mind sharing his time, and his bar-tab.

'You were right, Sean, that was a great meal.' Deanne couldn't remember the last time she'd eaten so much. Were the seams of her dress going to hold?

All those months of clean living damaged in one night—it was just what she needed. 'Thank you, Sean.'

Sean winked at her, and her breath caught in her throat. 'Either I'm getting a head-spin from smoking, or you girls are blocking my air?' She fanned her hand at her face. 'Why is it so hot in here?'

* * *

'Hi, Sean,' said Clare, sliding into the seat beside him, as her bare shoulders brushed against his arm that rested on the back of the chair. 'You've been watching over our girl, have you?'

'I was happy to help Deanne out.' Sean lifted his arm away from Clare and shunted along his seat towards the wall.

The bodyguard Lou flexed her set of scary biceps, while Clare's perfume cloud shifted closer, the more he moved away.

'Watch yourself, Sean, Clare will eat you alive,' said Deanne, while dodging Jane's attempts to extinguish her cigarette.

'Thanks for the warning.' Pity the bridesmaids had crashed their private party, where the hours had disappeared, as their conversation flowed with ease. He'd shared opinions he'd never told anyone before, blaming it on Deanne's slight head tilt and the full focus of her eyes that shattered all his defences. It was unfair. But it was the best interrogation Sean had ever surrendered to in his life!

He hadn't left Deanne's company for a second. Not that he could, now cornered by Clare, where it was obvious the bridesmaids weren't leaving without Deanne. *Pity.* 'Ladies, care for a drink?'

'Sure, Sean.' Clare fluttered her false lashes at him.

'You've got to be kidding me.' Lou mimicked Clare's eye action in exaggerated disgust.

'You're just jealous.' Clare frowned, jutting out her chin. 'Just because you haven't gotten laid in a year—who does that? Declare a vow of celibacy when you're not even religious.'

'Well, that's an interesting concept,' said Sean, the conversation reminded him of his sisters' bickering.

'We're all tired, ladies,' said Jane, getting to her feet,

'and it's time we got Dee home.'

'Got no home. And I'm not going back to Dad's, I'm not ready.' Deanne stared at her wine glass as her stature deflated.

'Hey, are you okay?' Sean couldn't help himself and placed his hand over Deanne's where an electrical pulse of pleasure shot beneath his skin.

Yet inwardly he cursed at the sight of her sad aquamarine eyes that made his stomach tighten as if he was falling through gravity. *Why did the bridesmaids show up and upset this poor woman?*

'OI.' Lou leered over the table at him. 'That's our job, lover boy. Leave her alone, Dee's been through enough already.'

Well, this was going to be tricky. Trapped in a booth, outnumbered, and surrounded by bridesmaids!

He had to admire their protectiveness over Deanne — which is probably why Deanne chose them to be her bridesmaids. 'Sorry ladies, don't mean to offend.'

'You didn't, and you've been great, Sean. But they're right, it is time to go.' With trembling hands, Deanne clutched her wine glass and gulped down a big mouthful, avoiding all eye contact. 'Where are you taking me?' She reached for the cigarette packet.

'Clare's place,' replied Jane, flicking the smokes across the table towards Sean, well out of Deanne's reach.

'Oh man, fun's over.' Deanne screwed up her nose. 'What've you got to drink at your place, Clare?'

Hitching up her strapless dress, Clare rose to her above average height, smoothing over her shiny black up-do. 'Nan gave us two bottles of scotch with your name on it.'

'They're the bait to get you into the car,' Lou said with a nod.

'Gotta luv my Nan…' Deanne stared at the table, sinking into her seat. 'I'll need it to pass out.'

'Come on, Deanne, I'll help walk you to the car.' Sean shuffled free from his seat.

Lou held up her palm like a stop sign inches from Sean's chest. 'We'll take it from here, mate.'

'Don't get me wrong, Lou, I'm sure you could carry a fireman up a ladder. But in those shoes?' He pointed to her swollen feet squeezed into heels that reminded him of a Geisha's bound feet gone wrong. 'But if I was as strong as you, Lou, I'd offer to carry you to the car, too.' Sean smirked at Lou who blushed—*huh, there really was a sensitive female under all that brass.*

Deanne's eyes widened. 'Lou, I've never seen you blush before.'

'Thanks, Sean, we could do with the help. I think Dee's going to be a handful,' said Jane, tugging on Deanne's arm, who wouldn't budge.

'Please, allow me. Remember your delicate condition, Jane.' He carefully guided Jane back. Then he held out his hand to Deanne, and for a man who rarely smiled—smirk, yes; smile, no—he couldn't help but grin at her. 'Time to go, sweetheart.' *Where did that come from?* Sean had never called anyone sweetheart before.

'If I must, I must.' Deanne stood, only to stagger back as if gravity pushed her.

Sean laughed with her.

'This is all your fault, Sean.'

Truly, she had such a beautiful smile—a smile he couldn't

get enough of.

'Sure, blame me, I can handle it.' Sean leaned down and his palm slid across the silky gown around her waist, as her soft hair brushed against his cheek. His shoulders stiffened to suppress the urge to dive into her shiny mane and absorb her seductive delicate floral scents.

Instead, Sean helped Deanne to her feet… and found he didn't want to let her go. 'Are you up for some dancing?'

Deanne laughed. 'Tempting. But I don't think I can walk straight. Although, I'll pinch those smokes to get me through the night. I'll quit again in the morning.' She reached for the packet and lost her footing.

'Careful.' Sean trapped Deanne to his chest, catching his own breath. She was close enough for him to appreciate the intricate specks of colours that made her eyes so spectacular. He could stare into them forever.

'I've got 'em.' Clare scooped up the cigarette packet, then glanced at the drunken Deanne. 'Nan's right, it's a good thing we came.' Clare nodded to Lou and Jane. 'Car's this way.'

* * *

Along the sidewalk, Deanne winced at flashing neon lights beckoning to customers to enter various nightclubs. Live rock bands competed with techno-rap music that echoed along the smoky streets.

Sean held Deanne close to his side, arms wrapped around each other's backs as they trailed behind the bridesmaids clearing a path through the thin crowd.

He pointed at their reflection in the shop window. 'For

a drunk bride, you walk pretty straight.'

'I live in heels.' Deanne touched her tiara that hadn't shifted all night. 'I can run in them too.' *Duh*, she'd done that earlier and refused to think of why.

'Hey, thanks for everything, Sean, I mean it.' She gazed up to meet his dark eyes that glinted between the strands of his long fringe. Her body broke out in goose bumps as she shivered under his stare. Or was that from the autumn air?

His palm rubbed her bare shoulder, tucking her in closer to his side, instantly warming her. She softened against his hard, muscular torso. Inhaling his intoxicating, aromatic rich spices, while her heart raced like she'd just sprinted the street. Why was she reacting like this?

Duh, major emotional crisis.

Plus, the smoking could explain the head spin—not Sean. Or was it?

'Thanks for dinner, drinks…'—she'd lost count on what she'd drunk— '…and your company,' she squeaked out the words, her throat suddenly thick and tight.

Was she choking up because she didn't want to go home and face all those people waiting to throw her some pity-party?

While the bridesmaids got busy opening Nan's car, Sean gazed down at her, his voice so soft and low. 'My pleasure, Deanne. I had a great night.'

Even though Sean's hands held her in place, her entire world tilted just looking at him, to revel in the strength of his embrace. She was meant to pat his chest, but her hand rested over his heart beating strongly beneath his shirt, her own pulse responding in an irrational rhythm.

'Pity the party had to end…' Her words slipped out, hypnotised by his intense dark brown eyes.

His lips hinted at a smile on the lips she wanted to kiss, the intense craving cooled and heated her body at the same time.

'He was a fool to have done that to you, Deanne.' Sean's lips brushed against her ear as his nose nuzzled against her skin.

Her skin shuddered from his touch. The warmth of his breath fuelled the pour of desire that spread throughout her body, humming through her veins, she swayed towards him.

Deanne's eyes closed to force back tears. Was she sad about what Darren had done? Or sad to leave Sean?

'Take care of yourself, Deanne.' His fingertips tenderly traced the side of her face.

Breath held, she was entranced by his handsome features and those twinkling dark eyes that saw everything hidden within.

Sean leaned down and brushed feather-light lips against hers.

Deanne didn't move, holding her breath as her pulse stopped, and the world was silenced.

But then her body trembled at the touch of his warm soft lips. She tasted the sweetness of the wine and moaned at the contrast of the slight bristle itch from his chin. The kiss, soft, firm and…*heaven*.

Her palms slid across his strong chest, over his strong shoulders, to wrap her arms around him. Her fingers slid through his silky hair that was short back and sides, yet thick and wild on top that gave her something to grip. And she wanted to grip.

Sean pulled her closer into his chest. His fingertips caressed her bare shoulders, sending an electrical warmth submitting her soul into surrender.

It was there an unsung rhythm rolled between them with the stroke of his unrushed sensual lips, the heat built as tongues tasted deeper than the physical. His kiss swept away her pain, and all was forgotten except for his tender touch.

Her whole world had become still, and all its noise disappeared. There was no past, no future, only the now focused within this one, perfect kiss.

'That'll do, Romeo. We'll take it from here,' said Lou, grabbing Deanne's arm, forcing Sean to release her.

Deanne gasped for air, blinking at the blur of lights as if ripped awake from a dream.

She'd never been kissed like that.

It was as if her entire universe had been consumed within his presence, all within this one magical moment.

Reeling with giddiness and confusion, she was startled as the slammed door woke her from this trance. Somehow, she'd been guided into the car's back seat.

Her fingertips touched her swollen sensitive lips, still tasting him on her thirsting tongue. She shivered, missing his warm embrace.

Had that kiss been real?

Deanne peered out the car window to the dazzling harsh lights of the boulevard, where Sean stood on the edge of the pavement. Pressing her hand to her twirling tummy, she swallowed air to slowdown her rapid heartbeat.

Unable to look away, she watched Sean's exhale highlight his cheek bones and his shaded strong jawline. He raked fingers through his thick blue-black hair and shared a slight grin, but his shining dark eyes communicated with her soul that wanted to sing for him.

How? When they'd only just met!

But she knew what he was saying to her, what they were saying to each other. This was their goodbye.

For Deanne, she thanked him with her returned smile and her eyes remained locked on Sean's until they were driven apart from each other's lives. Forever. But he would remain a memory as the one good thing from this day.

If she dared to remember him, and that kiss…

FIVE

Deanne woke to a stiff neck with her head hanging over the side of the double bed. Rain drummed on the roof which competed with a pounding inside her skull. Her furry oversized tongue made her dry mouth taste like an over-used ashtray, in desperate need of water.

Deanne rolled over on the mattress. Groaned and grunted as she sat upright as slowly as a Koala awakening in the branches of a bent eucalyptus tree. She stretched her arms, rubbed her nose, and scratched her head, blinking gravelly eyes until her focus cleared on the dress she was wearing.

Her bridal gown.

Falling back against her pillow, Deanne stared at the unrecognisable ceiling. She became paralysed by wave after wave of shame, disgust, disbelief, and sorrow. Bitter tears constricted her throat forcing her to gulp for small pockets of air. Her ribcage tightened as sadness swamped her drowning soul.

'Mummy…' Deanne knew her mum wouldn't show, the loss only adding another layer to her agony that led to a blubbering ugly cry.

Deanne heard the door open and recognised the slipper-shuffle belonging to her grandmother. She reached for those familiar arms that wrapped around her.

'There, there, child,' said Nan, rocking Deanne gently against her heart.

Deanne hurt everywhere. Burrowing into her grandmother's familiar lemon and vanilla scent, she hoped to erase her suffocating pain. Yet, she couldn't stop bawling, as Nan stroked Deanne's hair, the same way when she was a child.

How she wished to be that kid again. To never know what it felt like to suffer from a broken heart, free from fear and shame, to live a life of ignorant innocence.

Whoa horsey—a kid? That part of her past sucked.

Her torturous teens triple sucked.

As for her grown up experience, so far…

It was nothing less than an infinite suck-zone.

It. All. Sucked!

'Let's get ya into the shower?'

'Sure, Nan.' There was nothing left inside. Nothing but a fool stupidly blinded by love.

With head down, shoulders slumped, Deanne shuffled behind Nan to the bathroom.

'Let's get you out of that dress, child.' Nan put on the shower, then helped to undo the clasps on the back of Deanne's ragged-edged wedding gown.

When Deanne spotted the scissors on the cabinet and snatched them up. She gripped the cold plastic handles as the blades reflected off the overhead light. 'I'll do it.'

Before Nan could stop her, Deanne hacked at the loosened bodice and let the shredded material fall to Clare's bathroom floor.

'There, I'm free.' Deanne blinked at the hurt and hatred

in her voice. Was she truly free?

'Aww, now that's a bugger, child, it was a nice dress,' mumbled Nan, reaching for the material fragments.

'It's wrecked now.' Just like everything else in her life.

Deanne scratched at her irritated skin as if diseased from that cursed gown. She jumped into the shower and inhaled steam, as the jets of liquid heat pounded across her neck and shoulders.

'I'll get ya coffee ready.' Nan headed out the door, with arms full of ruined bridal gown.

'Ta. And don't throw that dress away, Nan, I'm going to burn it later.' Where she would curse the adulterer and his accomplice to an eternity of damnation.

Nightmarish visions of Katrina and Darren being together tortured Deanne's mind, unleashing fresh tears that mixed with running water. Shrouded in steam, she collapsed to the tiled floor and hugged her trembling knees. Defeated and defenceless, there Deanne surrendered to her own private hell.

Deanne's cutlery scraped against her plate as autumn rain pounded on the roof and chilled the air. Nan tinkered at Clare's kitchen sink, while Jane, Clare, and Lou sat at the dining table, sipping their coffee.

Nobody said a word.

Deanne sat at the head of Clare's kitchen table and ate with a vengeance. The food seemed to return a comfort she'd long denied. For what? A man? A future husband? The scum who'd controlled what she said, did, and ate.

Darren despised big women, which made Deanne

even more self-conscious, to become the spineless sucker who'd sacrificed herself for what?

Why?

Because Deanne had been too scared Darren would find out she was less than perfect and leave her.

Well hello sister, the results were in and the jury's verdict… delivered.

The kitchen gloves were off, and it was time to roll up those sleeves, because Deanne's appetite and mouth demanded to roam free from suppression and judgement. Bugger the table manners—*let's bring on the binge!*

She concentrated on shovelling food into her gob to avoid the looks of pity from the seated trio. She didn't want anyone else to join her sufferance parade. *No sir, this was a one-woman show, forever closed to the public.*

But her little party for one could do with a kick.

From the centre of the table, she snatched up the three-quarter bottle of scotch and poured a decent dash into her coffee.

Jane opened her mouth to speak, but Deanne glared at her, not in the mood for a lecture. She wasn't in the mood for company. Deanne was just in *the mood.*

Lowering her head, she clamped her eyes shut and clung to this new upsurging swirl of anger building inside. She relished how it curled around her chest like a smouldering fireball that leeched liquid heat into her veins. She needed this to fight against the hurt caused by those she'd trusted.

Why did they do this? What did she ever do to them?

To stop the tears, Deanne pinched her thigh and tried to reclaim that inner fury.

'Still got ya appetite, child.' Nan picked up her granddaughter's empty plate.

'Thanks, Nan. How's Dad and Jimmy?' It was automatic polite small talk, a sign she'd been well-trained. Yep, just like a well-coached waddling seal waiting for a reward after her fine public performance.

And her treat? The medicine she'd slipped into her coffee she sipped, almost purring at the warm explosion that spread across her chest.

Deanne checked the bottle's black label and found a new love. His name was Johnny. Johnny Walker, the bad arse in black. 'Black Johnny, so nice to meet your acquaintance.'

She clutched the bottle that awakened her inner rebel, as if Black Johnny was bringing her back from the black. It put her in the mood for ACDC to burst her eardrums and deafen all unwarranted thoughts.

Deanne unscrewed the scotch bottle and let the lid roll across the table while she added another heart-starter's kick-arse dash to her coffee mug. She stirred it with her finger, then sipped and sighed at the coolest coffee from the magic medicine of the Scots—or was that the Irish?

Nan raised an eyebrow at the coffee which contained more scotch than caffeine. 'They're worried 'bout you.'

Nooo! Deanne didn't need to hear that. 'I'll be fine,' replying with her automatic mumble as part of her well-trained clapping seal-act. Would she ever be fine?

Nope, she didn't want to think. She wanted out, and away from the four sets of eyes giving her that damned pity look you'd give a terminal cancer patient.

Why don't they just lead her out to the firing squad

now before she squandered any more oxygen?

Deanne then spied the cigarette pack on the side dresser. She jumped to her feet, snatching up the packet and the lighter.

Sean's silver lighter felt cool and weighty within her palm, remembering all about him. The flick of fringe shading his dark eyes, the handsome features of a man who was also very clever. But was their perfect kiss real?

Deanne winced at her reflection in the large mirror above the bench where red, swollen eyes stared back beneath a mass of frizzy auburn hair. Bulging cheeks offset the sallow, blotchy, freckled complexion. The borrowed t-shirt was ten times too small, it pronounced every stomach roll, magnifying her ballooning boobs. She saw nothing but a fat, ugly, fool.

Maybe she'd deserved what happened?

Deanne wasn't marriage material. If she'd been worthy as a wife, her future husband wouldn't have cheated on her in the first place.

To hide her body, Deanne grabbed the throw blanket off the couch, because it wasn't her place to cover mirrors.

She popped a coffin nail to her lips. Screw her health. *Screw everything.*

'Give me a few days and I'll be fine.' Deanne doubted you could put *fine* on a timeline, but hoped it was enough to keep the pity-party off her back.

But she didn't want to talk to anyone, except cosy up with her new BFF—the black label scotch—and watch the autumn rain that brought a chill to the air.

Deanne wrapped the blanket tighter around herself, tucking the scotch bottle safely under her arm, and with the cigarette packet and coffee in hand, she headed out the back door.

Before it swung shut, her smoke was lit, the bottle lidless, and misery had new company called Black Johnny.

From nowhere, Deanne heard the voice of a TV preacher with an American southern drawl inside her head proclaim:

'I now pronounce you shall be
for evermore with
Black Johnny
… and numb.'

Amen to that.

SIX

Nan dried her hands on her full bibbed apron as she shuffled in her house-slippers along the wide hallway. 'Is this all of Dee's gear from Darren's place?' Nan asked her grandson, Jimmy, who nodded as he dumped another box by the stairs. 'What about the furniture from her duplex?'

'Dee leased her place fully furnished,' said Jimmy. 'This is just her clothes and stuff. I'll put this gear in the spare room till Dee's ready. What do you think, Nan?' Jimmy straightened up the boxes against the wall and headed out for more.

Nan shrugged, it was Deanne's stuff to deal with, and there were some things a young lady might not want to share with her grandmother.

Jimmy soon returned, followed by his best mate, Petey, carrying a large brown box each, with Lou, Clare, Jane, and the neighbour, Chris, bringing up the rear.

'Good the see everyone's home again,' said Nan.

'Good to see you too, Nan,' said Clare, slinging an arm around the shorter elderly woman. 'How is Dee?'

'Too bloody busy seeing' out the end of a scotch bottle to care. Leave 'em boxes there, Jimmy. Might you're your sister wake up to herself and do something instead of drinking.'

'Don't forget about the chain smoking,' said Jimmy. 'I swear she's polluting the whole street. And you should hear Dee's excuse for playing a live chimney stack.'

'What?' They all asked at once.

'Dee reckons she's sending smoke signals to space hoping to get kidnapped by aliens.' Jimmy shook his head as the crew snorted and guffawed, trying not to laugh. 'I'm serious.'

'I wished that'd happen in suburbia, it'd be cool,' mumbled Chris. They all gawked at the Anglo-Indian neighbour. 'What?' Lifting his skinny shoulders towards his ears.

'Dee never smoked this bad before. Yet, I can relate,' Jimmy said with a deep sigh. 'I reckon we're cursed in this house when it comes to our love lives.' Jimmy stepped back, cringing to himself as he stared at the ground.

No one said a word.

At the far end of the lounge room, the wall mounted clock's tick echoed. *Tick-tock. Tick-tock.*

'Beer?' Jimmy nosed towards Petey, who nodded back. Both men turned to Chris who was too busy grinning and nodding at Lou. Jimmy and Petey looked at each other, shook their heads as if Chris had breached some unspoken caveman pact, and headed for the fridge in the kitchen.

Lou arched her eyebrow at the grinning and nodding Chris beside her. 'Go Christopher, its little boy's beer-time.'

'But...' Chris's smile was reduced to a pouty sulk. His shoulders drooped and he shuffled off without a word.

'Since when has Jimmy suffered with a broken heart?' Lou asked.

'Rebound divorce, remember,' replied Clare, putting her handbag on top of the pile of boxes.

'Dee believes Jimmy's never gotten over his childhood sweetheart,' Jane said, parking herself on the bottom of the staircase and stifled a yawn. 'Poor Jimmy, he's obviously feeling his little sister's misery, too.'

'Nan?' Lou asked the older woman busily poking around the boxes. 'Did you say Dee's been drinking for a week? Is that her excuse for not returning my calls?'

'The child says she's on her honeymoon, married to Black Johnny and got the time off work to drink,' said Nan, heading back to the kitchen.

'Who's Black Johnny?' Clare asked, assisting the pregnant Jane to her feet.

'Her new boyfriend,' said Nan from the far end of the hallway.

'WHAT!' The three women followed Nan.

Inside the kitchen, Reg sat at the wooden dining table, with the newspaper spread out before him. The other men milled around, leaning against the yellow kitchen cupboards, handing out beers, as the smell of roasted meats warmed the air.

Stifling another yawn, Jane took a seat beside Reg.

'Are you all right, luv?' Reg asked.

'You're always tired first trimester and then for the next eighteen years,' Nan said, shuffling her slippers across the chequered linoleum floor to peek at her roast in the oven.

'I'm okay,' said Jane, rubbing her flat tummy. 'Is it true Dee's been drunk for a week?'

Reg sighed as he shut the newspaper, pushing his glasses along his nose. 'All Dee does is sit on the swing under the tree, smoking and drinking. Jimmy had to carry her in a few times because she's passed out, drunk on the lawn. I haven't seen her this sad, since, since...' Reg lowered his head. 'Since their mother died. Then we were all miserable.'

'We can't let Dee do this to herself.' Clare started for the back door. 'Girls, it's time for an intervention.'

'Yeah, let's give it to her hard and straight.' Like a drill sergeant, Lou punched a fist into her palm.

'But gentle, too. Dee's been through a lot,' called out Jane, her corkscrew curls bouncing as she followed them out the back door.

'Good girls.' Nan grinned, then she whirled around to face the men. 'You boys, stay here and keep out of the way when Dee comes inside.' Nan then grabbed a towel from the cupboards and tucked it under her arm.

'The reason we're hiding in here, Nan, is because Dee's polluting the outside with that chain-smoking factory she's got happening,' Jimmy said, pointing his beer at the screen door.

'Why, Mum?' Reg arched is eyebrow above the rim of his glasses. 'What are you up to?'

'None you mind.' Nan suppressed her grin as she hobbled out the door after the three young women.

SEVEN

Opposite the silent beer shed, Deanne sat on the swing that hung beneath the wide jacaranda tree. It sat in the far corner of the large suburban back yard. With a smouldering cigarette in one hand and a lidless scotch bottle in the other, Deanne stared at the sky that reflected her mood. Cold and grey.

Just like that, summer had slipped by. Exchanged by an autumn chill, where the promising tang of more rain lingered in the air.

The back screen-door opened with its tell-tale squeak and the clip-clop of shoes on the back stairs, broke her out of her daydreaming.

'Oh man.' She screwed up her face, not in the mood for company.

'Dee,' called out Clare, making short work of the clipped lawn with her long stride, with Lou and Jane on either side they stood before Deanne.

Deanne sipped from the spirit bottle. *Okay, no harm in being polite.* She braced herself to put on a good performance, remembering to try and smile. 'Well, if it isn't the three Greatest-Girls-of-the-Galaxy. Pleasure to see you ladies. Wanna drink? Except you, Mother. Hey, when do we see the baby bump?'

'I'm six weeks, Dee,' replied Jane.

'It's the size of a sesame seed, or it's graduated to the width of an almond?' Lou shrugged her beefy shoulders at Clare arching an eyebrow at her. 'Come on, what's to show? We're comparing the kid to the dimension of nuts. You'd wanna boy after this conversation.' She chuckled. 'Besides, Dee's dad's gotta bigger gut. What stage would Reg be?'

'I'd say Dad's beer belly is in the late second trimester. It used to be bigger.' Deanne noted her own tummy and wondered what gestational stage was her own flourishing scotch-pot at?

'Peoples, please,' Clare said, tucking her sleek black bob behind her ears. 'Focus.'

'Oops,' Lou and Jane said in unison and turned to Deanne seated on the swing.

'Spoilsport,' Deanne muttered.

'Dee, we've brought your stuff back from Darren's place,' said Lou.

Deanne dragged deeply on her cigarette, trying to stop her hands from shaking, and exhaled fire from her lava-churning guts at the mere mention of his name. 'Did needle-dick show his face?' The words were like venom dripping off her tongue.

She was beyond sad now. Thanks to her new strong and silent boyfriend-in-a-bottle, Black Johnny, Deanne was bitter.

'Only Darren's parents were there.' Timidly Jane, clasped her small hands together. 'They said they were sorry, and that they're ashamed of their son. They're hoping you'll visit them sometime, later?'

'But *he* wasn't there, was he?' Deanne had vowed to never speak the name of the one who'd permanently splintered her biosphere. What a fool she'd been, and what a geek she'd become!

'Er...' Jane shrugged, fidgeting with her fingers.

'Chicken.' *Yeah, full use of vocabulary — not.* But she was too drunk to contemplate clever revenge plans, aside from the instant gratification of incinerating his property with the owner inside.

But she didn't want to risk the separation from her boyfriend-in-a-bottle whilst holidaying in prison. All Deanne had left was Black Johnny, who'd managed to smudge her reality's hard edges. She just wanted to be left alone and hope for amnesia.

'I told ya, Darren wouldn't have had the guts to be there. Not with Jimmy gunning to dent his perfect teeth.' Lou kicked at a tuft of grass with her sports shoes.

'Was my stuff in boxes or did you have to re-pack them?' Deanne asked. 'I'd couriered them over the day before the wedding. I wonder if they'll let me break my tenant's lease so I can move back?' Nah, it was too hard to think too far ahead, except where to find her next refill of her boyfriend-in-a-bottle.

'My gear should've been in one piece because I'd never made it to his house to unpack. I was planning to do it after we got back from our...' Deanne frowned at the dirt tracks she'd cleared by dragging her shoes while swinging.

'You know, he teased me by saying he'd put my things away on our pre-wedding night. Bet he didn't.' She dragged heavily on her cigarette, while reading the confirmation in their faces. Yeah, that was the night when her fiancé was too busy humping her cousin all while she'd been fretting over her part of playing the perfect bride!

Broken and twisted, that's where her soul was at now. It's all she had. And Black Johnny.

Taking another deep slug from the bottle, she sighed, slowly sliding her shoes across the dirt.

'You know,' Deanne said, still staring at the ground, 'he didn't have to do anything for his day-to-day life, because there was always someone who'd take care of it for him. His mother ran around after him, and so did I. I could never say no to the guy.' Her fist pounded her chest, as cigarette ash spilled over her grubby jeans and gazed up at her friends, her peers, and her jury. 'That's what I did— I'm pathetic! I was nothing more than an eager mongrel always fetching for him. And there he is telling me what to do, eat, drink, and wear—it was pi-ti-ful. Well, I'm not doing it anymore. I'm done. There'll be no more carrying anyone else's excess baggage around.'

'All your gear's here, untouched from when they were delivered,' Clare said as she slid her arm around Jane, both tearing up. While Lou stood dumbfounded.

'Thank you, ladies. I wouldn't have been able to go back there without ending up in prison. So, here's to the end of an era.' Deanne lifted the bottle to her lips and took a large swig, then let her body hang limp on the swing.

If she kept her eyes shut, she could ride the slight spin of the world and everyone else should soon disappear. And with luck, her honeymoon-of-hurt would fade away into some bad dream.

Lou stomped her foot. '*Enough, Dee.* You've gotta stop this.'

Deanne flinched on the swing's seat. 'How rude.' *Why were they still here?*

'Lou's right,' said Clare. 'You're killing yourself drinking and smoking. Remember how hard it was to become a non-smoker?'

'You can't solve problems through the end of a bottle, so give it to me.' Jane held out her small hand.

'Did you ever consider that I don't want to see my problems?' Deanne's knuckles whitened around the bottle's neck. 'Did you ever think that I might enjoy sitting on the sidelines to view my little life from the bottom of my boyfriend-in-a-bottle?'

Clare leaned forwards with hands on hips. 'Do you realise you've just called a bottle of whiskey your boyfriend?'

'I'm not prejudiced.' Deanne cradled the bottle to her chest. 'We're on our honeymoon.'

'That's pathetic,' said Lou. 'Hand over the bottle.'

'No. Don't break us up. We're good together. We don't argue, and he listens to my dribble and never judges. Besides, I'll stop when I'm ready, just not today.' Deanne took an angry swig from the bottle, followed by a deep drag from her cigarette, to blow smoke into their faces. She then winced at Jane. 'Sorry Mother, forgot, no smoking near the baby.'

'Dee, we're only doing this because we care,' said Jane, fanning her face. 'You've always been there for us when we needed someone, so it's our turn to finally help you.'

Clare pressed her palms together as if in prayer and took a step closer. 'We want to help you, and I know if you were in our shoes, you wouldn't stop helping us. Just like you've done for me so many times that I've lost count. Dee, we understand what you're going through.'

'How? Did you ever humiliate yourself in front of a room full of people? Did your fiancé get your cousin pregnant, only to discover this juicy titbit ten minutes before marrying that spreader-of-sperm? How can any of you relate.' Deanne's words loudly echoed across the backyard. Great, why not broadcast it to rest of suburbia.

'Leave me alone.' Deanne just wanted to be forgotten, to forget the heavy lump of regret that was like a weighty barbell resting across her shoulders.

'Eeenough, young lady,' Nan called out from where she'd been watering the plants. With towel over her shoulder, Nan flicked off the nozzle, and stormed toward them, dragging the hose behind her. 'It's time to move past this self-pity crap.'

'Only when I'm good and ready.' Deanne scowled at Nan.

Only for Nan to scowl with a glimmer to her grey eyes, she lifted the garden hose and unleashed a vicious stream of icy water all over Deanne.

'*What the hell!*' Deanne leaped to her feet with palms shielding her from the raging torrent.

Nan stopped the spray with a flick of the wrist but, kept the dripping hose aimed at Deanne.

'*What the hell are you doing?*' She was cold. Shocked. And saturated. Holding her diluted boyfriend-in-a-bottle in one hand and a limp cigarette in the other.

'Don't you bloody swear at me, young lady.' Again, Nan twisted the nozzle and showered Deanne, as if putting out an enraged fire.

'STOP, NAN. STOP.'

Nan turned off the hose, yet kept her loaded weapon, aimed and ready to spray again.

Deanne heaved furious steam through trembling lips. She was soaked from head to toe, freezing, and sober.

Oh no, I'm sober!

Worse, her emotions were awakening.

Great, now she was miserable inside and out.

Deanne squinted at the beloved water-witch, and clenched her trap shut in fear of another douse.

'Enough of this wallowing, self-pity crap. It's been a week,' said Nan, waving the dripping nozzle at her granddaughter. 'You're not the only poor-bugger-me who's dealt with a damaged relationship. Look at your father dealing with your mother's death. Your brother's still regretting his rebound-divorce while still pining for his childhood sweetheart. There's poor Chris from next door, who can't get no female unless he marries one of his mum's Bollywood-brides he's only seen in a photo. AND YOU—' Nan pointed the hose as Deanne who winced. 'You did the right thing when you outed that idiot and didn't marry him. You saved yourself, child. It's done. It's time to move forward.'

Deanne clenched her jaw, pursing her lips tight. She didn't dare go against the family's matriarch. Which brought the trained-seal-act back into action, considering Deanne was wet enough to be a seal. She just needed to eat fish twenty-four seven to seal the deal. *Ha!*

'Now,' continued Nan, holding out a towel, 'gimme that bottle and get upstairs to that shower. Then you can sort out them boxes taking up space in the hallway, coz it's time to get your act together, young lady, or so help me, I'll—'

'*All right, Nan, I've got the message.*' Deanne snatched the towel and glanced at the bottle she hadn't let go of all day. All week.

A week, huh?

It'd been a good relationship while it lasted. But then again when bad boys lead you astray, it's best to surrender them, and she reluctantly passed over her boyfriend-in-a-bottle to Nan.

Deanne's lips trembled from the combination of bubbling emotions and crisp weather, waterlogged, ice-chilled, and freaking sober. Everything just sucked.

'AUGH.' Deanne stropped past her friends, up the back-steps, ripped open the screen door and into the kitchen, where the men scrambled for cover. Fuming, she left a dripping water trail across the floor, and didn't dare stop or look at anyone.

* * *

Nan listened for the bathroom door to close with a bang and the shower started upstairs. It had to be done, even if her granddaughter was going to hate her for a month.

But more was needed.

With a shuffle of her slippers, Nan moved to the shed that occupied the corner of the yard. Inside the homemade bar, she switched off the tellie in the corner, and put Deanne's scotch bottle on the side table. 'Lou, I could do with a bit of ya muscle.' Nan signalled to the shed's wide-open doorway. 'Pull her shut.'

'Sure thing, Nan.' Lou pulled on the large roller-door. Unmoved in years, it squealed and groaned in protest until it closed.

Nan produced a key from her apron's deep pocket and locked it tight. 'This'll upset the boys for a bit.'

The back door's tell-tale screech led the sound of many footsteps.

Nan inhaled deeply and prepared for the next battle about to begin.

Leading the men, Jimmy rushed down the back steps from the kitchen, grasping onto his auburn hair. 'Why'd you do that for, Nan? Not our bar. You can't shut the Beer Shed, Nan. The dartboard. Me beer. The fridge. The barbecue. Out tellie. My beer! Dad, do something.'

'Mum, you're denying a man his beer-rights.' Reg tugged on the roller-door with Jimmy doing the same beside him, but it wouldn't budge.

'Our beer.' The four men mumbled, standing in front of the locked door. Their access denied.

'Come on, Nan, give us the key.' Jimmy held out his open palm.

'Nope, she's a shut-shop, and it'll be bloomin' well shut for a week.' Nan slid the key safely into her apron pocket, then stood with hands on hips like a bandy-legged-gunslinger ready for the quick-draw. 'I did this with ya father to move on with his mourning. And I'd done it when you got divorced, Jimmy. Now, it's your sister's turn. Until then, ya can drink at the pub.' Nan ignored the men's pleas and headed for the back stairs. She'd get her family back in order but knew the dust needed to settle first, now that the worst of the storm had passed.

A rumble of thunder rolled amongst heavy, low grey clouds; it made her wonder, *had it?*

At least now the healing could begin. She hoped.

EIGHT

Seated behind her office desk, Deanne held a rectangular silver lighter. She flicked open the lid, closed it. Opened it. Closed it. Staring out to space, her legs swung beneath her as she leaned back and gently rocked in her work chair.

'Hey, Sis.' Jimmy walked into Deanne's office, placing a brown paper bag on her desk. He then plonked down into one of the guest chairs opposite. 'How's it going?'

'Okay.' Not okay, but better. The wedding had passed months ago, and she was now back at work and unexcited over everything.

She flicked the lid of the lighter, closed it. Opened it. Closed it. While her legs swung beneath her rocking chair.

'How, um, are you?' Another feeble attempt at dialogue, considering she was now a master of small talk minimalism.

She'd even created a set of covert cultish commandments, where number one on that list was: no conversations. All forms of conversation were to be avoided at all times. If trapped in conversation, it might make people think that she cared.

Deanne had also learned that her award-winning performances as the perfect trained-seal, while living life on autopilot, kept all pity-party-players off her back. So far.

Deanne flicked open the lighter's lid, closed it. Opened it. Closed it. And stared into space.

'Haven't you stopped smoking again?' Jimmy unwrapped his sandwich. 'You know I don't like it.'

'I quit when Nan hosed me off.' That sober-dousing moment had generated history's cruellest hangover ever. It forced her to remain trapped inside the patchy pink bedroom, nicknamed the horror-titus, that was garnished with nightmarish childhood posters. Deanne still couldn't work out what possessed her to worship boy bands that sang like girls.

Living at Dad's again, it was is if she was being forced to re-connect with her inner child. Which was unlikely when she'd forgotten to laugh and had no more tears to cry. She was nothing but an empty shell.

Deanne flicked open the lighter. Closed it. And rocked in her chair.

'Are you sure you've quit smoking, when you're always playing with that lighter?' Jimmy took a bite of his sandwich and watched her as he chewed.

'Huh?' She didn't realise it had become a habit. The lighter was warm and solid in her hand. It had become her unrealised talisman, a trophy from the last time she'd laughed.

How much longer before she'd feel more than this constant state of numbness? Yet right now, she was too bored to care.

'You'll ruin the flint. Where d'ya get it?'

'It was Sean's.' Deanne placed the lighter on her desk and unwrapped her lunch knowing Jimmy wouldn't leave until she ate, as per Nan's orders.

At least Nan stopped spoon feeding Deanne while suffering from the world's worst hang over after breaking up with Black Johnny.

'That's not another bottle of booze you're marrying?'

Deanne's hand covered her heart as she sighed like an unemployed drama queen. 'Black Johnny will always be a part of my memories.' Because the boyfriend-in-a-bottle didn't lie or cheat on her.

'So, who's Sean?'

Good question. 'I met Sean after my fabulous exit at the wedding. He creates company security systems.' *Wow*, she remembered. 'Sean bought me drinks and the biggest feed I'd allowed myself in years.' Why did she let her ex dictate what she ate?

But now her family were ensuring she consumed calories that weren't in liquid form. It sucked.

Had her food habit declined so badly that Deanne was endangering herself of fading into a shadow?

Not a chubby chance at that, when she lived with cellulite-infested thighs and where mirror avoidance had become a daily necessity.

Deanne chomped on her tasteless sandwich, glancing at Sean's lighter. She remembered he was funny, clever, and charming. A real gentleman who'd looked after her, and hadn't been offended with her eating, doing, and speaking uninhibited. The man had truly witnessed her worst—in public—and still stuck with her.

But did that breathtaking perfect kiss really happen? Or had it been nothing more than an alcoholic illusion?

'Did that bloke give you the lighter?' Jimmy took another bite of his lunch.

'Clare pinched it, as per normal.' Deanne even managed a half smile. *Wahoo.* By Christmas she might be laughing.

'Good to see you're smiling.'

Just great! It was those type of comments that made her want to dent the table with her forehead. Instead, she shoved the sandwich into her gob.

'Do you want to give it back?'

'Giv wat buk?' Nan wasn't around to tell her off for talking with her mouth full. But give the kid a pat on the head for being good, she's eating. *Hoorah.*

Although she was redefining her lifestyle habits to merely existing. Which meant looking busy and avoiding all forms of eye contact, so no one noticed how dull her life had become.

But Jimmy would. It was one of the benefits of having an older brother who'd been-there-done-that-and-got-the-t-shirt.

What's worse was enduring his doomsday speech over their love lives being cursed, vexed, and hexed, that their family were destined to be forever single.

Yep, there was a lot to plan in her future, such as breaking curses and, finding her smile, *if* Deanne could be bothered.

'The lighter looks expensive?' Jimmy inspected the lighter. 'It's made of silver. Must've cost a bit.'

Deanne shrugged. 'Sean used it to light his cigars.'

Sean seemed handsome, considering her emotional state when they'd met. She remembered his glossy thick black hair, a little long on the fringe that he'd effortlessly flick out of his line of sight. The slight shadowy growth that hid his laugh lines, yet added detail to his strong chin and highlighted his cheekbones. He also had an infectious crooked grin and a scamp's shine to his dark eyes.

Sean also wore a tasteful tailored suit and silk tie, and he seemed at ease spending his money entertaining her that night. He'd definitely charmed her, making her laugh so much she'd forgotten all her troubles.

But had it been real, or was her memory playing tricks?

'I might give it back … then I might not.' She didn't want to do anything. Even doing nothing was a hassle.

Perhaps it was time she did something for a change? Maybe.

NINE

Deanne pushed through the wooden doors and strode into the bar that didn't look shadowy, but cosy and clean. Except for a couple in the booth by the stained-glass front windows enjoying a midweek no-rush-lunch, the place was pretty much deserted.

She was impressed with herself for recognising the place, with its dark green walls covered in framed ancient newspaper headlines. The dark polished wooden floors, the low hanging glow of the stained-glass light shades, and the brass railing that ran along the base of the bar she remembered.

The place had a classic charm of some prohibition era to it, with its collection of ancient polished wooden barrels displaying glass cases of polished iron handcuffs and truncheons in the corners. Maybe her memory hadn't been so grog-sodden after all.

Then she spotted Mickey, the only bartender she knew by name, with his clipped salt and pepper hair.

But she'd forgotten his large stature and stern untrusting expression. How come she didn't remember that?

Blaming it on the alcoholic illusion, she hesitated, biting her lip, and glanced back searching for the door.

'Can I help you?' Mickey asked, leaning against the

inner side of the bar, while keeping one eye on the television in the corner.

'Hi, um, Mickey.' Should she dash for the car?

No.

She was here for a reason and cleared her throat.

'I'm here to say thank you.' With a deep breath, she stepped forward as his grey eyebrows lifted. 'You might not remember me? Um, bridal gown, tiara, veil, trying to sell you an engagement ring for a drink?' She waited for some embarrassing response while fighting to keep her posture from sinking to the floor.

'Deanne. Beer with a scotch chaser, hey luv?' Mickey grinned, placing two shot glasses on the counter, and reached for the bottle.

'I shouldn't.' But she was oh so very tempted. 'I'm on my lunch break.' She waved a hand over her uniform—a long-sleeved, blue-collared shirt with the family hardware logo embroidered on the pocket. Not to mention her dad would kill her if she got busted drink-driving the work ute.

'If it doesn't get me into any trouble, I have to say, you look a lot better from when I last saw you walk through those front doors.'

She remembered Mickey's first words when they'd met telling her *she was the saddest thing he'd seen all day.* Today, it felt like the first true compliment Deanne had received in months. 'I'm good,' she said. 'Well, I'm better now. Thank you.' Hello, she was smiling. A weak one, but it was a start.

'Are you sure?' Mickey poured the whiskey and held out the shot glass. 'My treat?'

Deanne sighed, her resistance was futile against Black

Johnny and took a seat.

Mickey placed the glass in front of her, then poured one for himself.

'It's tough.' The words spilled out. 'I'm getting there.' Her self-admittance was the naked truth, and she swallowed her scotch in one hit.

Oh, hello lover. She purred with eyes closed and savoured the liquor's wave of warmth. *Damn*, that boyfriend-in-a-bottle had a way of enhancing her world from the inside out.

'So, did you marry the guy?' Mickey asked.

'No.' She caught her frown to remain expressionless. But then she sighed, looking up at the big man, the stranger who'd helped her when in need—Mickey. 'No, I didn't marry him and moved back home. Which sucks—no, that didn't sound right—I love my family, I'm just suffering with privacy withdrawals.' And dealing with the shock-factor of her patchy pink childhood bedroom, along with her family's morning rituals.

Her dad's morning habit was hogging the royal throne room with the door wide open for circulation while he read the newspaper. Jimmy's choice of torture was his morning shower ritual where he simulated strangled banshees underwater. And Nan was always watching, serving stodgy starch as a side dish to the massacred meat served amongst a soup of salt-enriched gravy.

But they were her family and she loved them to bits, even if they annoyed her at times.

'Workwise,' she said, 'I'm currently exploiting the intricacies of the same-same-repeat-cycle used by, um, monks.' Although the excursion here had been a huge detour away from her usual thick cocoon of work-sleep and repeat lifestyle.

'And the fella?'

'He moved to Queensland. Banished would be a better word.' Was she talking too much and having a conversation? Which went against the first vow of her secret-cult-commandments.

'Is this your tavern, Mickey?'

'About five years now. I moonlight here as part of my retirement plans.' Mickey leaned against the bar and sipped his drink. 'You know, word got out about your bridal visit and business picked up for a bit. The other pubs along the strip reckoned I hired you as a publicity stunt.'

Deanne laughed.

Not only was she dabbling in dialogue, but she was now laughing. Was it Black Johnny, Mickey, or this bar that was aiding in the re-emergence of her old self?

Even her fingers tingled.

Had Deanne entered the de-numbing-zone?

And for the first time in a long time, she allowed the conversation to flow.

'Well, I'd better get back.' Deanne emptied her beer, pleased she'd made the effort to visit. Mickey was easy to talk to and non-judgemental, and this was the last place she'd laughed.

Glancing at the booth where she'd dined and drank for hours one night many months ago, she asked, 'Does Sean still come here?'

'Sean's a regular.' Mickey raised his eyebrow. 'You're not keen on him, are you?'

'Pft. Hell no.' Deanne shook her head as she

rummaged around in her handbag. 'I'm done with men. I've even divorced my boyfriend-in-a-bottle, Black Johnny.' She pointed to the bottle that rested on the bar. 'My friends were worried I was losing my mind calling him that.' Or her twisted personality had been indulging in a rare off-the-leash moment.

Mickey grinned, holding up the black-labelled scotch. 'Boyfriend-in-a-bottle, huh.'

'I would've joined a convent, but I couldn't leave Black Johnny home in the corner to collect dust. It'd shatter him.'

Of course, the publican would laugh at her silly scotch jokes.

She was also aware how much alcohol had mystified her memories, which would mean her perfect kiss with Sean wasn't real either. 'So, I've sworn off men forever.'

'Good.' Mickey gave a curt nod. 'Young Sean says females are a costly hassle.'

That wasn't nice. 'I know Sean spent his money on me, but I did offer to sell him the engagement ring.' That Nan had hidden until Deanne was ready to ask for it, which was probably never.

'I wouldn't let my daughter date him.' Mickey grabbed their empty glasses and slid them onto the glass tray. 'Though, in all fairness, Sean treated you well that night. Got to hand it to the lad, he pulled you out of the doldrums by making you laugh.'

Deanne smiled, realising it was this tavern that caused her to smile. Not Sean.

Although Sean had treated her like a lady and made her cheeks ache from laughing. He'd been noble towards her when she'd been at her worst.

It was so different compared to her family who'd practically force-fed Deanne to get back onto her feet to shuffle through the daily grind where everything was the same, day after day.

Mickey washed his hands and dried them on a towel. With head tilted, he resumed his lean against the bar opposite Deanne. 'Are you sure you're not keen on Sean? Because I'd warn you off him.'

'Thanks for the warning, Mickey, but I've sworn off men for life.' *To live eternally as a nun.*

Now, all she needed to do was find the right religion to stalk. Even if she was already proving to be an unsuitable candidate, breaking her own secret-cult-commandments by indulging in conversation.

'But I came here for a reason.' Deanne held out two envelopes and the silver lighter. 'It's a thank you card, with a cash tip inside.'

Mickey cocked a grey eyebrow at her. 'You didn't need to do that.'

'I know.' She smiled at the only barman she knew by name, who'd been her champion back then, and today. 'Can you pass this along to Sean, please? Inside, I hope I've put in enough to compensate him for his trouble. Please tell Sean, I'm sorry my friend borrowed his lighter.' That somehow ended up being her security blanket. 'I've had it re-gassed, and a new flint thingy done to it.' Still in disbelief she'd bothered to get the lighter serviced. Why?

Because two complete strangers had helped her out in her time of need.

Maybe this was her soul-cleansing step forward? Considering she'd managed a smile, held a conversation, laughed, and bared her soul to a bartender. Huh, she hadn't done this since…

Yeah, white gown, in tears, broken-hearted, and living in shame.

Her shoulders deflated as did her mood. It sucked.

'I'll make sure the lad gets it.' Mickey took Sean's envelope and lighter and placed it securely behind the bar. 'I'm, ah…' He hesitated, scratching at his salt and pepper crew cut, while holding open his thank you card. 'I'm touched. I really am.'

'Thank you for your kindness that day.' Hell yeah, the man made her smile, and the numbness shifted across her face. Was this what if felt like to when Botox injections wore off?

'You too, Deanne. Come back anytime.'

'I will. But I won't be wearing the wedding gown for any future publicity stunts,' she said, heading for the solid wooden doors.

Pity she didn't see Sean again, but then that might be a good thing.

Mickey waved his card at her. 'Hey, what happened to the dress?'

'I burned it playing with matches. I blame my ex-boyfriend-in-a-bottle for that, he was such a bad boy who'd showed me such a great time.' Both laughed as she exited into daylight, with hope that she'd finally left her sulky old shadow behind.

TEN

Yippee, another fascinating day in hardware. Not.

Seated at her desk, waiting for her computer to boot into life, Deanne closed her eyes hoping to ignite some sort of enthusiasm over something. But in a hardware shed? Come on, it was the same story, every day of the week.

Deanne didn't play with the tools, build, or fix stuff. Not when her father and brother relished playing handymen. Besides, there were enough tradesman in-store for technical expertise. So really, there wasn't much to get excited about.

But hey, she showed up, and that was a good thing.

Deanne leaned back and slowly rocked her office chair as her fingertips rubbed together. She missed holding Sean's lighter that she'd returned a few days ago.

Did Sean get his lighter?

She wasn't expecting a thank you from him, and she'd never left any details to contact her. Which was a good thing, because there was no room for men in her life, especially when she might have been under some alcoholic illusion that messed with her memory over some special kiss.

Her computerised calendar's alarm *dinged,* as the reminder flashed across her screen. It was to remember

Darren's birthday.

'Bastard!' With a fiery flash of fury, she stabbed at the delete button.

And felt better for it.

Even if her fingertip tingled.

Opening her electronic calendar, the urge to vomit was strong. 'Oh man, I'm never playing little Miss Freaking Efficient again. What was I thinking?' She winced at her entire reminders list that was all about Darren. It was notices for anniversaries, functions, even membership renewals, but it was all Darren's stuff.

Nothing about her.

So, she deleted one reminder.

Then another.

And another.

The more she deleted the more her inner strength grew with each slam on the keyboard. Was this a form of therapy to have Darren's history wiped out?

Whatever it was, it allowed for a slight weight to shift around her soul as a sly smile emerged.

'Morning, Dee,' said Janice, strolling through the open office doorway in her flowing skirts.

'Hi.' Deanne glanced up from her devilish deletions to the always-cheery office manager, which was annoying for those practising depression.

'You're looking better. There's even a bit of sparkle to those lovely eyes of yours.' Janice's many assorted bangles click-clacked as she placed the mail inside Deanne's in-tray.

'I'm deleting the ex.' Deanne slammed the delete button and the keyboard bounced.

Satisfied she'd deleted the last reminder, Deanne smiled up at Janice. *See, I can smile.* 'How are you, Janice?' Again, she broke her covert-convent rules by engaging in conversation.

'Can't complain.'

'Janice, have you ever been married?' What the hell were her lips doing, forcing her to engage in conversation!

'I'm divorced, twice. The first time I had to get married. I guess that's why I won't do the nuptials with Reg, even though I adore the man, I enjoy my space and he's the same. Don't you dare believe in any of Jimmy's bull about your family's relationship curse.'

Huh? Deanne blinked, her mouth opened, then closed it, as the heat prickled across her cheeks for prying, while making a mental note to slap Jimmy around the head for spreading rumours.

So, they'd suffered some bad luck when it came to intimate relationships. Or was Jimmy right in saying they were under a curse that destroyed their love lives? *Yay,* didn't that make her want to ride a unicorn over a rainbow.

Gawd, she needed to move out of her childhood bedroom, and fast.

Deanne sat forward in her chair and scooped up the mail. *Yep, look at me. I'm engaged in my labour-intensive employment—not.*

Amongst the usual off-white, business sized envelopes, she spotted a light blue coloured envelope.

'Your dad's a bit worried,' said Janice.

Deanne gave her well-trained auto-answer for the zillion, trillion, billionth time. 'I'm fine.'

Shoot, Janice was still watching. Okay, smile, but show

no teeth in fear of frightening folks or to give cause for Janice to scream for Dad. Avoid eye contact. Shrug shoulders. Seem busy. Wave duck-egg blue envelope in the air, which was enough to shoo away their always cheery administrative guru.

Deanne didn't desire company, nor want conversation. She was unsure of what she wanted. Perhaps a good place to start would be to jump off this sarcastic slide by remembering people were not the enemy. They were just … nosy and overcrowding when they hovered around her as if waiting for her to break down. Again.

Maybe she should check into rehab, imagining her first circle group: 'Hi, I have a boyfriend-in-a-bottle. No, he's not a genie, I wish. But he's a bad man, who corrupts good girls. But he's a silent soul who keeps all your secrets, and he doesn't judge, which allows for easy participation in the smile avoidance programme.' *Black Johnny was the man.*

Yeah, right. Nan was already worried Deanne needed AA, and if anyone heard her head space, they'd speed dial for strait-jacket-central and book her in for a padded room with a view.

Deanne grabbed her letter opener, a gift from her father and Jimmy for her tenth-year anniversary employed within the store. Yep, she'd accrued long service leave, even at her age, which wasn't too hard considering she grew up in the place. Hmm, the option of three months lying on a beach, never returning, was enticing.

She glanced at her letter opener. It was Jimmy's first engraving attempt that left an illegible childlike scrawl across the blade. The thought melted her with his efforts and knew she could never leave her family behind. The same way they'd never left her in her needy period, even though there had been times she'd wished they did.

The letter opener sliced through the envelope like a hot knife cutting up an ice-cream cake, because Jimmy sharpened it, often.

Oh Jimmy, such a soft-centred, simplistic soul, who'd found love and then lost it. If Jimmy hadn't moved past his broken heart in... *oh no, four years!* How could Deanne dare to hope of surviving after a few months?

Deanne unfolded the single sheet of matching duck-egg blue paper, and read:

Why did you have to ruin everything?

How? Ruin what?

She checked the letter and the envelope. It showed no other names and no return address. It was definitely addressed to her, but its contents made no sense.

'Hey, my life's already in ruins.' Although, the whole positive mantra for betterment each day did produce the teeny-tiniest tidbits of improvement.

Deanne grabbed her keys and unlocked her desk's bottom drawer. She then frowned at the contents, licking her lips at the sight of her black label Scotch bottle, Black Johnny. It was kept purely for medicinal purposes, along with a half dozen mismatched shot glasses.

She knew she wasn't an alcoholic, having googled the symptoms, nor a closet drinker. She was just an anti-social, social drinker.

One day she might return to being a sociable person, but not today.

Then she sighed at the open drawer. The bottle didn't bother her, it was the other stuff that choked up the space inside. She watched the blue note drop from her fingers to land on the pile of Sorry-cards.

The Sorry-cards came from Darren.

They'd started showing up at work a few weeks after the wedding, because all of Darren's other Sorry-gifts were destroyed by the family before it breached the front door of the house—Nan's orders.

It surprised her at the amount of coloured cardboard that almost covered her scotch bottle's label.

She'd blocked the ex's emails and numbers, burned all photos, and dumped all the gifts he'd ever given her. She'd even deleted every reminder on her calendar, her finger was still tender from her keyboard punches. So why did she keep these mementos in the drawer?

Perhaps it was because in the entire history of dating Darren, he never provided her with one romantic card. He never wrote her a love letter. In fact, his limited affectionate materialistic tokens were strictly kept for Valentine's Day or her birthday. Even then it was the usual non-romantic slap-stick humour.

But not like this, where twice a week she'd receive some handwritten *Sorry* pleas, heartfelt notes, even some love poems all from Darren, begging for her forgiveness.

Her shoulders drooped as she slumped back in her chair. Deanne shed no tears. She hadn't cried since she'd divorced Black Johnny and spent a week in bed enduring the world's worst hangover, where she'd consistently wept with her head over a bucket. But it'd been months since the wedding, so why couldn't Darren leave her alone?

And when would the dull pain around her heart and nauseous churn in her stomach go away?

Would she dare trust another male again?

'Hey, sis?' Jimmy paused mid-step at her open office doorway. 'Are you okay?'

'I'm *fiiiine.*' With hindsight, Deanne should've recorded her well-rehearsed speech, to then charge a dollar whenever she hit play. She'd be a billionaire by now.

'I've heard that story before.' Jimmy winked as he approached her desk.

Deanne sat back as her jaw dropped, staring up at Jimmy. Could her brother see through her protective shield and read her mind?

Oh man, get ready for the incoming guest booked for the padded-room-with-a-view.

'How goes the Lowes Construction tender?' Jimmy angled his head at the paperwork strewn across her desk.

'It's there.' Deanne could talk shop, it's what kept her going. And no, her brother wasn't telepathic, he just understood her too damned well. After all, they were siblings that shared oodles in common, and both had experienced broken hearts.

Perhaps Jimmy's curse did exist?

'Is the proposal finished?'

'I've only just received the final building chart for the structural materials list and need to do some more number crunching to include their changes.' A lot depended upon this proposal that would secure the family business's future.

This project was also her baby that had kept her busy. It was part of her avoidance programme against personal thoughts, people, home, and her horrible childhood bedroom.

'Word is,' said Jimmy, dropping into one of the guest chairs, 'Brinestones are our main competitor. If they win, they'll build a warehouse in our area, and you know what that'll mean for the family business…'

It was why she was trying so hard. 'It'd be nice to know what Brinestones are doing to outbid them.' And a crystal ball which worked better than Wi-Fi for unlimited downloads to binge-watch her future and to fast forward past the crappy parts. Then why not chuck in a real genie in a bottle, called Black Johnny, with a real six-pack-stomach and not the beer bottle variety. But a real magic-man who granted wishes to unchain her from her daily soap opera drama, where daydreams don't come true… *Boo hoo.*

Deanne was still waiting for her alien abduction from her dad's backyard. Where Chris, the neighbour who never left, was her space-buddy. Chris even provided the binoculars and popcorn as well as no embarrassing wedding questions. He was also the only one who let her drink and smoke unhindered.

In fact, Chris had even tried to teach her Morse coded messages via tobacco smoke.

Obviously, the smoke signals hadn't arrived at their pre-destined galaxy, but it had made for thought-provoking conversation—or drunken scotch-dribble—on the questions about the universe. Such as—

(Cue drum roll here…)

Was it possible for cigarette smoke to travel at light speed, and would aliens be able to interpret those smoke signals?

She sighed and smiled at another memorable Black Johnny good time.

'I've got some news you'll want to be a part of,' Jimmy said.

'Would that involve kidnapping...' As Deanne refused to say that prick's name. '... A certain male, who I'd chain to a wooden post in the middle of the outback, where I'd keep him near-naked and smeared in peanut butter to be skinned alive by peanut-paste-licking dingos. And...' She twirled the letter opener like an air-pen writing on an invisible board. 'On his waxed spray-tanned chest we'd engrave *I'm a cheater who doesn't deserve to breed and breathe.* Then we'd leave him for the blowflies to lay their flesh-eating maggots for the scavenger birds to pick at his bones.' The mental image made her smile. Quick warn the pity-parade because the final stages of her grieving process were well underway.

Jimmy raised an eyebrow as he plucked the letter opener from her fingers. 'Tempting thought, but no. I wanted to tell you our latest spring shipment has arrived.'

Deanne looked up at her brother. A handsome, sweet man, who deserved eternal happiness. She was totally bias on his nomination for the bestest big brother award, because he was also strong enough to scoop her up from the trenches, or from dew-covered backyard lawns while plastered.

But his worst fault was his annoying voice in the shower that was part of the household week-day-wakening routine. She'd prayed for corrective measures for his tone deafness, or to win funds so he could have private singing lessons or build a second sound-proofed bathroom. Because his singing was torture, and she swore his screeching had recorded new heights on the first day of her Black Johnny break-up recovery tour.

But they were family.

It was a shame they also shared broken hearts as an ancestral trait.

At least Jimmy had managed to get married, even if it lasted less than six-months. Perhaps there may be some truth to Jimmy's curse on marriage after all?

'Hello?' Jimmy waved his big hand in front of Deanne's daydreaming stare. 'Didn't you hear me? I said, they're unpacking the truck and I thought you'd want to check out the new spring collection.'

Deanne blinked at him, then smiled. 'Oh honey, I'm so there.' She slammed shut her desk's bottom drawer. Locked it and slipped the keys into her pocket, as the words *unseen, unheard, un-thought* echoed in her mind.

It was springtime and she was so over her winter woes and all things male, including incurable family curses against marriage.

ELEVEN

Sean walked through the tavern's main doors and headed for his favourite seat. 'Still moonlighting behind the bar, Mickey?' Sean rested his elbow on the countertop and watched his bourbon and coke being poured. The scent of yeasty-ales and cigar smoke lingered, as low music from the TV entertained a few customers seated at the far end of the bar.

'I've got some staff on holidays. Don't worry, I've still got me day job. Here, this came for you.' Mickey placed the drink, envelope, and other items in front of Sean.

'Hey, it's my lighter. Where'd this come from?' Sean picked it up and smiled.

Normally he didn't smile. Smirked, yes. Smiled, no. 'I haven't seen it since…' He smiled again and flipped open the lid. 'Hey, it's been re-gassed with a new flint.'

'The bride returned.'

'Deanne was here. When?' What the hell was going on with his heart rate to suddenly start jumping?

'A few days ago. She gave me my own thank you card, too.' Mickey pointed to the mirrored wall where the card stood with pride. 'Deanne gave me fifty bucks for my kindness.'

Sean opened his card that held two crisp hundred-dollar bills and read aloud, *'Dear Sean, thanks for your kindness and generosity in being a gentleman towards a lady in need. Kindest regards, Deanne.'* Sean smiled wide. Yes, the woman made him smile. 'Better put this on my tab, Mickey, and a tip for yourself.' He held out the cash and re-read her card. *Huh, this never happened.*

'Thanks Sean, might start paying for my own drinks, eh.' Mickey chuckled, sliding the notes into the till.

Deanne's generosity and thought in the repair and return of his lighter surprised him. Her effort meant more than the money. The amount he'd spent on her didn't matter because it had been an absolute pleasure. It was as if they'd enjoyed an impromptu first date without any of the awkwardness. 'How long did Deanne stay?'

'Enough for a drink.'

'Scotch with a beer chaser?' Sean remembered everything about her.

'Yep, she's a sweet kid. Members of the public don't go around thanking people anymore, not like she's done.'

'How'd Deanne look?' Sean couldn't forget the incredible sorrow shown within her emotive eyes, that whenever he saw the sea, he was reminded of her. Weird how a woman he'd met only once still affected him. 'Was she still sad?'

'It's a huge improvement from last time. Although, she admitted it's been tough. Still just as pretty, even in her work uniform.'

'Did Deanne marry the guy?' Sean held his breath waiting for an answer. Did he need to know?

'Nope.' Mickey grinned as Sean exhaled. 'Said he'd runaway to Queensland. She's back at work and sounded bored.'

'So…' Sean slowly traced over her handwriting. 'Is Deanne okay?'

Mickey pointed to the main doors as he spoke. 'When Deanne first walked in here, she looked like she wanted to turn around and run right back out again. I'm proud I got a laugh out of her before she left.'

'I suspect it'll take her a while to get over it.' Best he left it alone.

'Yeah, pity it happened, when she seems a nice kid.'

Sean glanced at his lighter. 'Deanne was really nice.' Those oceanic eyes reminded him of a Caribbean tropical coastline. But their kiss was unforgettable.

'You said Deanne was in a uniform. Did she say where she worked?' Sean sipped his drink and glanced at Mickey, waiting for the right reply.

'Deanne's too nice and honest for someone like you.'

'Hey, I've just given you a hundred-dollar tip and you say that—I'm hurt,' Sean said in a mock insulted tone, pressing his hand against his chest.

'She is, you know. I like Deanne.'

'So do I.' Surprised at his admittance, that had no financial gain. How could this female cause such an uncharacteristic reaction? 'I just want to thank Deanne.'

Why was he bothering? Not when women had always been taxing on Sean's pocket and sanity, and he'd only just freed himself of all those burdens.

Sean inspected his lighter, its solid weight perfectly balanced in his palm. A gift he'd bought himself and assumed it had vanished forever, yet, returned in pristine condition. 'Deanne's gone to all this trouble; it wouldn't hurt to see how she's doing?'

'She told me she's over men, where I'd doubt even you would have any luck in charming your way there, mate.'

Sean stood straighter as his grin grew, liking both challenges. First, get information from the barman. Second, find Deanne. 'Come on, Mickey.'

'I've known you too long, which is why I warned Deanne about you. She's too nice for your kind.'

'People change.' Sean refused to give-up his new challenges, and he'd get what he wanted. He always did. 'Mickey,' he said, sliding a fifty dollar note onto the bar.

Mickey hesitated for a moment, then snatched the cash and shook his head. 'I don't know how you suck me in.'

'Because you care, and we've been friends for a long time.'

'Friends, huh?' Mickey's eyebrow arched, but his eyes shone. 'If that's what you'd call it.'

'Come on, Mickey, what do you remember about Deanne?' Because Sean remembered everything.

'She had a hardware emblem embroidered on her work shirt.'

'Hardware?' Sean screwed up his nose. Sure, they'd drunk a lot and discussed many subjects, all except Deanne's job. He'd never pictured that about her.

'Family hardware, with a common name so it's not a franchise. Might be based in the outer suburbs.'

'Shouldn't be too hard to find. Have you got your vintage phone book handy, let's see if we can jog your memory? You're slipping, old man, when you'd never miss a trick.'

Mickey shook his head, grabbed the phone book from under the counter, and together they went through the yellow pages.

Mickey tapped his finger on an advertisement. 'That's it. It's the same emblem on her uniform.'

'*Harrison's Family Hardware*. Deanne Harrison.' Sean tried to suppress his grin. 'I think my trade-tools are overdue an upgrade.'

'Doubt they'd stock the specific tools for your profession, Sean.'

'Hey, I'm a legitimate business man who employs these annoying females who complain all day long, paying all this crap called company tax, and payroll tax and —'

'Sure, you are. I hope?' Mickey pointed his large finger at the young lad. 'You'd want to be.'

'I've retired from that other stuff.' But Sean missed the adrenalin rush from the old game.

'Deanne's an honest kid who shouldn't get tangled up with the likes of your kind.'

'My kind? I'm just a business man with business cards to prove it. Now fetch me another drink and stop insulting your customers.'

With lighter in hand, Sean thought of the sensitive beautiful woman with sad sea-green eyes. He hadn't stopped thinking about Deanne since they'd met, remembering her smile, her laugh, everything. But most of all their kiss.

Until now, he had no idea where to find her. Would he dare?

And would Deanne be ready?

TWELVE

Through the main warehouse, Deanne walked beside the leading nursery hand, Andrew. He hitched the plant tray higher against his chest. 'I'm glad you let me back, Dee.'

'Only because you're the best horticulturist we've ever had.' Polite conversation and smiling were total rule breakers in her secret-cult, but *woo-hoo*, she was making an effort. Her brother had been right for her to check out the nursery's new spring plant collection. It was like a spring-Christmas, that went for days with each new truck delivery of plants making her smile. *Wow*, had her winter de-numbing programme begun?

'Brinestones offered me the job,' said Andrew.

'I knew it, they poached you… What are they like?'

'Big store with welcoming people. They say nice stuff about this place.' Andrew plucked a dead leaf from one of the potted plants he carried.

'You're still not admitting they poached you?'

'My wife completed the application without my knowledge.'

'Sneaky.'

'She wanted the extra money for the new house that she still lives in, which would make her my soon-to-be-ex-wife, while I live with Mum.'

'Are you carpooling together?' Andrew's mum, Beatrice, ran the in-store café like it was her own home kitchen, which should be re-named *Gossipers Cafe* because Deanne didn't need to prepare staff newsletters, she'd just tell Beatrice.

'Yeah, morning shift. Mum makes brekkie here and the coffee's better. I never should've left.'

'Do you remember your reasons for leaving?' Deanne looked up at the guy who was tall, tanned, and geeky. As kids, they'd made cubby-house castles from cardboard boxes and wooden pallets. They'd invented car park wars and ride-by-duels using irrigation pipe as jousting sticks. They'd dressed-up as plastic-wrapped knights riding shopping carts, that were their mutated stallions created from various pinched materials. It was a great time where their innocent childhood imaginations were allowed to run riot within a well-stocked hardware store.

'I've never worked anywhere else before I went to Brinestones,' said Andrew.

And that was a big fat ditto from Deanne's end too. 'Do you remember what I said?'

'Yeah.' Andrew grinned. 'You'd wished you had the guts to leave here too. But this is family for you.'

'True.' Deanne shrugged. She loved her family. Yet, living and working alongside relatives while going through her own emotional turmoil was trying. 'I do get to exert the perks from the Boss-man.'

Andrew laughed. 'They don't say that about you at Brinestones.'

'Do they know I'm a slack, spoilt, demented daddy's girl?' If only they heard her internal voice chatting utter nonsense.

'You're not, and never have been. But you're always working, Dee, even on weekends.'

'You don't see me when I'm upstairs, streaming my favourite shows.' Why hadn't she thought of this option sooner? When her dad's place was a suburban oddity because they didn't have a television inside the house. The TV lived in the beer shed, permanently on the sports channels for the beer-belching-boys who were destroying the ozone layer.

Nan didn't like TV, she preferred to listen to talkback radio inside the house she ruled, and the boys controlled their beer shed — when Nan didn't do the lock-out. Which cost Deanne a beer carton, per day, as penalty-fines for Dad and Jimmy's denied access. It would've been cheaper getting the locksmith, they employed at the warehouse, to replace the beer shed's locks.

'If you surfed the net, it'd be to search for ideas for the hardware store,' Andrew said, nudging her with his elbow.

Wow, she sounded boring. Sad, but true. Was it another fall-out from the wedding?

But Deanne also had to remember she wasn't the lone wolf for heartache around this place. 'I'm sorry your marriage had um…' She caught Andrew's wince. 'Beatrice mentioned marriage counselling?'

'Trust Mum and her gob.'

'Beatrice means well. And come on, we're duelling buddies, or flunked science geeks. Remember when we shut down the shed from the chemical spill, we thought would make a cool ice-skating rink?'

'That's Jimmy's blunder.' Andrew again chuckled.

'Your brother was building a rocket that spilled everywhere.'

'Ah, yes. Good times.' She wistfully smiled at the memory. Maybe all she needed was this little injection of team spirit. 'Are you going to try marriage counselling?' Yep, tips from a bride who hadn't even survived a single day of marriage. *Whoop-tee-do*.

'I'm considering it.'

'Hey, I'll give the approval for time off and I'll keep this just between us.'

'See that?' Andrew smiled wider, carrying her box of plants. 'You'd never get this sort of treatment from Brinestones' management.'

'Aww.' Hand to her heart, she suppressed the urge to hug the man as they approached the checkouts. 'Thanks Andrew.'

'No sweat, and thanks, Dee.' Andrew nodded with a grin, placing the box on the counter, and returned to the nursery.

Deanne looked at the two girls behind the checkout counter, Tracey and Patricia. 'Hi.'

'I'm... Um—*on break*.' Patricia dashed around her counter area and scampered like a fugitive on the run, heading for the exit.

Her crime was poor friend selection being BFF Roomies with Deanne's runaway cousin, Katrina. If Patricia wasn't a good worker, and if Deanne was a bitchier person, she'd give the girl hell.

Although Deanne couldn't remember if she'd seen Patricia at all these past few months. So why did the girl runaway now?

Had Deanne reinvented herself as the mean ogre scaring away warehouse employees?

Sure, the first month back at work had been torture, with everyone staring at her, while overhearing the many whispers.

You'd think after all those years as the most talked about fat kid at school, she'd be used to those same stares now as the jaded bride.

But as an adult she'd scowled and snapped at a couple of smart-arsed staff members who'd learned their lesson to steer clear from her at all times.

That was until Reg and Jimmy gave her *the chat* for becoming a bitchy boss, allowing her personal matters to interfere within the workplace. Deanne had never been so embarrassed.

Well, a different kind of embarrassment.

Who knew there could be so many kinds of embarrassment—she knew them all.

Still, they'd better not bring up her wedding incident at their annual staff Christmas party or she'd fire them—using the paint gun from aisle nine, filled with kerosene from aisle twelve. Then light them up with the barbecue flame throwers from aisle four, where she'd drag the fold-up chairs from aisle two, and watch 'em burn.

No way!

No wonder Patricia ran as soon as she'd spotted Deanne. *I'm such a bitch in need of anger-management, stat.*

'Want me to put this on the account, Dee?' Tracey ran the scanner gun over the plants' labels.

'Ta. How's things, Tracey?'

'Fine, thanks. How're you holding up?'

Deanne had contemplated tattooing the reply on her forehead to deflect the typical BS pity looks she'd interpreted to say: is she fetching rope from aisle nine, the ladder from aisle ten, to Bungee-jump over the office balcony by the neck and hang like an ornament displaying hand-tool specials over the main warehouse floor.

'I'm fine.' She even smiled because the trained-seal-act was now in session. Hold on, it was the best she'd felt in months.

'Are you okay, Tracey?' Why not ask the same, damned, prying question, that Deanne got asked countless times a day?

Although, she'd heard through the usual channels, being Andrew's mother, Beatrice, that Tracey wanted a career change away from dental drills and whining customers with bad breath as an ex-dental receptionist. Tracey's sea-change to hardware was to help her recover from a relationship split.

She had to remember that other people were hurting too. And right about now, a career change sounded tempting.

'I'm okay. They're pretty flowers.' Tracey pointed at the plants.

'Nan's going to luv them.' Deanne picked up a small pot of African violets. Hoping she'll give Nan something else to hose down instead of the granddaughter.

Even now, whenever Nan turned on a hose Deanne made sure she was well out of firing rang. Which was another reason Deanne stayed at work all the time—to avoid Nan's watering times.

Would she survive living at her childhood home until

the tenant's lease expired on her duplex?

The bigger question was would her family allow her to leave? Was she ready?

At least Nan cooked, did laundry and all the household chores by choice. Deanne also carpooled with her brother and being back home she easily saved money having no social life. There were plenty of advantages for residing at the ancestral dwelling. No wonder her brother hadn't left since his marriage dissolved.

Then a new realisation hit Deanne—all the occupants at her dad's house were either divorced or widowed. Was it Jimmy's curse that had her destined to be single, forcing her to live with her family forever?

'I'm going to borrow a pot for my desk.' Proud she was doing something for herself, while she tried to work out how to find a gypsy who broke curses.

Deanne walked along the large aisles she used to skate through as a kid, carrying her pot of African violets. She gave a polite smile to customers, tradesmen, and staff members.

In the ceramics aisle she stood before an assortment of glazed pots trying to choose one for her desk.

'Well, don't you look even more amazing than last time.'

She turned around as a gasp escaped her. 'Sean?'

Complete with his crooked grin that sent shivers speeding along her spine that slammed to a stop at her nerve endings. Was she suffering some sort of alcoholic hallucinogenic throwback?

Sean flicked his long fringe from his vibrant eyes and her heart ka-thumped. It lumped over like a car trying to start on a flat battery, catching its spark that ignited the blood acceleration through her internal runway of heated veins.

It wasn't good. Her body shouldn't be reacting like this.

'You remembered me.' Sean's grin deepened.

How come she remembered Sean? It'd been months since they'd met, when she could barely recall what happened last week.

'What are you doing here?' Deanne gripped the pot plant to her chest, while her pulse's turbo kicked into a higher gear.

'I could give you some lame excuse about looking for supplies. When, honestly, I came here to see you.' Sean took a step closer to inhale deeply. 'Mickey was right.' His eyes combed over her from head to toe, then back up again. 'Your hair,' he said, reaching for a ringlet, 'it's like silk.' He pulled gently on the curl and watched it spring back into place. 'It's almost like untameable bed-hair. It suits you more than the tamed up-do you wore when we first met.'

She had no idea how to respond to that, because no one had ever said that about her hair. Ever.

Sean shared a grin and placed his hand on the shelf close beside her. 'Do you work here?'

'Ah…' Blank. *Work?* 'Yes.' *Think. Breathe.* 'Um, families it. My, them, Dad—'

'Family business?'

'I just said that. Didn't I?'

'I thought Harrison's Family Hardware was a marketing gimmick.' Sean pointed at the emblem on Deanne's shirt pocket.

'It's not a gimmick, my grandad started this place. And it's not just my family, there are other families that work here too.'

Sean smirked at her, stepping in closer. 'Are you into plant strangulations too?' His finger stroked her hands clutching the pot.

On impact, little electrical sparks spiralled beneath her skin. 'What?' Deanne gripped the plant against her chest that spilled dirt over her shirt.

'Oh no.' She dumped the pot onto the shelf and dusted herself off. Her face burned while she cringed at her stupidity and at the dirt that crumbled down her cleavage.

Sean leaned his shoulder against the shelf, watching her every move. 'Thank you for the card and returning my lighter.'

Why was it so hot in here? 'You were kind enough to help me out and I'm sorry my friend stole your lighter.' She brushed off the soil. Checked inside her shirt, the shelf, the plant, looking anywhere and everywhere but at Sean.

'Which friend?'

'Clare.' Her friend would laugh at Deanne's awkwardness. And with that thought it gave her some much-needed backbone.

* * *

'Here, you missed a spot.' Sean's fingertips swept dirt from the side of her delicate throat, admiring the details in Deanne's smattering of freckles across her nose. Along with the green flecks amongst the blue in her sea-changing eyes, through to her dainty chin and plump, flushed cheeks.

He'd imagined Deanne had been under some bridal beautician's enchantment when they'd first met. But seeing her now, Deanne's natural beauty was far more appealing than having it hidden by layers of makeup.

'Can I help you?' Deanne's voice shook.

'Yes.' Sean explored her laugh lines, and her full luscious lips void of any lipstick. 'I need to check something.' With gentle fingertips, he clasped her delicate chin. His head dipped and he pressed his lips against her soft, warm lips, and tasted her sweet, hot, moist mouth. His tongue swirled, lapped, lunged, as his hands slid around her, bringing her closer.

Adrift in her taste and in her perfumed floral scent, he felt her silky hair brush his skin. Her supple frame yielding and warm, while his heart pounded a base beat beside her heart's rhythmic tempo, and his once-numbed internal desires had awakened.

But Sean resisted, pulling back to gaze at her. 'Mm… Better than I remember.' *Hell yeah.* Why had it taken him so long to find out?

Because he didn't know where to find Deanne until she'd returned to Mickey's bar in her work uniform. Good girl. His girl?

Whoa tiger. He expected a face slap for what he'd just done.

But he couldn't walk away, not even to step back free from swinging distance. Instead, Sean's fingertips feathered across the edges of her beautiful face and brushed a rich red, silk ringlet that coiled around his index finger like a python in a tree. 'I prefer your hair this way.'

Stopping himself from the temptation to rub his face in those curls and inhale the aroma.

He scrutinised her sweeping conflicted emotions, the display of shock with a flash of stormy sea green versus a cool Caribbean blue in her eyes. He wanted to lock onto her sensual red lips again, but instead he waited and watched.

Deanne panted, somewhat breathless. She brushed his hand away from her hair and stepped backwards, until her back pressed against the shelf. 'We've met once. Months ago. You… Just… Kissed me. In the warehouse. At work. Here. *Why*?'

'Because I wanted to.' Sean grabbed her hand to delicately toy with her fingers. 'Please have dinner with me?'

She slow blinked. Then blinked again. 'What?'

'Dinner. I'll buy you another steak. I don't know this side of town, so where do you recommend?'

'What? Why?' Deanne pulled her hand away.

'Because I want to.' Sean leaned against the shelf, watching her blush deepen.

She stood straighter, jutting out her dainty chin as the frown darkened her fiery eyes. 'You have the expressions of a cat eyeing its prey, until you pounce and leave the carnage behind. Well, I'm not some toy. How dare you kiss me in less than five minutes of meeting me—again. Do you think you can just do whatever you want?'

'Yes. So don't fight it, sweetheart.' Again, he grabbed her hand, and pulled out some cash from his pocket 'You can have this back. You gave me too much money in the thank you card you gave me. We can make dinner your shout, if you want?' Yet, before he could give her the money, again she pulled her hand away from his.

'No, that's for you. It's compensation with interest for taking care of me. Mickey warned me about you, he said you'd considered all females an expensive accessory, so keep it.'

Sure, women were expensive to keep, but this was new, and he liked it. 'Take it back.'

'No.'

'Fine.' Sean rolled his eyeballs towards the ceiling and Deanne followed his line of sight. Then in a flash, he dropped the cash inside her collared shirt.

Whoops, had he gone too far?

Why was he doing this to her? It certainly wasn't giving Deanne any reason to like him at all when he was acting like such a tool.

With palms up he stepped away from her. 'I'm so sorry I did that.'

Her hands slapped her top shut and she scowled at him. 'You should be. I'm not some hooker! You can't pay me.' She yanked out the money and shoved it into his top pocket. Glaring at him she snatched up her pot plant. 'And don't touch me again.' She turned on her heel and headed down the corridor.

'Why not let me make up for it and have dinner with me. Please.' Sean enjoyed the challenge. The way her eyes burned like emerald fire, her skin glowed and hair shone, then there was the whole curvaceous figure of a goddess. But how her hips swayed with each step in those heels, wearing that simple navy skirt, made him hungry. 'Please, I'll behave.' Even if the view was so worth his careful observations, he didn't like Deanne walking away from him and started to follow.

'No. I've sworn off men, marriage, and dinner dates, forever. Now go away.'

Sean did as he was told and stopped to watch Deanne stride fast across the warehouse, run up the stairs then through the windowed corridor leading towards the management offices. She'd ran away from him.

Damn, that wasn't part of the plan.

He had a lot to make up for and wasn't about to give up.

* * *

Through the windowed corridor that led towards her office, Deanne glared down at Sean standing in the warehouse, wearing an amused expression. Stuff his sexy smirk that wanted to make her toes curl.

The heat rushed through her, disgusted at Sean, and at her own body's two-faced reactions that she slammed her office door shut behind her.

She plonked the pot plant onto her desk and took deep breaths to recover. She then snatched a clean tissue from the box, dabbed it in her glass of water and began cleaning the spilled dirt off herself.

Even though she was annoyed at Sean with his arrogant ambush and request for dinner, she knew she wasn't ready and wanted nothing resembling a rebound relationship like her brother had experienced.

Jimmy believed in one true love per person and

proclaimed all other relationships were nothing more than a cure for anti-loneliness. Her dad and Nan had never re-married, which only added fuel to Jimmy's belief in his curse.

Yet, Sean's kiss with his feather light touch of his warm lips against hers, the strength of his embrace, and the electrical sparks when her skin brushed against his, made her whole-body sigh at the memory.

But he'd kissed me! In the smack centre of a staff-filled hardware store, he'd kissed her. *Oh, no?* She hoped no one saw it, and face-palmed herself feeling the heated flush fan out from her cheeks.

Her office telephone rang. Deanne straightened up her work shirt, took a deep breath, and lifted the handset. 'Deanne Harrison speaking.'

'You have such a beautiful phone manner, sweetheart.'

'Sean?' Deanne frowned at his taunting tone, but her heart betrayed her by starting to pitter-patter. She slammed into her seat, suddenly suffering from weak knees.

'Please let me make up for my rude behaviour before and join me for dinner?'

'No.'

'Come on, you'll enjoy yourself. Or come back downstairs and I'll shout you a coffee.'

'No, I'm busy.'

'The lady who made my coffee says you're always busy and that you have no life. She doesn't mind a chat, does she?'

Deanne could just picture the biscuit-baking-Beatrice chatting with anyone while making coffee. Which reminded Deanne to ask her father and her brother on their thoughts of her getting a sign that said *Gossipers Café*?

'I do have a life.' *Not much of one.* 'I'm busy.' The tender for the new shopping centre had kept her focusing on anything but her dismal private life.

'Are you a locked away princess in your off-white tower? Or are you free to join me for a coffee?'

'I am not a princess trapped in a tower,' she snapped back at him, shocking herself for her rude behaviour. She'd never behave like this to anyone.

'The word is that you don't have fun anymore?'

'What do you care,' she growled. She had no emotional control when it came to Sean. What had she become?

'Believe me, I wouldn't have bothered driving to never-land to visit you if I didn't care. And I wanted to see if our first kiss was as good as I remembered. It made your hair curl, didn't it?' Sean laughed as her frown deepened. 'It's not all about you. I needed certain hard-to-find-tools they don't make anymore that you happen to have in stock. It's also Friday night where I'm told you don't normally work on weekends, but do now because—'

'Stop prying into my life, Sean.' Now embarrassed at how much Sean knew about her lacklustre lifestyle. It was almost a creepy stalker-ish behaviour.

Yet, compared to Darren's entire dating process, which had been old fashioned courting and snail paced slow, Sean was too fast. And with her level of inexperience, Deanne was unsure if to be frightened or flattered?

'I'll sic my big brother onto you,' she blurted out. *Way to go with the twelve-year-old trash-talk.* But it was all Sean's fault.

'Your brother is too busy chatting-up the ladies at the tradesman's' counter.'

At her window, she barely split open one of the horizontal slats of her venetian blind, to peer at the main warehouse entrance. 'Nope, not my brother, that's Brian from painting.' Would Jimmy mind performing big brother duties against Sean, considering Jimmy still had the desire to use Darren's face as a punching bag.

'Can you see me from your off-white tower, Princess?'

'It's an office, not a tower, and I'm not a princess locked away by a fire-puffing dragon.' Oh, great, was she suffering side-effects from moving back into her childhood bedroom?

'There's plenty of fire in your eyes. Hey, isn't that a line from some song?'

'Stop. I can't see the café from here. No, I will not have dinner with you. So no, no, no, no, no, no, no, and no.' She poked her tongue at the handset, only to cringe at her childish behaviour.

Sean's laugh only made her scowl more. Does this man not take a hint?

'Do you want me to come upstairs?'

'No. You're unbelievable.'

'Want to find out how unbelievable I am?'

'Do you want me to call security?'

Sean laughed louder.

'You're such an irritating—*ugh.*' Deanne's inner fight dissipated, realising her ridiculous behaviour was only amusing Sean more.

Yet, her reactions and actions were unpredictable and spontaneous, when she'd never been like this. Except when they'd first met and had dinner. Sean was an obvious fool to want to endure dinner again. Especially, when she'd been an emotional mess, gorging on her first decent meal in months.

'That bridal gown didn't do you justice, and before you complain, you did not look like a puffy marshmallow. Its fault was that it hid your curves, and sweetheart, you've got some lush curves and a great set of legs.'

She glanced at her hips and ballooning thighs. At school she swish-swashed from the noise of rubbing polyester trousers that echoed through the corridors. Which gave fodder-fuel for the bullies' chorusing *here comes thunder and her tree trunk thighs*. Deanne hated her hips, thighs, and curves. She'd missed out on her parents' genetic beanpole frames that her brother received. Instead, she inherited Nan's lineage. Thankfully, she was taller than Nan, otherwise Deanne imagined she'd be a human beach ball.

'I'll pick you up at what time?'

'No. Please go and pursue someone else.' Deanne slammed down the phone, fell back into her seat and crossed arms over her chest in a huff. She was no longer the dummy bowing before a man because she couldn't say no. Never again would she agree to run their endless errands.

Admittedly, she'd been doormat-Dee for Darren. But this little red hen swore never to do that again because she was over men forever.

Yet again, her office phone rang, and Deanne snatched up the receiver. '*Leave me alone.*'

'*No. I will not,*' Clare shouted back.

'Sorry, Clare, I thought you were someone else.' Deanne rolled her shoulders, stretching her neck from side to side, surprised how worked-up she was.

'Are we talking about dumbass Darren? Is he still sucking-up and sending you those Sorry-cards? Don't you dare cave in girl, you memorise those feelings and what he'd done to you.'

'No, not *him*.' A shiver of hate passed over Deanne's spine, refusing to speak that man's name again.

'Who then?'

'Sean.' Deanne sighed, shaking her head over the whole incident, she sunk deeper into her seat.

'Who's Sean? Because girl, you sound gooey.'

'Do not.' Deanne straightened herself in her seat. 'Sean was the guy I had drinks with after I bolted from the wedding. Remember, you girls found me with him, in that bar.'

'Oooh, that Sean.' Clare almost purred. 'Sean's sexy.'

'He's pushy, sleazy, and creepy-stalkerish.'

'Why? What did he do?'

'Not even after a minute of conversation, Sean kisses me. But now he won't leave until I agree to go out with him.'

Clare laughed. 'I remember when Sean kissed you. You were left speechless in the car.'

'Not speechless. Drunk.'

'We all saw your reaction.'

'Intoxicated means being unable to make proper responses.' Pity she didn't suffer from drunken-amnesia, then she wouldn't have remembered the way to Mickey's bar.

'Lou said you'd use that as your excuse. Jane and I think Sean swept you off your feet because we'd found you laughing and having a great time, when we were expecting a suicidal bride. Instead, you were your old carefree self, the true version of you before you started dating Darren. Considering what happened that day you'd met Sean, he must've done something right to make you laugh. I hope you said yes to dinner?'

'No. I'm not ready yet.'

'Bull. Jump back on I say.'

'You would.'

'I'm not ashamed of what I like, which we know is art, men, and sex. And you shouldn't be ashamed of yourself for who you are and what you've survived. You're stronger for it. Oh boy, now I'm mimicking Lou.' Clare giggled.

'Lou would be so proud to hear that.' Deanne could just picture the body-builder-of-beauty posturing over that comment.

'So how was Sean's kiss?' Clare asked.

Deanne sighed as she leaned back and rocked her chair. Her feet swung beneath, while fingertips grazed against her tender lips.

'Dee, you there?'

'I'm here… It was better than the first time.' Deanne didn't lie to her friends. But she'd never been kissed like that or experienced these new unnamed feel-good emotions. 'You've heard the cliché of time standing still?' She gnawed on her lower lip, surprised she'd said it. But when Sean kissed her, her mind did go blank where she'd willingly drowned within that moment. It was as if nothing else mattered except his lips against hers, and his muscular arms wrapped around her body warming her. His power was strong, sensual. Safe even.

Deanne shook her head. 'Forget I said anything, because he then shoved money down my shirt and called me a princess locked in her tower, and dragons were mentioned. Who talks like that?' Had she challenged Sean's ego with her newly learned ability to say *no* to the man? Wow, she'd said *no* to a man. *Wahoo,* look how far she'd come.

'Are you kidding me? You would have to be the queen of geeky conversations, especially when you and Chris talked for hours about alien abductions,' said Clare. 'Not to mention, questioning the properties of light speed while inventing UFO smoke signals from a cigarette. And do not get me started on your boyfriend-in-a-bottle.'

'Ah, yes, Black Johnny. Good times.' Deanne grinned. How could she not.

'So, hey, if the guy's talking dragons and fairy-tale princesses and not afraid to say it, you should go out with him.'

'No. I won't be going out with Sean or any other man.' Her nostrils flared and jaw tightened, and she so wanted off this soapbox derby's landslide of emotions. What happened to slow and steady, where each day was the same? To live life under the constant repeat of routine, which did not include the art of swapping spit with strangers whilst at work.

'What did you ring for, Clare?'

'Drinks tonight, remember?'

'What drinks?' Deanne glanced at her vacant desktop

calendar that would never evoke any Darren-days again, because she'd deleted everything.

'At Jane's shop. She's got that author's book thingy and we promised we'd help do the food and counter sales. We're still trying to talk her into having a baby shower. But get this? We're the backup team for the birth because Jane is scared Petey's going to faint in the birthing suite.'

'Petey won't faint, he's a horror movie junkie.' Was Deanne ready for a girl's night out?

But then again, a night with the Greatest-Girls-of-the-Galaxy might be just what she needed.

'Jane's organised Petey to be our chauffeur, and champagne's being provided as our fan fees. Did you read his book?'

'I have no idea who the author is.' It wasn't on Deanne's survive-the-day list. 'What time?'

'Six o'clock. Petey's collecting me first to help drag you out.'

She pictured the tattooed, bearded, burly plumber relishing the chance to play caveman and toss her over his shoulder to carry her to the car. Her brother, Jimmy, being Petey's BFF, would no doubt follow while taking photos. 'I'll be ready.' Not.

Deanne spied another one of those duck-egg blue envelopes amongst her paper cluttered in-tray.

Not another anonymous hate-note to add to her downward spiralling mood?

With her engraved letter opener, she slit the envelope open, removed the matching coloured paper and with phone cradled on her shoulder to her ear, she read:

Simple. Straight to the point.

The point being?

'Aaand honey?'

'Yes.' The purr in Clare's voice made Deanne's ears prick to attention. Or was this a reaction to the depressing duck-egg blue's minimalistic message?

Deanne unlocked her desk's bottom drawer and threw the letter onto the breeding pile of pleading Sorry-cards.

Nope, men sucked. Affairs of the heart sucked. And right now, she craved to stay in her unsentimental one woman show. It was safer that way.

'You should take Sean's offer for dinner,' said Clare. 'If he makes you breathless from one kiss, imagine what more he could do for you?'

'Goodbye, Clare.' Deanne rolled her eyes and hung up the phone in a huff. She then slammed her bottom drawer shut to hide her Sorry-cards that reminded her of how much Darren had hurt her.

He'd betrayed her trust.

He'd used her.

But the main reason she hated Darren the most, was because he'd made her hate herself.

THIRTEEN

Using the back of her gardening glove, Deanne wiped the stray hair strands from around her face. Pleased in what she'd created in her elbow bending mission of the day, planting an assortment of flowers beneath the shaded jacaranda tree and silent swing.

The result had turned this once hollow corner of misery, into a vibrant colourful display with rich floral fragrances from her spring plant selection. With the sun on her back and the fresh air lifting her spirits, she knew she was definitely on the road to recovery. Who knew playing with dirt could be so rehabilitating?

The side gate opened and Reg, balancing a beer carton over his shoulder, strolled down the path. 'Hello, luv. We're having a barbie tonight. Remember?'

'Dinner is already prepped and waiting your cooking delegations. How was non-golf?'

'I won another boyfriend-in-a-bottle in the raffle today.'

'Where is he, Dad?'

'In the car. He's a bad boy who'll only lead you astray, and I don't think you're ready to rekindle that kind of commitment, kid.'

'Yeah, the separation's been hard for Black Johnny.'

She shared an exaggerated sigh. 'You're right, Dad, it might be best if that bottle stayed in your care.'

'We'll stash it at work, that way we can both keep away from Nan's eagle eyes.' He gave her a wink.

'Good point.'

'You've done a great job there, luv.' Reg pushed up his glasses to inspect the transformed corner of pink, purple, and yellow mass. 'So, during your tree-swinging-honeymoon, you were actually designing the beer shed's garden view?'

'Call it forward planning.' They both grinned at her BS. 'Give it time to settle, then it'll be fantastic. I hope Nan remembers to water the plants and not just humans. Which reminds me, Dad, why haven't we installed an automatic irrigation system when we sell the stuff?'

'Your Nan enjoys playing with the hose. She says it's her exercise routine to do the stairs every time she shifts the sprinkler around the lawn. Trust me, your brother tried, and he copped the full spray in the face, the same as you, luv.'

'Did Nan ever get you with the hose?'

Reg chuckled. 'A couple of times.'

'It's a strange custom being hosed down by the family's matriarch.'

'At least it's family, and it's so… *us.*' Reg's laughter followed him as he headed for his homemade bar and loaded up the beer fridge. 'Your brother's bringing a new mate over for dinner.'

'Remember Chris, Petey, Jane and her rockmelon tummy are coming.' Lou's nickname for Jane's baby bump had now graduated to fruits. It was no longer being compared to nuts and seeds, but never vegetables—ever.

'Chris, huh. That's different for the neighbour to visit. Are you two going to talk alien constellations again?'

'Why not.' Why did she mention Chris when he practically lived here? 'We might use beer bubbles to try and create an ET dialect.'

'No need when we can do that later in what we humans call beer-bubbling-bull. Just don't tempt your brother because he can burp-count to twenty these days.'

Deanne winced at her brother's escapades; it was like she'd never left. Was she ready to move out?

Her father never believed in paying other people's mortgages when it came to renting. Maybe she should get another property?

Her head tilted, with the garden trowel hovering in the air. Had she recovered enough in her grief process to move forward?

'Hey, Dee. Nice job,' called out Jimmy as he sauntered down the concrete path beside Chris, both carrying a beer carton in their arms. 'Nan will appreciate it. Which reminds me to get her a new hose.'

'It's *so* pretty,' said Chris.

Jimmy raised an eyebrow towards his offsider. 'I worry about you sometimes, Chris.'

'I'm just admiring Dee's work. What's your deal?'

'My deal… Firstly, I'm not having a thirsty argument by letting this beer get hot.' Jimmy walked into the beer shed with Chris following.

'Some things never change.' Deanne blew at a bothersome springy hair-lock and started to pack her gardening tools away.

'Now that's a view that'd stop traffic.'

Deanne whirled around and frowned. 'Sean?' Her heart ka-thumped, she struggled to swallow the lump in her throat. 'Why are you here?'

'Well, you won't answer my phone calls. You don't return my messages. You won't even say thanks for the flowers I'd sent you. Nice legs by the way, the view's got my heart hip-hopping.'

She felt naked the way his dark eyes combed over her body, making her flush with embarrassment.

Great. Here was Mr Tall-dark-and-not-so-terrific when she looked like she'd rolled in the mud.

She stood to brush away the dirt from her legs, avoiding eye contact. 'What are you doing here?'

'You really are gorgeous and down-to-earth. Literally.' He lifted the oversized shirt back onto her shoulder, to tenderly brush away the dirt softly from her jaw.

She clenched her tongue between her teeth to contain the shiver that spread from his touch.

'Well, if you won't let me take you out for dinner, I'm coming to you.' He stood so close she could smell his divine spicy cologne.

'H-how are you even here?'

'Jimmy asked me over for a barbecue. He seems all right, and that's saying something because normally I don't like people. But I like you.'

Deanne gasped. Sean did not just say that.

'So, are you going to sic your big brother onto me for being so rude to you last time?'

She pursed her lips, peeking into the shed where her brother was standing with her father. 'Maybe I should.'

He bowed his head slightly. 'Again, I'm sorry.'

Not another guy saying *sorry* to her.

Although technically her ex never said sorry, they were in the forms of cards and notes mostly written by florists or Hallmark. In all the time they'd dated Darren never said sorry once. Yet, here was a man she'd technically just met stepping up and apologising openly.

'Did you get the flowers I sent?' Sean asked. 'They were supposed to be the romantic dozen red roses.'

'Thank you. The flowers were nice.' She had no need to be an outright bitch, yet Sean brought out the worst in her.

Even if he was a sinful smart-arse in a perfectly proportioned package, exuding his own brand of sex appeal. Sean could have any female he wanted. So why her?

'Thanks. I've, um, never received a full dozen roses before.' Chewing her bottom lip, she swore Sean beamed at her like a lion in charge of his pride. *What the hell?*

Sure, the roses from Sean were beautiful, but they'd arrived at the same time as another one of Darren's mood-killing Sorry-cards that got added to the pile.

What happened to her dull boring daily shuffle of life?

'I like flowers.' She exhaled heavily, while her tongue struggled to fight against the thick cottonwool filling her mouth. With hands clasped behind her back, she stubbed her sneaker's toe in the dirt, knowing her cheeks were glowing.

How come her body only seemed to overreact when in Sean's presence?

'I can tell.' Sean nodded at to the patch of petunias,

daisies, and other floral varieties that brightened her once dull corner of pain.

Deanne peeked at Sean in his jeans, casual shirt. Then he did that hair flick exposing those intense black eyes that gave her his full attention, and that sizzling sinful smile — it sucked. Why didn't Sean go play elsewhere, and not be here looking far too handsome for this backyard. 'How did you get here?'

'I drove in my car, came in through the front door, where I'd received the warmest greeting from your Nan. So unlike the granddaughter's welcoming.'

'You know what I mean.'

'Sweetheart, what you try to say, yet project, can be interpreted in various ways.'

'Huh?' Was she naked? Or did Sean have x-ray vision?

She wrapped her shirt around herself tighter, wishing she'd worn jeans to hide her legs. What gave Sean the power to magnify her self-consciousness while dulling her brain?

'Dee,' called out Jimmy, strolling towards them, 'have you met Sean?' He handed a beer to Sean. 'Want a beer, Dee?'

'I'll get my own, thanks.' How the hell did Sean get here? And why was she feeling like hunted prey, stalked by a male predator in her family's backyard — *not cool.*

Ripping off her gardening gloves, she headed for the shed where her father held a beer out. 'Thanks, Dad.' Should she ask her dad to evict Sean?

'Sean's staying for dinner. He reckons you both met in the warehouse last week?' Jimmy said, following Deanne.

'Yes, we did.' She raised the stubby to her lips and

chugged back her beer.

'Slow down, luv,' said Reg, raising his eyebrows at her, 'there's plenty there.'

'Must be thirsty from gardening,' said Chris, seated on the stool, with his elbows resting on the bar. 'Don't you play with plants at work?'

'Dee would work full time in the nursery if we let her,' said Jimmy.

'You'd get bored out there, luv.' Reg pushed his glasses higher along the ridge of his nose. 'And we both know it.'

'And because I couldn't handle Latin, chemistry, or complex mathematical equations for water volume ratios...' Deanne was well aware of her strengths and weaknesses.

'Dee's got some of the brains, where I've got the brawn and all the good looks.' Jimmy flexed his arm muscles.

Deanne giggled at Jimmy's pathetic performance of a bodybuilder's pose, considering her best friend, Lou, was a master at the sport, with her own gym. 'My brother's brainlessness has been publicly declared, peoples. Do not forget this moment.'

'Why bother with paper shuffling when we have you, sis.'

'Because you're a shed-dwelling, beer-guzzling, hands-on kind of guy.'

'But the women love me for it,' said Jimmy with a cheesy grin.

'You wish.' Deanne screwed up her face and shuddered.

Reg chuckled from behind the bar and said to Sean, 'You'd think they'd grow out of their sibling rivalry by now.'

'What do you do at the store, Deanne?' Sean asked.

'Dee's job description is HR, plus dealing with all the management stuff that no one wants to know about,' said Jimmy, with a wide smile. 'When we all know she just sits in her office and surfs the net, painting her nails.'

Deanne held up her dirty, nail-polish-free fingers. 'Gee thanks, just call me Girl Friday.'

'Nah, Dee does the technical managerial stuff.' Jimmy's large hand forced down her straw hat and mussed it up as if her head was an orange juicer. 'Dee's focusing on the construction works in the new suburb.'

'What's happening there?' Sean asked.

'Just over yonder in the new suburbs,' replied Reg, aiming the remote control at the television mounted in the corner for the footy channel, 'they're building a new shopping centre where Dee's tendering for the supplier's contract.'

'I'm trying.' Deanne readjusted her hat and stared down at her drink. It was a much bigger job than she'd thought. If awarded, the benefits would be huge for the family business.

'Are you confident in winning, Deanne?'

Deanne peeked up at Sean from beneath her hat's brim and shrugged. This was the biggest and most complex tender she'd ever done. The number crunching was a brain-strain, she'd put everything into it because work had been her safe distraction from her misery. Although, she'd assumed hiding in her father's backyard was safe too — except Sean was here.

Yet the way Sean showed genuine concern made her

plonk onto the bar stool. Her body just melted as if she was a bar of chocolate left on a car dash-mat under an Aussie summer sun. All that hard-learned resistance against him leeched right out her.

'Dee's gotten most of the supplier contracts for smaller jobs,' said Reg. 'But it's our first main industrial job we've decided to go for. We're hoping, if we win, it'll slow down any corporate competition supplying to this area. But it's a tricky task because we don't have the buying power that those franchises have with their suppliers. We couldn't compete.'

'I bet Dee would love a copy of the opposition's tender proposal to give us a head start,' said Jimmy.

'Wouldn't we all want to see what they're putting forward,' Reg said, pushing his glasses up his nose.

'That'd be cheating.' Chris scowled from his barstool.

'Who asked the neighbouring bean-counterer?' Jimmy grinned as his hazel eyes sparkled.

'I'm the voice of reason, shed-dweller,' said Chris with his nose in the air. 'People pay me for sound accounting advice, you know.'

'Settle, petals.' Deanne waved her hand like an umpire between her brother and Chris to keep the peace, because the boys had the habit of arguing like brothers.

'I'm off for a shower.' She needed to get away from Sean. Feeling his dark eyes scrutinise her every move, she had to focus to not trip up the stairs. Why was Sean here?

But it wasn't her place to say no to certain visitors because Sean was Jimmy's guest. Was she ready to move out and move on with her life?

What life?

FOURTEEN

'I'm heading off.' Sean stood from the outdoor wooden table that faced the corner jacaranda tree shading Deanne's new floral garden bed. 'Thanks for dinner, it was great.' He shook hands with Deanne's father Reg, her brother Jimmy, and their neighbour Chris.

'Haven't had too much to drink 'n drive there, Sean?' Reg asked, cradling a schooner glass in his lap.

'Wouldn't risk it.'

'No worries. Come again, anytime.' Reg held his beer up in salute.

'Might take you up on that offer.' Sean grinned wider, flicking the fringe from his eyes.

Jimmy crossed his legs at the ankles. 'For future reference, the beer shed rules are BYO beer or leave your money on the fridge. Better yet, you can just deliver the beer we like and leave.'

'Don't mind Jimmy. Dee will walk you out.' Reg shook his head as he watched Sean walk up the path. 'I reckon that Sean's got a thing for your sister?'

'Wouldn't be the first bloke.' Jimmy said.

Their voices following Sean as he leaped up the stairs. He gave a polite wave at the last of the party crew, stepped inside to find Deanne wiping down the kitchen benches.

'Aw, aren't you the ultimate goddess of domesticity.' It was like a flash of some future he'd never imagined for himself—one of a home.

'Are you leaving?' Deanne turned away to pull out the plug in the sink.

'Your dad said you were to walk me out. Why? Don't you want me to go?'

Deanne dried her hands on the tea-towel keeping her back to him. 'Thought you'd settled in for the night. Most of Dad's and Jimmy's guests do.'

'You can ask me to stay, and I will.' Sean stepped closer.

She frowned, ready to make her escape with the same side-stepping routine she'd played all night.

'Well, you can walk me to my car to make sure I've left.' He grabbed her hand and led her through the house.

'Just to the front door so I can slam it. Lock it. And chuck away the key.'

'Can't banish me that easily.' Although, he probably deserved it.

'Why are you so persistent when I keep saying no to you?'

Sean walked Deanne out the front door and down the path towards the street. All while maintaining a firm grip on Deanne's hand as she tried to shake him loose.

Sean stopped on the darkened sidewalk beside his car and turned towards Deanne. 'This is why, sweetheart.' Pulling her close, his hands cupped her face and his lips collided with hers. She struggled to pull back, but he endured until she surrendered, and her supple lips parted.

Sean again found the purest of pleasure from her hot

mouth with its sweet richness of chocolate and wine that was intoxicating to him.

Her curls were like silky water slipping between his fingers, and Sean became the exultant diver, free-falling inside a tidal surge of sensations that swamped him.

He felt the fight flee from Deanne, as her arms slid around his shoulders. His skin tingled against her touch, sending sizzles of electricity that added power to his pulse, feeling her heart quicken against his own heart's erratic beats.

It was raw, yet sensual.

He was strong; she was fragile.

Her body trembled and he embraced her closer, chest to chest. The passion pressed against clothes as their kiss deepened.

Then with a wince, Sean stopped as his hands cradled her face, not wanting to leave the touch of her soft warm skin.

'That's why.' He swallowed hard. Aware his self-control was diminishing against the intense hunger for her soft body. Her subtle fragrance was so fresh and sweet.

Yet, he found himself fighting against his own resistance as he embraced her. He wanted the feel of her skin against his. To be with her. To make love to her.

He flinched with a hasty inhale that was accompanied by a miscued heartbeat, all from these unfamiliar thought patterns.

Sean had never made love to a woman.

Yet, he'd never experienced such passionate desire for any other woman. Except with Deanne. And only Deanne.

But he'd gone too far last time, even now he'd again

breached her boundaries, and didn't dare make that same mistake twice.

If he had, would she forgive him?

Was this union worth all this hassle?

What about the personal risk for both parties?

Sean's forehead rested against hers and feathered kisses over her slightly swollen lips. Resisting the temptation to drown in her completely, he stepped back from her body heat. The cool air bit at his skin as his body screamed out to hold her, to keep her warm and safe from the night.

He needed her.

But did they both need this?

'Goodnight, Deanne.' Then Sean let her go.

He had to.

And as much as he wanted to, he didn't look back.

* * *

Speechless and light-headed, Deanne swayed slightly on the sidewalk watching Sean's car drive away.

Only then did she remember to breathe.

Her brain had slowed, yet her heart hammered like it'd been through a marathon. Blood propelled through her veins and stimulated a healing all-over warmth, while her toes scrunched inside her shoes, as her scalp tingled.

She had this sudden urge to do some sort of swoon and collapse on the world's floor. She'd never understood the swoon's true meaning until now.

Unless it was a gooey, warm, caramel sauce, combined with a decadent indulgence of a sensual, swirling, chocolate bath that allowed for a full body immersion—*oh, yeah*. Now that was her personal interpretation of the poignant swoon, and she liked it.

Deanne watched Sean's car disappear around the corner as her cheeks lifted and the walls around her soul softened with her smile. There was no one to witness this miracle and she didn't care because this was her moment.

Light-headed, she didn't want to think, but to defrost and just feel. This new tingling sensation beneath her skin, it was almost electric, along with a giddy, soft, stomach spin of warm desire. It was as if her whole body floated like a passenger in a hot air balloon, miles away from all obstacles, drifting beyond the emotional stormy clouds of her past.

Deanne opened the front door and gazed back to the darkened road where the shadows were softened by the street lights. Above, thousands of stars twinkled in silence as she whispered, 'Do I deserve to be happy? Do I deserve to be loved?'

It was a question she left in the air.

But she knew she was well on that road to recovery, because she hadn't felt this fantastic since…

And let the door whisper shut behind her.

FIFTEEN

Hunched over her desk, Deanne inspected her proposal sprawled out in front of her. When there was a tap on her open office door. It broke her focus.

'These arrived for you.' It was Jimmy, carrying a large bunch of colourful spring flowers.

'They're beautiful.' She smiled so wide her cheeks tingled.

Jimmy placed the fragrant bouquet on her desk and handed Deanne the sealed envelope. 'It's good to see you smiling again. So, who are they from?'

Deanne opened the envelope, with a giddy churn to her stomach. Why was she having such an emotional response to the flowers? Were they from Sean?

She hadn't spoken to him since Saturday night, but, dammit, just the thought of him made her glow.

But as she read the card her smile disappeared. 'That arsehole.'

She dropped the card as if burned by acid, to pick up the flowers, and dumped them into the hallway bin.

Jimmy reached across her desk and read the small, coloured card:

'Dee, I miss you.

*Today, would have been the third
anniversary of our very first date. Again, I'm
sorry, please forgive me?
With all my love,
Darren.'*

'Mine, thank you.' She snatched the card from Jimmy, unlocked her bottom drawer and flung it on top of the continuous growing pile of Sorry-cards.

Displayed on top of the cardboard pile was her morning delivery of another anonymous duck-egg blue letter that read:

'You don't deserve someone new when you've hurt the ones who've loved you. You have no heart, and destroyed my life. I should be destroying yours.'

Deanne frowned at the duck-egg blue letter's pathetic poor attempt at prose. Was Darren playing a game of Jekyll and Hyde?

She eyed the word-processed blue letter amongst the other correspondence. Darren's Sorry-cards were all different styles of handwriting, probably written by the florists.

However, all the letters were on a duck-egg blue, luxuriously thick paper. The messages were typed in the same font, with a simple and direct text. They were hateful blame letters obviously designed to be cruel. But she didn't get it?

Was this cousin Katrina's doing, considering she was the female felon in the deceitful duo?

Deanne had never asked about Katrina.

Did she need to know?

Deanne reached for her medicinal scotch, a reflex action at the mere thought of the sordid love triangle. It was a self-proclaimed Black Johnny moment, and her boyfriend-in-a-bottle was in da-house.

It was like pulling out Excalibur, as the black label bottle was freed from the confines of the coloured cardboard that spilled like large confetti pieces within the deep drawer.

Why was she keeping all of those Sorry-cards?

Deanne dug deep under the cards for the glasses, hearing Nan's natter against drinking alone and poured a shot for her brother, who never said no.

'Are you okay, Sis?' Jimmy reached for his shot glass of scotch. 'Pity I never punched Darren for what he'd done to you.'

'Not your fault, Jimmy. And, no, I don't feel all right.' *Huh.* It had to be her first time she'd openly admitted it.

She threw back her shot, swallowing it down in one gulp and held the glass to her forehead. Eyes closed, as the warming liquor slid down her throat and ka-powed straight to her soul. 'Damn that's good. Why did I ever leave you, lover?'

She glanced at the pile of letters from her ex-lover, overcrowding the open drawer. 'I wished Darren would leave me alone.'

And Sean had done just that. She hadn't heard from him since last weekend's sneaky entry into her family's backyard. It was like the guy had just disappeared.

Did Sean enjoy a challenge? Was he the type to tease her with false promises as part of his pursuit to break her resistance?

Yes, she'd crumbled. Hating how she'd so willingly surrendered to Sean, where the chase for her affections was won the second she'd melted in his arms and understood the swoon.

It was obvious Sean's challenge had been accomplished. Game over. Move along, nothing more to see here.

And what a fool she'd been.

The first blow had been Darren's deceitful betrayal leaving her to survive the emotional crisis and personal shame. Then there were the constant Sorry-cards as heart sucking reminders. With the added bonus of receiving nasty little blue notes from her ticked-off cousin, Katrina. When would everyone forget what happened to her?

But nope, she'd probably be destined to become some haunted ghost story whispered about between the warehouse shelves. To be remembered as the old spinster who ran away from the only man dumb enough to want to marry her—the man who'd impregnated her cousin.

She needed to change the subject. 'There's a rumour about you asking Tracey from checkouts to dinner? It's headline news, honey.'

'I'm testing out a way to break the family curse. Are you ready to date again?'

'I'm contemplating life in a nunnery as part of my Superannuation plans. It's where I'll maintain my man-less forever lifestyle in my one-woman-show, selling tickets to star gazers while I spin tales of alien abductions. Then I'll invest my fortune back into Black Johnny's birthplace to keep him as my constant companion for life.' Deanne smirked at Jimmy's laugh, but it was no laughing matter, she'd actually researched this venture.

'Jimmy, it's been almost four years since you'd divorced Casey, I believe it's time to date again.' Perhaps, her family really was cursed against relationships? Especially if Jimmy was looking for a way to break it.

'All around the shed, is it?' Jimmy asked, holding out his glass for a refill.

She nodded. 'I'm pleased you're going out. It's a big step from your usual pub hook-ups?' Maybe her brother had finally recovered from his heartbreak, when his first love, Fleur, married another man. Jimmy reacted by marrying Casey, within a month of meeting each other. They'd separated within six months and were divorced before their first wedding anniversary.

Did this make Sean a rebound? *Nooo*—they weren't having a relationship, full stop. Three kisses were just a momentary connection. It wasn't dating. It was nothing. *Nada.*

Jimmy tried to hide his smile. 'Yeah, it's true I've asked Tracey. I'm thinking of taking her out for a counter meal at the pub.'

'Don't you dare. Go somewhere nice, Tracy's a nice person.' Who was she to play cupid when her own love-life was a mess.

'Fine, I'll take Tracey to the Chinese place down the street.'

'Good for you.'

'You know what else I think is good? That we make a managerial decision and have a boardroom meeting in the beer shed. Now I've tasted the medicinal, I think we should escort Black Johnny home.' Jimmy stood, draining the last of his glass, and passed it back to Deanne. 'I also think we should add beer to this conversation.' When his eyeballs bulged at the sight of her open bottom drawer. 'What the hell? Is that all of Darren's deliveries?'

Deanne slammed the drawer and locked it. 'Don't ask.' Because she still couldn't understand why she kept them.

Jimmy held his hands up in surrender, walking backwards to the safety of the door. 'You definitely need a beer and dribble session, and as I'm your delegated driver this evening, we're leaving, right now.'

'Done.' Deanne picked up her bag and walked out the door, in need of some light hearted shoptalk in the beer shed. And perhaps a quiet natter with Nan to find the location of her scheming cousin to stop sending those pathetic duck-egg blue hate-letters in the mail.

It was progress—but was it in the right direction?

SIXTEEN

On dusk at the lookout, Sean sat at the stone table. He put two thin manila folders beside a couple of water bottles, takeaway coffees, and checked his watch again. Was he late?

He looked over at the circular clearing that opened to a hilltop vista where olive-leafed eucalypts fluttered in the breeze. Their trunks were dressed in rough to smooth paper curls of peeled bark in various browns, through to cream reflecting the sunrise. As the sun climbed higher, the view widened to show the new suburban sprawl in various stages of development.

Footsteps crunched on the gravel coming up the road, he wiped his hands on his jeans and waited. Thanks to Jimmy, who happily told all about his family's routine, this was his golden opportunity.

It was now or never.

Deanne came jogging up the hill, her cheeks red, her ponytail swinging with each stride, she sprinted to the top then skidded to a halt. Her eyes widened as her mouth opened in surprise that was soon swapped with a frown.

Even sweaty and in running gear she looked amazing. But the frown she wore he hoped to fix, or she was going to hate him forever.

He'd may as well get it over with...

'What are you doing here?' With hands on knees, she tried to catch her breath.

'You're such a creature of habit, with a routine so perfected I bet you sleep-walk through life.' Because she looked annoyed at him for breaking that routine.

But he was here for a reason.

Sean sipped his coffee to swallow any second thoughts and leaned back against the stone table.

'Why are you here? And where the hell have you been?'

'Aw, you missed me.'

'Are you stalking me?' She scowled at him, crossing arms over her chest.

'No. Stalkers don't bring coffee.' Sean pointed to the spare cup on the table then held out a bottle. 'You might want some water first. It's water, not vodka.'

'Thanks.' Deanne took a drink and with her back to him she faced the view.

'So, that's the shopping centre, huh?' He pointed to the large area cleared below.

She shrugged her reply.

'Well, aren't you a chatty person in the morning? Or you don't like your routine challenged? Change is recommended. I've got something for you.' He was rambling and knew it. Why was he putting himself through this?

'What?' She peeked over her shoulder at him. 'Busy week. I mean, have you been busy? Because I'm always busy.'

'You keep busy, so you don't have to think about yourself.' *Damn, that came out wrong.*

'What the—' Deanne spun around to glare at him.

But at least he now had her attention. 'There you are, with your whole fire-breathing goddess glow of a damned fine morning look.' Stunning wasn't even close to how fine she looked. 'It's hot with that fire in your eyes and the sunrise behind you…'

The plastic bottle crackled from her death-grip. 'A fire-breathing, what?'

Sean leaned back against the table, trying to hide his smile. 'You've got my number, why didn't you call me?'

'Am I a simple point score in some twisted male's trophy game, for you kiss then runaway to the next female?'

'Wow.' He walked towards her, drawn to her. 'You did miss me.'

'Don't you dare?' She threw her hands up, preparing to push him away.

'I'm a sucker for a dare.' He grabbed her wrists to stop her walking back towards the crumbly edge of the look out.

'Admit it,' she said, trying to wriggle her hands free. 'You like a challenge?'

'Hope you dare me not to kiss you, because I won't. I can't.' He just couldn't help himself and pulled her body to his chest, entrapping her with his arms, and his lips pressed against hers.

The instant contact was made he felt her surrender as her lips caressed him into heaven from one unbelievable lip-locked moment.

Then he let her go.

He had to.

Was she going to be angry with him? Again.

Sean gently cradled her face with his hands. 'I missed you too.' Her reaction was worth watching. It amazed him, whenever he kissed Deanne, Sean shared her same pleasure. It was such a seductive pull from all these new emotions, his soul had no choice but to willingly surrender to her.

'Why do you do that?' Deanne stepped back with her face screwed up. 'Just lure me in, then let me go?'

'I took off this week for work…' Sean pressed the takeaway coffee cup into her hand. He then grabbed his own coffee and returned to his seat at the table, pleased the fiery glow in her eyes was simmering. 'And I did it to try and distance myself from you.'

'What?'

'It's the truth, lying is my pet hate. I've never lied to you before and won't now, or ever.' Sean saw the confusion in her aquamarine eyes dousing her anger. Watching her face and interpreting her emotions could easily become a fascinating lifelong study for him.

'Why?' Deanne took a step closer, like a timid bird getting gamer for the seeds being offered. She sipped her coffee, gazing over the rim as her hands slightly trembled.

Sean saw everything.

He inhaled deeply, preparing to spill all. 'Because, sweetheart, you are in my head, and I can't get you out. I'm meant to have a soulless heart programmed to let no one in, but somehow, you've breached those borders. And as much as I try, it won't let you go.' She'd become his Siren, calling out to lead him to his peril, and he wanted to jump in.

Sean gently grabbed her fingers, making her sit beside him and without thought, he caressed her thick curls gathered in her ponytail. 'It's nice how the sun catches your hair.'

Deanne swatted his hand away in annoyance. 'How can I believe it's not another game you play? It's so easy for you to charm women. I've watched you smooth talk the girls in the café, you even did it to Nan in my dad's backyard.'

'Well, you're the only one I want to kiss, to keep on kissing, when I've never been a kisser. And you're the only one I've ever bothered to chase.' He raised the back of her hand to his lips. 'My attraction to you was instant when you walked into the bar that night, and I thought I'd never see you again. Yet, you returned which allowed me to hunt you down.'

Her eyes flared at the word.

'Yes, I'll admit it was a game at first, and I love a challenge.'

'I knew it.' She tried to tug her fingers free, but Sean wouldn't let go, sandwiching her small soft hand between his palms.

'I understand why you have no trust in anything male, including me, after what you've been through.'

'Ya think?' Deanne squinted at him.

'That night, when you walked into the bar looking like a fallen angel, you'd thrown this invisible lasso that tightened around me.' Sean swallowed, nothing else stirred, as if everything held its breath. He'd never thought or spoken like this before. He couldn't help it and knew it was because of Deanne. 'When you told me, what happened with your ex and your cousin, I could relate.'

Deanne frowned. 'No way? How?'

'I understand what it's like to be betrayed by those you love and trust. You see, my parents were married for fifteen years. Then my old man suffered a heart attack and Mum rushed to his side at the hospital, only to be met by my father's lover.'

'Oh, no?' Deanne mumbled as her stature softened.

'My father was having an affair with the same woman for ten years. When they released him from hospital, he never came home. He'd left us for another woman. My mum, me, and my three younger sisters, were left to fend for ourselves. Mum's face was pure shock, and I know I wore that same look of disbelief, while my little sisters were confused. We couldn't understand how or why he'd left us when we were meant to be his family.' Sean gazed at the valley and swore the silence grew louder.

Deanne gave his hand a gentle squeeze. Her small gesture gave him the courage to continue this conversation.

'Mum was a mess. I'd never understood heartbreak until I witnessed my mum's desolation.' He dropped his head hating the memory that had hurt, not just him, but how much it had crushed his mother. He could still see the tears she'd shed silently at night that shredded his heart back then, where those same invisible scars he felt today gripping like a hot poker burning in his chest. 'Mum devoted herself for the love of a man and he did that to her. *He. Deserted. All of us.*'

Sean saw shock and sympathy within Deanne's eyes, it took away his pain. If only he could do the same for her.

'It's why I understand what you've been going through,' he said. 'You wore the same expression my mother had. But with you, I saw more. Felt more.' Twisting one of her irresistible curls around his finger, Sean bowed his head to gaze into her eyes that reflected the spring sunrise. He admired each lash, the delicate laugh lines that surrounded her sweet mouth where she gnawed on the bottom lip he wanted to kiss.

'I know this isn't normal, especially for a guy like me, but I'm going to say *Sorry* now, in case I stuff up un-intentionally or upset you.' Because he sure had a habit of doing and saying the wrong thing to her. He was normally all stand-offish with people, it's what kept everyone away, until now. 'I swear, as a promise to me, I will not hurt you the way you've been betrayed. Believe me, that pain my mother went through, I endured it too. I swore I'd never let anyone hurt me the way my father did. To trust no one, and to let nobody in here,' he said, tapping a fist to his chest. 'I tried to walk away, swearing to never come near you again. But when I'm away from you, I can't stop thinking about you.' It was the most he'd ever told anyone, and it scared the crap out of him.

'It must've been terrible for you, and your poor mother to bring up four children on her own.'

'Mum's okay now.' He held Deanne against his chest, with his chin lowered to her soft hair, it was like resting on a silk bed beneath a summer breeze.

'Is she okay? How long did it take your mum to recover?'

Sean didn't want to scare her off, but wouldn't lie, not to Deanne. He never wanted to cause her any grief about trusting him, and understood it had to be earned. 'It was tough. But Mum's great now. She's in Italy on a boat cruise for singles.'

She arched her eyebrow at him. 'Italy?'

'Yeah, on her way home in time to give me a haircut.' He flicked the hair from his eyes. 'My two older sisters are married, and my baby sister and her partner live with Mum. So, they're all good and no longer my financial responsibility.'

'Oh.' Deanne winced as if sucking on a sour lime. 'Is that the expensive female habit Mickey mentioned?'

'Yep, the four of them.' He grinned at the way her eyes gave away her secrets.

'Did you ever see your father again?'

'By pure chance our paths crossed once.' He sat back, picking up his coffee.

'What happened?'

'I pulled into this roadhouse, coming back from an interstate, err, business trip.' Sean sipped his cup and then wiped his mouth. 'I fuelled up my car and went in and ordered a coffee to go, when he called out.'

'So, you talked and forgave him?'

'Do you forgive your ex?' Her death glare was his answer. 'It'd been that long; we'd forgotten all about him being so busy with our own lives.'

'Did your father say why he left?'

'I didn't give him the chance.' Sean hid his smirk behind his cup.

Deanne's eyes narrowed at him. 'What did you do?'

'Why do you assume I did anything?' He chuckled.

'Did you talk?'

'Nope.' Sean placed his cup on the table, looked at her squarely and said, 'I punched that man so hard I broke his nose, grabbed my coffee, and left without another word. And you know what?' He leaned towards her, inhaling her sweet aroma deep into his lungs.

'What?'

'It felt good too.' He laughed.

Deanne's hand covered her mouth as if to catch her laugh. 'Did you tell your mother?'

'I don't keep secrets from Mum.' He never wanted to keep secrets from Deanne and hoped she'd handle the rest of this conversation. But it was all for a reason.

'Didn't she lecture you about the wrongs of violence?'

'The guy taught me how to fight. It was his way of toughening us up, carrying on about life lessons. Instead, he'd toughened us up in one fast lesson by leaving us to fend for ourselves. Do you know where we lived?'

'Umm…' She winced. 'No.'

'Try Slumsville, in Scum Towers. Five of us crammed into a two-bedroom unit. I slept in the lounge, guarding our front door with a baseball bat in case some idiot tried to break in—and they did. Until the rest of the tenants learned quick to leave us alone, once I'd knifed this prick trying to rape my sister on the stairwell.'

Deanne gasped as her eyes widened.

Sean grabbed her hand to calm himself down. 'It didn't happen. I stopped it by stabbing the junkie. But then my sister and I spent weeks worrying we'd gotten Hepatitis or AIDS, which we didn't.'

'Thank goodness.'

'What I'm trying to say is, we may have been brought

up tough, but with us, family came first. Nothing and no one else outside of our family unit mattered. The man who was our father was no longer a part of our family unit. He left us. So, I punched him for doing that to us. Mum reckons I should've booted him one.'

'But he's your dad. I love my dad.'

'You're lucky to have a decent father,' he said as his fingers interlocked with hers. 'I have nothing left for my father. He doesn't deserve the honour. No man walks away from his family responsibilities, and if he does, he's not a man.' He scowled at the view. They sat in silence, sipping their coffee.

Sean then reached behind for one of two manila folders resting on stone table top. 'Anyway, besides avoiding you, this is why I've been busy this week.' He handed the documents to Deanne. He was taking a huge risk and hoped she would come along for the ride. But there was only one way to find out...

* * *

'What's this?' Deanne held the file, while Sean's life story had her mind reeling. Hold on, the guy just proclaimed he cared for her—big time.

Whoa. Her knees wobbled and her belly rolled.

Did she have the courage to trust his words?

Why would he make it up?

What did Sean have to gain in lying to her?

The questions rattled off one after the other, but she was too scared to ask, because she'd never been allowed to ask before.

'Focus, sweetheart. I want you to take a look. But I really need you to look at that paperwork with an open mind.'

Was he after her opinion for business? Business she could talk about. She could do paperwork, after-all she was the prim and proper paperwork queen of their family business.

She flicked open the folder's cover and scanned the opening the page. She gasped as her eyes widened, leaning in closer to check that what she was seeing was real.

'This is…' As the pages turned, she scanned columns of figures and architectural drawings. She took in the headers, subtitles, dot points, and the content. *No way!* 'Is this the Brinestones proposal for Lowe's shopping mall?'

Sean sipped his coffee, watching her over the rim of his takeaway cup.

'How did you get this?'

Sean didn't answer.

'How?'

Sean's grin was as sly as his shrug.

She frowned at him, searching for answers in his handsome face. Why was he so smug about this? 'Did you steal this?'

'It's a photocopy. But I must say, I'm enjoying your complete lack of accusational tact,' he said with a chuckle.

'This is stolen!' Deanne dropped it on the table as if it was radioactive.

'Do you want me to explain the intricate details? Unless you prefer being stuck as the woman of routine, who never ruffles feathers? Boring. Safe. Conservative. Don't you ever take risks?'

'What? No. Risks are dangerous,' she said, screwing up her nose at him.

'Boring.' He rolled his eyes. 'Guess that must be part of your good suburban middle-class upbringing.'

'Are you calling me a snob?'

'You're not a snob. You're adorable. Even with this conservative outer shell that hides that Siren's soul that's too scared to colour outside the lines. Or can you?'

'You're a crook!'

'You see that…' He waved his crooked finger at her. 'That's the reaction I'd predicted. But then I thought, nah, she'll want to learn more, to listen with an open mind. Which is what I'm hoping for—'

'This is illegal.'

'It's a photocopy that can be burnt in a second, sweetheart.' He pulled out his lighter from his pocket.

That bloody lighter caused all of this. If she hadn't returned it, Sean wouldn't be here.

Deanne scowled, with hands on hips and with a lowered voice she said, 'This is not a game. Do you realise what happens if I'm caught with this?'

'That's why I brought it out here and not to your office. Your brother is right, your movements are so predictable I could set my watch to your routine.'

'Not predictable. Or boring. Or safe… *augh*.'

'You just growled at me. Go, baby.' Sean laughed.

'YOU'RE A THIEF.' Her words echoed around them.

Forcing air through her nostrils, she gritted her teeth. The man was irritating, with his smug grin, shiny eyes, and sexy hair flick, when she was meant to be outraged at the thief.

'Prove it.' He laughed at her reaction.

'Go to hell.' She shifted from her seat, but he grabbed her hand to stop her from leaving.

'Look, I won't lie to you, and I need you to believe me when I say I'm retired. I quit that game a long time ago and rarely do it now, except for the odd love job. Or if the challenge is too tempting to let slide.' He gave her a schemer's wink.

She tugged her hand free. 'Did you just admit—'

'It's how *we survived!*'

Her mouth clamped shut as she stepped back from his raised voice filled with power.

'Dad left us with nothing. So, I did it for food and clothes where I'd learned to shoplift. Pretty soon I became an accomplice to teams when I was this skinny runt of a kid, because I was hungry enough to climb through windows to unlock doors to let the crew in for my measly cut. Because those pricks ripped me off.'

'What? How?' The man was too smart to be conned.

'Because I was unable to sell to fences when I should've been in school. But that was my start until I got smarter and bigger. Then I worked my way up because the small stuff wasn't worth the risk, and I wasn't comfortable stealing from people's homes. Instead, I went for businesses covered by insurance. Which led to specialist jobs that paid more. What you'd earn in five years, I'd pull in one job.'

'Why are you telling me your life story that just keeps on coming?'

'It's called open communication and I'm putting it all out there. No secrets. No lies. I don't keep anything from my family. And now that you've breached my inner circle, this means I trust you enough to tell you anything you want to know. You just have to ask.'

'Should I be honoured?' Did she have the courage to ask when she'd never asked questions of any male before? Her ex was to blame for that.

'Take the honour, sweetheart, you're privileged with inside information.'

'Er, hello.' She pointed to the stolen tender document.

'That was easy.'

'Do you normally steal? No way, I've never met a thief.'

'Everyone's stolen at least once in their life. I bet you did it too?'

'No.' She frowned. 'We're always mindful of shoplifters.'

'You're rare. Must be your privileged background.'

'Is that an issue with you?' She pursed her lips tight.

'Right back at ya, baby,' he said with his dark eyes sparkling from the sunrise. 'Do you want me to tell you what I used to acquire?'

Deanne gnawed her bottom lip, barely shrugging her shoulder.

'You are such a chicken. Well here we are, sweetheart, about to cross into those grey areas of life. It's okay, I won't ever take you to the dark side, but I'll show you the light.'

A snort-laugh escaped her. He had such a knack at lightening a heavy subject. 'Are you a preacher?'

'Not in my lifetime. Aren't you curious?'

'You're admitting you're a thief?'

'I said I acquired items. Different.'

'Ooh aren't we all technical-shmechnical.' Again, her

inner geek was alive.

'Smart arse. Try jewellery. Rare stamps. Coins. Sculptures. Historical artefacts. Paintings and lots of other pricy stuff that was worthy of my attention.'

'Are you for real? What would your mother say?'

'Mum called me that overused cliché of a modern-day, Robin of the Hood,' said Sean. 'I'd steal from the rich to give to the poor—which was us, where it put food on our table and clothes on our back.'

'Your mother knew?'

'I'm pretty sure I just said that. Mum's my alibi.'

Deanne blinked rapidly, to sit hard on the stone bench.

Sean chuckled and pulled her hand into his lap as he toyed with her fingers. He then took a deep calming breath as if for the both of them, and said, 'I preferred working on Corporations and the mega rich. Aware it'd only cause an inconvenience because they're compensated by their insurance.'

'But…your mother lets you do this? My dad wouldn't let me out after dark.'

'I wouldn't let you out after dark on your own either,' he said, giving her hand a squeeze. 'I promised Mum, once I'd made enough, I'd quit. And I did. I also swore to this old cop who kept trying to bust me—who's a mate now— that I'd retire from that game. Which I have.'

'And do what? My family thinks you work in security.'

'I do. I started my own company for the challenge in creating security systems to keep me out. These days I'm hired to break into other corporations where I use their mistakes to perfect my products that my sisters—who all work for me—sell to the market.'

'So, um.' Deanne scratched her head. 'That file...' She pointed to the file on the table.

'This job, I did for you. I can see you don't believe me, not that I blame you.' He looked up to the sky as if searching for answers. 'Look, my sisters deal with the clients in our security company, because I generally don't like people as a rule. They deal with the sales details and send me in to test out other systems. That's how I met Brinestones' director, drinking coffee in his office, where he had to call his own security people to show up.' He then inhaled deeply, and said, 'I thought this would be a great way for you to learn about me in one quick conversation. Where I'd rather survive your rejection now, instead of later.'

'All part of some grand plan, huh? Yeah, right.' She pulled her hand away from him.

Sean massaged the bridge of his nose. 'I understand it's a lot to handle before breakfast, but it's all true. I chose to have all of this out in the open so you can then decide to be with me before we got any deeper. I want you to know upfront because I don't want any secrets or lies between us.'

Us? Her brain just wasn't registering when normally she'd be zoned out on her morning jog. 'Oh, come on, this is an overload of information.' Oh no, she really didn't react well to her routine changed—not like this. How did he know?

'You don't believe me? When I've just confessed everything to you.' He gasped in mock horror, pressing a hand over his heart.

'How can you be so casual in telling me all of this? And

your mother knew?'

'My mother didn't like it and didn't want me doing it, but we had no choice.'

'Cunning is what you are. I now understand why you're two steps ahead in everything.' Deanne wagged her finger at him. 'You'd learned to scope people, right? Cased premises and checked out their routines before robbing those places.'

'Where'd you learn that?'

'I read books and watch movies.'

'I bet you had a nice education in a clean, suburban school, where you never had to worry about finding food for the table.'

'Um, no. I mean, yes.' She shook her head while feeling guilty of her own childhood compared to Sean's. 'Same school.'

'Pegged that.'

'But I got bullied.' She then glanced at him sideways and asked, 'How did you cope?'

'Food,' he said with a wide grin.

The girl with food issues blinked at Sean, wishing she had an immunity to food—and his grin. 'Food?'

'Mum cooked, and we'd take the time to sit and eat. Food was what I'd risked myself for the most. Mum worked part-time as a cleaner at nights, while I took care of my siblings. Mum covered the rent and power, while I scored the extras. But it was my sisters who started our food habit. You see, back when we walked home from school, they'd pick these flowering weeds to decorate our kitchen table. They'd fold paper napkins, polish the mismatched cutlery, and even write place settings. Then we'd sit there and make out our mashed spuds were these priceless pies served to us while we were sitting at a fancy seaside restaurant. When, in reality, we were right next to a drug den, living on the wrong side of poverty.'

Her stomach spun as if on that ledge with him. 'And now?'

'I still like to sit and share a meal. I always make the effort for Mum. Besides, you've got to eat, so why not make the time to enjoy it. I bet you scoff your food at your work desk?'

Deanne shrugged. 'Sure. Don't most people do that?

'I'm not talking about other people, just you. Breakfast?'

It surprised her that a man wanted to know what she ate. 'Um, in the car on my way to work.'

'Dinner?'

'At the table.' Her lips twisted trying to remember. 'No, standing at the bench, if I'm hungry, before bed.'

'When was the last time you sat and ate a meal that included actual dinner conversation?'

'Last Saturday night, when I last saw you.'

'You did miss me.' He planted a loud smooching lip-whack on hers, making them both smile. 'Your eating habits suck. We'll work on it.'

'No!' Deane was well aware of her food issues. Surprised she'd again said *no* to Sean. 'My ex did that, always taking charge of me.' Darren had made her feel so self-conscious about her weight, her clothes, everything, where now she liked being her own person, away from anyone's control. It had taken her months to get to this standard.

Sean held her chin, trapping her with his stare. 'I won't do that, not to you.'

Her fight disappeared, she had to look away. She sipped her coffee, still feeling his touch that warmed her all over. *How did he do that?* Did she dare believe him and this whole conversation?

'Guess what else I found while visiting your competition?' Sean picked up the second folder. 'Don't answer that question, you'll just chicken out.' He placed the folder in her hands.

'I'm not a chicken.' She stepped back, needing her own space, but was surprised how cold she felt away from his body heat. But then she was in her running gear, it was still early morning, and she was lacking all forms of imaginative pathetic excuses for her body's reaction to Sean. *Not fair.*

'No, you're a conservative good girl with some fire and fabulous curves.'

'Is that wrong?' She was unsure if she should be flattered or insulted.

'If you enjoy living in a cocoon that rolls in the same circle— Yeah, best I stop before I upset you further.' Sean cleared his throat and then nodded towards the documents. 'But you'd better look at that stuff, I believe it's yours. Go on, I dare you.'

Deanne was unable to help herself; his taunts pushed her buttons.

Was she a girl of routine? *Yes.*

Predictable? *Okay, predictable was good.* It's not like her day job was as a professional gambler.

But was she boring? Boring was safe—but boring.

Her eyes widened at the thought. Hold on, was she boring?

'Am I an easy pick-up for you?'

He shook his head. 'You've resisted.'

'The challenge thing, huh.' Again, she pursed her lips tight.

'Even though I know I went way over the top in the hardware store where my behaviour towards you was inappropriate—'

'Sleazy, stalkerish.' She waved at the empty carpark area where he'd interrupted her morning run.

'Yeah, that.' His forehead lowered, flicking the fringe from his eyes. 'I'm sorry, but I seem to lose the filter for my mouth when it comes to you.'

She could relate. 'Nice to know you're not perfect.' Although, he was pretty damned close.

'It seems that ever since I've met you, all I want to do is look after you. To take care of you. Buy you gifts, when I don't do gifts, unless it's for family from their handwritten wish list. I'm trained that way. Besides my family, you're the first female I've ever bought flowers for. I've never had romantic thoughts until I'd met you, let alone voice them. And here I thought I'd gotten rid of the last of my female responsibilities, yet I'm willing to sign up for more, with you as the treasure hidden within the depth of this suburban sea. You are my crown jewel that's more precious to me than any pile of gems.'

Deanne blinked. Blinked again. Sean did not just say all that? 'Gifts?' Her mind flashed to a future of checking Police websites to see if her gifts from him were stolen.

'Stop that.'

'Stop what?'

'I'd never give you anything stolen.'

'You're giving me that.' She pointed to the paperwork.

'That's different.'

'Jeez, talk about grey lining.' She rolled her eyes.

'You'll understand once you've read that file. Trust me.'

'Do you trust people who say that?'

'No. Never. In fact, I rarely trust anyone, and I've always lived by my instincts. But it seems my non-existent heart wants to trust you. So, this is a huge risk for me. Okay? Remember, you've entered the inner circle, standing at the right hand of man.' He held out his right hand to her and smiled wide.

'You're so full of it.' She involuntarily smiled with him. How did he do that, make her feel better so fast, and so effortlessly?

'Part of the charm in keeping it real.' He gave another schemer's wink.

Deanne took a deep breath and held it as she opened the folder and began reading. 'Oh. My. God.' Deanne dropped onto the bench seat as her stomach recoiled in horror. 'It's my proposal. This is my work. The proposal I've been working on for months. My. Work! It's even got my final figures from yesterday.' Deanne looked at Sean in disbelief. 'It was faxed an hour after I left the office with Jimmy. How did you get this?'

'Well, it wasn't through the front door…' Sean reached for her hand and toyed with her fingers.

'Stop! I don't want to know.' She pulled her hand away and went back to looking at her *own document*. 'Who did this?'

'I have no idea, but they had older copies of your proposal in their office where it looks like they're updated every few days. And you're too honest to not look at theirs. But I can't resist your lips when you twist your mouth like that, it makes me want to straighten them out.' He then kissed her, hard.

It took everything to push him away, the heat of his mouth, the taste, and the touch was overpowering. It was heavenly, yet scary all at the same time. But she did. 'Hey, I can't think when you do that.'

'For real?' His eyes grew as wide as his smile.

'I did not say that.' Damn, she'd never live it down now. 'Back to this.' She used the document to fan herself from the man making her body burn.

'I'm never forgetting what you just said.' He then slid his arm around her shoulders. 'But here's the thing, they must be worried enough to pay your staff to send them your work.' His eyes darkened and his expression hardened. The fun mood was gone even from his voice. 'Who else has access to your office?'

'I don't lock my office.'

'So, it's open slather to anyone?'

'I remember Jimmy pulled the door shut when we left last night. We've never locked our offices and we don't store cash or jewels in hidden wall safes, but we do sell safes and security systems.' She gave Sean a sly grin.

'Cheeky thing.' He slightly squeezed Deanne around the shoulders. 'Who else has keys to your office?'

'The cleaners. Floor supervisors. The spare keys are kept downstairs in the floor manager's office, but they've been with us for years and wouldn't do this?'

'Yet, one of your staff is selling your secrets, sweetheart.' He pointed to the page in front of her. 'Not that it'd be too hard because your shed's security sucks. And, I'm amazed the amount of trust you have for your staff. Do I have your trust yet?' Sean lay his head on her shoulder where his dark eyes shone beneath his fringe, it was almost irresistible.

'Are you going to whimper like a puppy?'

'I should get you a puppy as a running companion, they're cute. Then it'll grow up to be a loyal and protective dog for you.'

'I still haven't finished my morning run.' That had been blown out to something else entirely.

'Let's focus on this matter, first.' Again, he tapped his finger on the document.

Sean was right. 'At least you're trained to bring coffee.'

'I aim to please. So, who worked the warehouse floor last night? Do you have any locksmiths in your store?'

'Sure. Brian and his apprentice, that's his son. I saw them coming back inside as we were leaving. They go out on site regularly in their van.'

'Is there anyone else in the warehouse who can cut keys?'

'Another supervisor, but he's on leave. There's Andrew from gardening, he trialled it for a stint before going into horticulture. Andrew grew up in that place, he wouldn't do this. His mum, Beatrice, runs the café they're like part of the hardware family.'

For a third time, Sean tapped on her stolen document. 'Well, someone did. So, who else can cut keys? Was this

Andrew working on site yesterday?'

'We shared the afternoon coffee break discussing plant stocks.'

'Exciting stuff.' Sean half-rolled his eyes. 'Is there any other staff member trained to cut keys?'

'No. You're required police clearances for that trade.'

'I can cut keys and my record's clean,' he said with a sly grin.

'Are you qualified?' Deanne arched her eyebrow at him.

'The question you should be asking, sweetheart, is how great am I?'

'Are we still talking about key cutting?' She squinted at his crooked grin as her body shivered, even as the heat coursed through her veins. It sucked how Sean did this to her.

'I'm awesome in all departments.' He nuzzled into her neck.

'You're so full-of-it.' She squirmed as her resistance started to crumble.

'I've never found a lock I couldn't undo. So, do you wear a chastity belt?' He placed his hand on her bare thigh.

'Hey!' She slapped him with the document.

'How many times do I have to tell you I love a challenge.' He ducked as she swiped the folder at him.

Then her whole demeanour changed, and the inner flirt was squashed. In its place was disappointment and disenchantment that she knew so well, ever since the wedding. 'It's not fair,' she said, staring down at her proposal. 'All that time wasted.' It'd been the one thing that stopped her wallowing in the depths of depression.

'Hey, hold on a second—' Deanne swivelled around to grab the other folder, containing Brinestones' tender, and ran her finger down the pages. 'They've used my work. It's my own details.' She showed Sean the comparison. 'They've just switched the index sequence.'

'It could be a coincidence, if they've used the same sources as you for their research.'

'Not all. The guys who did the original plans for this project helped me.'

'You mean you, *Miss Innocent, let's play-it-safe in the land of boring life-of-routine,* had insider information? Why, Miss Harrison, I'm flabbergasted.'

Deanne tried not to laugh but he was so damned cute, and sexy. 'These guys drink with Dad when he's non-golfing.'

'Non-golfing? Don't you mean Reg plays golf?'

'No, Dad non-golfs.'

Sean arched an eyebrow at her. 'Which means?'

'Dad suffered a heart scare from stress and was told to take up a relaxing hobby. So, he took a few golf lessons, then proclaimed it was all too hard and would rather sit in the air-conditioned bar, win meat trays, watching the other golfers outside while Dad non-golfs at the golf club.'

Sean laughed. 'I like his style.'

'Dad is meant to be exercising.'

'It's his life, let him live it the way he wants. Obviously, he has contacts within this golf club?'

'Yeah. Which kind of justifies his membership.'

'Smart man.'

'Anyway, these guys volunteered their advice.'

'Why? Because they know how hot you are?'

'What? No way. Have you ever stopped and listened to yourself?'

'See, I'm doing it again.' Sean shrugged with an apologetic smile. 'Or do you want me to tell you that you have an approachable manner enjoyed by the warehouse clientele, where you and your family are well-respected, and so is the whole work environment.'

Now it was her turn to arch her eyebrow at him. 'Excuse me?'

'I did my research. It's what I do.'

'Andrew said the same thing.'

'Key-cutting-Andrew?'

'Head Nurseryman, Andrew. He used to work at Brinestones and just came back to us.'

'Oh, really?' Sean narrowed his eyes at her.

'Andrew wouldn't do this.'

'How do you know what people are like after hours? Is he flush with cash?'

'The poor guy's going through a divorce, well, counselling first.' She sighed at the question Sean posed. 'Andrew has only just moved back into his mum's, paying off the mortgage he got when at Brinestones for the higher wage.'

'Don't you pay your staff the big bucks?'

'We'd like to. But we do contra deals, offer discounts for items, and allow for more family-friendly flexibility and holiday time. Andrew's main reason for leaving us was because he's worked with us ever since he was in school.'

'Like you?'

'Yes.'

'Did you want to do anything else?'

'I wanted to run a plant watering business for a while.'

His brow crinkled. 'Say that again?'

'I'd cruise around visiting office complexes watering hired pot plants all day.'

'Sounds cruisy.'

'I know.' She gave a deep soulful sigh.

'Does your job stress you out?'

Deanne rolled her shoulders as she stretched her neck from side to side. 'There's this weight knowing I have all these families depending on me. It's not just the place's reputation, but Dad's approval, and Jimmy's too. It's taken me a long time to earn our customers' respect instead of being known as a Daddy's girl. People forget I grew up there and worked after school, on weekends, and every school holiday, it is a family business, you know. But I don't want to mess this up for my family and for all of our employees. Yet, I'm scared I'll fail them all.' She'd already failed herself; she didn't need to do that to her family too.

Sean slipped his arm around her shoulders. 'With this proposal, are you worried you might've stuffed up?'

'I've never worked on anything this big before. I haven't worked on formulaic models since university, and this is way more than Dad's ever done. Jimmy's the same, he'll tell you he's a hands-on warehouse manager and he's happy there. It's why I approached the tradies to help with my research.'

'You actually asked questions?'

'Sure. It's work.' Deanne never had problems in asking questions when it came to work. But when it came to private matters, she didn't want to know. Damn Darren for training her to be that way. Or was it a family thing to never pry in people's private business?

'I'm sure Brinestones has a team of high-flying experts, where I've only done small stuff in comparison. But if we won this tender, our business future's guaranteed, and I know this stress will disappear.' She hoped.

'You could be flattered they've had to resort to such tactics to find out what you're doing.'

'Yeah, right,' she mumbled, slumping low in her seat.

Sean gave her shoulders a slight squeeze. 'Hey, I admire how much you care about this business. It's obviously more than a store.'

'It is. But what can I do?'

'Let me help you?'

'What?'

'I'll only do this for you.' Sean sat taller and nodded at her with that sexy-serious look he wore so well. 'Can you give me a list of your staff members working last night? Including those with access to the supervisor's office and the locksmiths.'

'I can do that. But—'

'Just leave the details to me. By the way, you did nice work on your proposal. I've done a few before.'

She gave a half shrug, unsure if her work was good enough?

'That was a compliment, sweetheart.'

'Do you realise what this means? We treat these people like they're part of our extended family. I don't believe this.' Deanne dumped the documents onto the table, to pace the dirt, wringing her hands together. 'All my work—for what? I'm too trusting, because for weeks it's been sitting out in the open on my desk for anyone to see. It's still there, right where I left it last night.' Deanne covered her mouth with her hand, blinking furiously to stop her tears. She turned her back on Sean to face the vacant land designated for the shopping centre.

'Hey…' Sean came up behind her, slipping his arms around her. 'Why not tease their end game?'

'What? How?'

'Set up false figures and leave it out for them to copy. Easy as. Everyone in the store will be expecting you to hang there all weekend if the deadline is Monday, because you have no life. So, do two. Carry the updated proposal or lock it up in a safe and keep a fake proposal on your desk as part of your normal life of boring routine.'

'There's no time to work on two documents when I need to rework the whole thing because it'll look like I've copied theirs.'

'Do women in safe-land suburbia have their own language where I'll need to enrol in some interpretation classes?'

'Smart arse.'

'See, I understood that.'

'Listen, if two businesses competed and their information was identical, it'd look suspicious.' She thrust her palm up to stop Sean interrupting.

Gravely dirt crunched under her running shoes as she paced back and forth, with the view spread endlessly below them. But she didn't see any of it as her mind worked fast. 'If the smaller business won this contract, the corporate giant could exercise their right to scrutinise all tenders submitted. Don't you get it, they're the big fish who has the power to fry us when they take one look at my proposal and assume, I've plagiarised *their* work.' Her hands clutched the top of her head as her stomach dropped. 'It'll ruin me. Us. Everyone, my entire family—'

'Hey, I won't let that happen. And I missed that clever point you made.'

Deanne stamped her runner into the dirt, raising a small dust cloud. 'Will this crappy year end already?'

Sean grabbed her hands. 'Okay, here's what we'll do. I'll take you home and destroy these documents.'

'Getting rid of the evidence, huh?' She gave him sideways look.

'Sweetheart, I'm trying to help you. I'll scribble up a false proposal for you. I also want those employee names, and then I want you to start work on a new proposal. You're not giving up on this by letting them win the easy way. Okay? Because I'm not going to give up on you.'

'Um…' The challenge laid out before her was made of land-sliding rubble, where she was just beginning her mountainous climb.

Yet, to risk her trust in this guy and let him help her, was unheard of. It was almost terrifying.

Where was her one-woman band now?

'Can you work elsewhere? Home?' Sean asked.

Her work was her way of hiding from the world, it was all she had left. 'I'll need my charts, notes, and laptop. I can't work from home, Nan's strict on her rules. I might go to Clare's office and use her boardroom. How do we find out who did this?'

'Let me tackle that. Right now, you work on your own proposal, and I'll work on catching your mole.'

'What's that saying, to catch a crook you send a crook?' She narrowed her eyes at him.

'I'm retired. I was also a perfectionist who never got caught, which is why I make more money creating security systems keeping out thieves. I have other talents, you know.' He kissed her cheek, nuzzling into her neck. 'I can do so much more…'

Her breath hitched as her skin broke out in goose bumps.

'Unfortunately, we don't have time for this right now.' He took a deep breath as if to control himself, and stepped back, looking at her.

They both stared open-mouthed at each other. Their breathes erratic.

'You have got to stop teasing me like this,' Sean said, but he pulled her close, as his sensual lips locked against hers that made love to her in ways that was so hot, sweet, and seductive, while still fully clothed and just kissing.

'Stop. I've got work to do.' For the first time Deanne resisted. Pushing Sean away, she tried to catch her breath. Even though her body was like liquid lava building towards its own volcanic eruption of passion and lust, she needed to focus.

How did he do that?

But right now, she needed to concentrate and that meant not being near Sean. 'Can you drop me off? I'll call Clare to see if her boardroom is free.' She headed for Sean's car with her mind racing at warp speed. She had a plan and almost felt game enough to do it too, and could only hope it worked for everyone's sake.

SEVENTEEN

Deanne sat at her desk with her head cradled in her hands. Footsteps accompanied a whistling tune that carried down the corridor.

Janice's whistled stopped in the corridor. 'Darren's not bothering you again, is he? I heard about the flowers yesterday.'

'I'm okay.' *Not.* Considering Deanne's other escalated drama-filled morning, her ex's floral arrangements were no longer on the radar.

'Where is my father?' Deanne could do with some serious daddy-time right about now.

'He's gone to check out a new plumbing gadget. Reg will be in around ten, then he's going non-golfing this arvo. Here's your mail, honey.' Janice dropped the paperwork into the open tray and spun around on her well-worn wedges. Her multi coloured toenails shone under the fluorescent lights as she headed for the open door. 'Do you want me to fetch you a coffee?'

'No thanks, I'll collect one at my usual time.' Was Sean right about her living in a sleepwalker's world of repetition? Was her routine so deeply ingrained it overtook her existence of being?

Alone in her office, Deanne sorted her in-tray, performing the trained seal-act. After all, she'd been showing up to this warehouse for over ten years and had the engraved letter-opener to prove it. Did that make her boring?

All thoughts stopped when she spotted another duck-egg blue envelope.

She frowned, holding it up to the light, trying to see through the thick parchment.

Last night, Deanne spoke with Nan, seeking answers to some very painful questions. Her cousin, Katrina, had been shipped off to some relatives on the mother's side, living in some remote region near Broome.

The postal mark on the duck-egg blue envelope came from the local post office. Not from Western Australia.

With her super sharp letter-opener, Deanne sliced the envelope's lip with ease, and unfolded the matching duck-egg blue paper.

The note read:

I hate you and I will ruin you.
You have ruined me and I will enjoy watching you fall.

'Screw you.' Deanne wanted to screw it up and jump on it.

After this morning's information overload, she was tempted. But current events demanded that her personal emotions be shoved to the cooler side of the oven, to concentrate on the crappy note in hand.

Deanne was positive Katrina was hiding in Western Australia. Darren was camped out in Queensland. However, the local postmark on the envelope suggested it was from someone else within their midst.

Duh, Sherlock she wasn't.

She chewed on her bottom lip, squinting at the note searching for clues. Could it be the same staff member leaking her proposal?

If Sean—regardless of how—hadn't found her tender with the opposition, she would've been seriously stuffed. Ruined even.

But who'd do this? Why?

Deanne unlocked her bottom drawer, pushed her beloved medicinal Black Johnny aside, and rummaged through the pile of colourful love letters, notes, and Sorry-cards. The different sizes and shapes of the mish-mashed clash of colour made her wince. She still didn't know why she kept them.

She plucked free all the duck-egg blue letters and spread them across her desk.

Letter one:

Why did you have to ruin everything?

Letter two:

Do you have no heart in the lives you've ruined?
So now I'm going to ruin you.

Letter three:

You don't deserve someone new when you've hurt the ones who've loved you. You have no heart, and destroyed my life. I should be destroying yours.

And today's winner, letter four:

I hate you and I will ruin you.
You have ruined me and I will enjoy watching you fall.

They reminded Deanne of a schoolyard taunt. They were easy to read one-liners. Not intelligible. Not a sonnet. Not even a riddle. Or where they?

Deanne sat back and stared at the blue paper. Obviously, someone was against her, but who? And the big billion-dollar gameshow question was *why?*

When there was a sharp knock on her open door and Deanne propelled from her chair. '*Augh.*'

'What's wrong?' Sean kicked the door shut with his boot's heel, placing two coffees on her desk. 'What are these?' He pointed at the blue letters.

Deanne blinked a few times, before realising Sean wasn't a mirage.

Why was she suffering with these delayed reactions when she was normally quicker than this?

'Um, I've been receiving these for a month. I'd assumed they were from the ex, thinking he was doing a Jekyll and Hyde thingy. But he's hiding in Queensland. Then I thought they were from my cousin Katrina who's absconded to Western Australia. But I just opened this one that came from the local post office.' She showed Sean today's trophy in literary excellence. 'Is it the same person who's sending my proposal to Brinestones? Why set me up?' Her panic rose, she began to pant, as her knees trembled collapsing into her chair.

'Hey...' Sean crouched beside her, grasping her

trembling hands. 'Calm down, I won't let it happen, okay. Take a deep breath, come on, sweetheart.'

She exhaled slowly, staring into the depth of his dark eyes as if to draw on his strength.

'Better?'

She nodded. Somehow, he did make her feel safe. 'Jury's still deliberating.'

Sean shared his signature grin that did wonders to her heart rate. 'It's a lot to digest for someone from your background—'

'I don't live in a bubble.'

'I'm pretty sure we discussed this only a few hours ago and called it a cocoon?'

'This morning was a major info-spill, that's still yet to be processed,' she said, twirling her finger above her crown.

'Which you will process carefully, and I'm open to questions, anytime.' Resting on his haunches, he flicked the fringe out of his eyes. 'So, here's hoping you'll actually ask me questions that you seem to hesitate in doing.'

'Do not.' She did too, especially when it came to personal stuff, not business.

'So, let 'em rip.'

Deanne tugged her fingers free to drag them through her hair. 'Will they hurt me when I don't know what I've done to deserve this? Am I in danger? Worse, is my family in danger?'

Sean pulled himself up to read the blue letters. 'They're simple sentences. No fancy words. So, I don't think we're dealing with a mastermind? I wish I had all the answers; but we'll find them.'

'I need to tell Dad and Jimmy about this.' Deanne tried to stand.

'No.' Sean held her in place. 'These letters were meant to distract you, and they're doing their job.'

'Huh. You're right.'

'Remember that.'

'Please focus.'

Sean winked at Deanne. 'I agree that this could be the same person faxing your stuff to Brinestones.' Sean narrowed his eyes at the letters. 'They're playing mind games, but they don't mention your family, just you. And I'm betting it's someone who works here because of logistical access.' Sean exhaled long and slow as he re-crouched down in front of her. 'Now, I can't say this any nicer, but you can't tell Reg or Jimmy. They talk too much and might leak it out to the person we're looking for.'

'What are you saying? My family would demand we go to the police. But we can't, because then they'll ask how I found out that my proposal was being sent to Brinestones, then Dad and Jimmy will suffer a major dummy-spit if they learned the truth, which might give Dad a heart attack, where Jimmy would follow for the sympathy.'

'They're both dating staff members.'

'I trust my family. Why should I trust you? How do I know you're not the one setting me up?'

Sean laughed. 'You don't, do you. Your inner fire, sweetheart, do you realise what it does to your eyes?'

Deanne leaned towards him and said through gritted her teeth, 'Be serious.'

'No. You need to lighten up. You know I'm here to help you.'

'Why?'

'Call it my sufferance of some Robin Hood syndrome. I copied info from the rich, being Brinestones Corp—which was your own work.'

'Real blurry edge of grey, honey.'

'By the way, you're the only one I've ever called sweetheart.'

'Huh?' Her jaw dropped.

'But it's good to see you're already learning to smudge on the details.'

Deanne frowned. 'I'm not a crook.'

'Neither am I. Remember, I was paid to break-in. Crooks have no morals.'

'And the rest?'

'Okay, so I copied from the rich and supplied the info to you. Though, you're not poor. You're honest and hardworking, and so is your family that employs another fifty families inside this hardware store. Besides, I like the little guys winning, because corporations care only about profit margins. Most of all, Deanne,' he said, as he stroked her hair, 'I get to gain your trust and be with you.'

Was this man volunteering to play hero? Her hero?

Deanne blinked up at Sean as her irrational emotions collided with her over conventional mind. Yet, it was a moment of crystal clarity that cut through the chaos.

Had she finally woken up from her life of dreary sleepwalking day-to-day existence?

But then she realised something else…

She believed him, not sure if to trust him, but she believed him, and gave Sean a light smile. 'A thief with a conscience?' He was far too sexy to be her hero.

'Something like that. Glad to see you're smiling, because I understand the pressure, you're under.' He pressed his lips to her forehead. 'Better?'

Deanne nodded, her mind awake and now churning in top gear. 'Please explain why I can't tell Dad and Jimmy? Janice has been Dad's girlfriend for six years. And my brother hasn't even gone out on his first date. Hey, how come you know about Jimmy's date?'

'I overheard Beatrice talking about it downstairs when I fetched your coffee.'

'Gossipers Cafe.' Again, she reminded herself to order a sign and wrote it on a post-it.

'Can you see my point?'

She gave him a half shoulder shrug. Then shook her head. 'You do realise this is a family business. Duh, Daddy's the director.'

'You can't say anything to Reg or Jimmy. Not while we have the rare element of surprise to bait this person. Your family's reaction may tell the world what's going on.'

'How? Are you going to fingerprint the fax machine? How rude is this crook to use the one in my office?'

'Convenience, while not being spotted with the paperwork.' Sean checked out the bulky contraption on her side bench. 'Who uses faxes? It's a bit outdated, don't you think?'

'Tradies. Some are quite slow to adapt to modern technology. Trust me, I had to teach a few tradesmen how to use their smartphones.'

'Do you play with gadgets and take over the television's remote control, too?' His eyes widened in mock fear.

'Only if I have to.' But then in her dad's house, the only TV they had was always on a sports channel that was kept in their precious beer shed. 'You'd be a gadget-man.'

'I'm a man who enjoys his toys.' Sean wriggles his eyebrows beneath his fringe.

'Why are we talking about toys when—'

'Lighten up. I'd hate to see you handle a fire.'

'We're due a fire drill.' She snatched another post-it to make another diary note for herself.

'You need to focus. And I need to nut out the final details. But look what I did this morning.' He removed a roll of paper from his back pocket. 'I took the pleasure of dodging up your documents. You just need to enter my adjustments, print it out, and then concentrate on the new one. Did you get those staff names for me? And take this.' He handed her a coffee.

She sipped as she checked his figures scrawled all over her worksheet that she'd spent months working on. Now stolen. *Not fair.*

'Won't the staff be suspicious of you being in here?'

'Are you worried about being seen with me?' Sean gasped, but his eyes sparkled with mischief. 'Do I need to find you a paper bag?'

'Why can't you wear the bag?'

'Good to see you're playing the game.'

'It's the coffee not the company.'

'I'm trained to fetch,' Sean said, giving her a sweeping bow.

Aw the man was too cute. Sexy cute.

'Your staff will assume I'm a customer. Your brother knows I'm interested in a trade agreement about some refurbishments where I've hired Petey, Jane's husband, to do the work for me.'

'Since when?'

'Last Saturday we swapped numbers. Unlike you, he called me.'

'Why Petey?'

'Because I'm a charismatic—'

'Please, there is only so much oxygen in the room.'

Sean chuckled. 'I've heard Petey does good work, and he's available. And...' He paused to sip of his coffee. 'There's the baby factor too.'

'Aw. No way you're real and so generous?' The guy was practically perfect. So why was he still single?

Because of the thief element!

'It's rare. So, enjoy this moment and tell no one.'

He made her smile. *Prick.* 'Who else have you been talking to? Are you a spy, too?'

Sean threw his head back and laughed, taking a seat in the visitor's chair. 'I've discussed options with your dad about beefing up this warehouse's security system. But honestly, I don't care what people say about me, if I'm happy and my family's taken care of, that's all that matters to me.'

Deanne leaned across her desk. 'Did you know, the staff spotted you kissing me in the ceramics aisles.' The heat crept up her face like steam escaping a boiling kettle, only to hide her shame behind her hands. 'I hate being talked about.'

Sean laughed louder. 'Are you twelve?'

'Go away,' she said, peeking through her fingers. Why did this man stir her up so much? What happened to calm, steady and normal? Oh, that'd be with boring Mr. Dependable, the cheating ex, banished to Queensland.

'Hey…' He pulled her fingers away. 'I happen to admire your sensitivity—which I hope you never lose. But no one has the right to affect you unless you let them. You shouldn't care what people say on the outside when you need to care about you, on the inside.'

'Are you preaching again?'

'Maybe I've missed my calling in life.'

'Boy, didn't you take the wrong turn, big time.' She giggled, getting up from her seat. 'So, what do we do first, Captain?' She even gave him a salute.

Although she wasn't used to taking orders from an outsider, so far, Sean made sense. And he was tall. Handsome. Smelt nice. And her body swayed towards him, surrendering to his invisible spell.

'Well,' Sean said with a grin as his arm slid around Deanne's waist, 'it's business and pleasure.' He delicately held her chin as he pressed his lips tenderly against hers, drawing them in where everything was forgotten, except their kiss…

'Phone call, line one, Dee,' Janice's voice cried through the intercom.

* * *

'Buzz kill,' mumbled Sean. He was getting into that kiss but stepped back to let Deanne to answer the call.

Relieved that her panic had passed, and her head was back in the game.

Sean picked up the blue letters from Deanne's desk

and considered his options.

With Deanne's publicised private life, a mess, it meant hammering her professional reputation. The woman was already sensitive from her wounds and knew this would destroy her.

Why would someone set up Deanne like this?

Slipping the folded blue letters into his pocket, Sean was going to call in a favour from an old mate for help.

But how far would this person go to hurt Deanne?

Pity the fool when Sean caught them because Deanne was now under his protection, and he'd do everything in his power to keep her safe.

EIGHTEEN

Deanne locked herself away in Clare's spare office with charts and plans spread across the table. Folders and files were scattered in some form of chaotic order across the floor, while she tapped the details into her laptop and sipped on her coffee. 'Augh.' She screwed up her face at the cold coffee.

She rubbed her gritty eyes, wondering if it was worth making a fresh cup when it was one o'clock in the morning?

Yet it seemed only a few hours ago when she'd begun recreating her proposal.

Back then, Sean went through her staff rosters, narrowing it down to a few possible suspects. With her false proposal left, as per normal, on her desk, while she hid in secret at Clare's office.

Where had her life of routine gone?

Her life's plan was meant to be all slow and gradual by sticking to the plan: going to school to get a job, get married, have a family, and watch her kids repeat the same cycle. Normal. Slow. Expected.

Boring?

Now Sean was making her question everything, to wake up and look around her.

And what about Sean, himself, what does she do

there?

Deanne sat back, swinging her legs under the seat. A soft smile curled the corner of her lips at the memory of their kiss.

But what were his reasons for helping her?

And was Sean's life-story true?

Most of all, was he honestly romantically into her?

Sean was charming. Handsome. Intelligent. Cheeky. But a cunning ex-thief. Not what you'd expect from the package.

He was clever. Too clever. The way he spoke to people easily gaining their trust, while scrutinising the minutest details. The man missed nothing and remembered everything.

It rattled her.

She was used to people not seeing her.

She was used to people forgetting what she'd said, because she lived on the sidelines always taking care of everyone else but herself.

Yet, Sean took care of her. He ensured she ate and drank over lunch, even delivering her dinner at this office. He'd held her hand as they talked, teased her, yet listened to her ideas while giving her his undivided attention.

Was she being manipulated again, the way her ex had done?

Back then she'd questioned herself about dating Darren, and look how fairy-tale-fantastic that turned out for her. Was Sean the same as the ex? Was she ready to risk her heart again?

Deanne sighed, stopping her thoughts, and leaned over her documents. Her work was her focus. There was no time for wallowing in emotional questions when her work was all she had left.

'Sweetheart, haven't you done enough for one night?'

'Ah!' Deanne jumped, to land back in her seat with a ka-thump, staring at Sean leaning against the doorway. 'What the—'

'Sorry, I didn't mean to frighten you.'

Her heart still pounded as her pulse raced, but was that from Sean or from the scare? 'How did you get in here? The place is locked up. Why are you here?'

'Aaaand you're wide awake now.' Sean chuckled as he walked towards her. 'The how is that I came in through the front door, which is a simple bi-lock. The security system in this place is pathetic. The why is because I'm here to take you home. Come on, grab your bag.'

But before she could react, Sean lifted her like a helium balloon, instead of ten tonnes of bone and blubber. 'But I've got work…' Still trying to shove her intellect into gear that Sean was volunteering to take her home. He was here to check on her, to take care of her. *No way!*

'It's almost two in the morning and you won't be any good if you stayed up any longer. You're beautiful now, so we won't call it beauty sleep, but your bright brain needs rest to function properly.'

Her mind stopped as she blinked. Did Sean say she was beautiful?

'Come on, you.' Sean handed Deanne her bag and left everything behind—not like she had any choice in the matter.

Sean parked his sedan in front of Deanne's family home where all the houses were shrouded in darkness. Streetlights held back long shadows from the road, while everything around them slept. 'Are you okay?'

Deanne felt like she was seventeen again, being dropped off from a date at her dad's house. Although, she'd never been privy to that herself. Her limited dating career commenced after her eighteenth birthday, when she'd lost weight, moved out of home and into her own duplex.

'Is it normal for you to walk into a locked property at two in the morning and drag out some woman?' Deanne asked.

'No. I was worried you'd lost track of time, so I drove over and spotted your work-ute parked at Clare's office. When I saw the lights were on, I knew you were still busy inside.' Sean stroked the side of her face. 'Why?' he said, beating her before she'd said it.

'Am I that predictable?' She was starting to resent at how easily she could be read.

'You've never allowed yourself to be unpredictable. But this is why.' Unclipping his seatbelt, Sean clutched her curls, leaned over and brushed his lips against hers, while his hands gently pulled her closer and he kissed her long, deep, and deliciously slow.

Deanne pushed back into her seat. 'Goodnight Sean.' A little breathless as her lips tingled and her heart hammered out its own rap dance. She gazed into his dark eyes that weren't expecting her to stop, and she felt proud of her unpredictability.

'Night, Deanne.' Sean's fingertips brushed her soft

jawline.

With this sudden need for spontaneity, or perhaps the rush of desire that hit Deanne, she found her nerve and grabbed Sean's shirt and pressed her lips against his.

Passion flowed into her bloodstream like an unstoppable spark that followed an undrawn line to ignite like grenade fire when their two souls collided. Tongues ravished as heat rose and arms wrapped around shoulders. He pulled her closer, but she was trapped by her seatbelt.

Sean latched onto a handful of hair, pulling her head back as his hot lips traced along her throat. The force of his actions dragged her deeper into a spiral of sizzling pleasure that flooded into her soul.

Searching for body heat, she lifted his shirt and purred as her fingers caressed his bare skin and tight, hard muscles that only made her hungrier.

Seatbelt unclipped; Sean pulled Deanne towards him. 'Come 'ere.'

'Ow, the gear stick.' It slammed against her knee. She wanted to climb on top of him, but her skirt restricted her movement.

'You're mine.'

Deanne felt the growling rumble from his chest as he swiftly pulled her onto his lap. 'How did you—' The steering wheel pressed against her back and her head knocked against the cold driver's window.

'You talk too much, sweetheart.' His mouth covered hers, as he pushed back his driver's seat. The buttons on her shirt were undone in the blink of an eye, and he eagerly pulled down her bra cup. His hot mouth and tongue latched onto her breast, lavishing her hardening nipple.

'Oh, sheeezusss.' She hissed through her teeth. Clutching into his thick black hair, his rigid body pushed beneath her, she was desperate to be with him.

A bright flash of light swept through the window.

'*Oh, no.*' Deanne hid her naked torso against Sean, they froze.

She peeked at the car driving past. It was a taxi. It pulled up a few houses behind them, let the fare out and continued around the corner, while breathless pants filled Sean's steamy car.

'I'd better go inside.' Deanne shuffled back into the passenger seat, while her heartbeat echoed in her ears. Her shaky fingers fumbled with her shirt's buttons. She soon gave up and tied it into a loose knot. Brushing fingers through her messy hair, she licked her tender lips.

Then she realised she'd just made-out in a car, like a sweaty teenager, in front of her dad's house. 'Oh man.' And dropped her head in shame.

Sean took a deep breath and let it out nice and slow as he straightened his shirt and thrust his fingers through his tousled hair. 'Not that I'm against the old-fashioned fumble in the car...' He grinned at her, wrapping one of her rouge ringlets around his finger. 'But I'll want room to move when I make love to you, but first you need sleep.' Sean reached across and pushed open her door. 'Go to bed, sweetheart. Move, or I'll want to tuck you in, then you'll never get any sleep.'

Closing the passenger door behind her, she swayed like a zombie on the sidewalk.

Sean started his car. Lowering the passenger window, he called out, 'Go to bed, sweetheart.'

Deanne turned on her heels, holding her shirt shut as the night air nipped at her hot skin. In a euphoric dream-state, she stepped up to the front door. As if on autopilot, she closed the door to the outside world, and only then, in the protective shield of home, she smiled.

NINETEEN

Sean drove from Deanne's house and made his way across town, dressed all in black for a reason. If Deanne asked, which she never did, he'd happily explain everything.

If he hadn't planned tonight's urgent little escapade, he would've happily escorted her to bed. But he was here now, and slowed down as he entered the deserted car park.

Sean killed the sedan's lights and drove along the front of the *Harrison's Family Hardware* warehouse. He parked out the back, where he was hidden by a tower of wooden pallets that created elongated shadows across the bitumen.

He grabbed his black backpack from the car's boot, slipped on his gloves, and headed for the fence line.

With ease, he clambered up the wall of mesh and over the barbed wire to land effortlessly within the deserted nursery. It reminded him of an atrium jungle.

Sure, he could've asked Deanne to let him in, but where's the challenge in that?

Sean unlocked the glass sliding doors, then tricked the alarm cable inside the door's groove using a specialised aluminium plate to keep the circuit running. He slid the door open and stepped inside.

Too easy.

Sean stood still and stared deep into the shadows

filling the silent warehouse. The red light on the security cameras blinked, fully aware of their systems blind spots. After all, this was his day job.

How would Reg and Jimmy handle it if they found out that Sean was breaking into their premises at two thirty in the morning?

How would Deanne react?

It was too late to wake up Deanne now, because he was here for a reason that seemed pretty lame right about now. It was a huge reminder as to why he never mixed business with pleasure.

He couldn't believe he'd breached his own retirement rules, especially when there was no financial gain when it came to Deanne, or this shed.

Sean didn't do hardware. He did corporate buildings, high-end security vaults, and billionaire's mansions. Not warehouses.

'Because she's worth it, mate.'

Hell yeah, Deanne is worth it. It's what he'd hoped to achieve from his tell-all-session with her this morning.

Although, what he was doing now didn't seem like the right thing to do.

Why was he always messing up when it came to Deanne? He was a man who rarely ever made mistakes—especially when it came to his job?

But he was here now and all suited-up for the occasion. It'd be a shame not to finish what he'd started.

With a shrug, Sean effortlessly passed the motion sensors in the main warehouse area. Keeping to the shadows he climbed the stairs and headed for Deanne's office.

Dumping his pack on Deanne's chair, and with pen light in mouth, he set about his task. Not stealing anything, instead Sean installed his own hardware within a hardware store, chuckling at the irony.

After packing his tools away, Sean checked the fax machine's slight re-programme was still working. Satisfied, he checked that the fake document was spread out over her desk.

He sat in her chair and tapped away on his smart phone to activate his installations, when he spied the letter opener and its inscription:

'Congratulations on ten years and a job well done, luv Dad & Jimmy'.

Sean guessed the barely legible kid's scrawl was Jimmy's. It made him grin because that's what families did for one another.

Sean then remembered Jimmy talking about the pile of Sorry-cards from Deanne's ex, Darren.

The name was itself fanciful—Darren and Deanne. D&D lives here. Just imagining the perfect mirrored D&D monogramed swirls, etched onto stained glass above a house's wide wooden front door as the journey's end of a stone path, bordered by a white picket fence. Should he retch now?

Did the Sorry-cards exist?

Sean didn't get it. He'd been trained to leave no trace, to not write letters or notes, and had never been a romantic, not until he'd met Deanne. Was this what Deanne responded to? He had to see.

'Don't do it.'

Even as he cursed his curiosity, Sean unlocked the bottom drawer. Aware he was prying when he'd never bothered before. He never cared what people thought before.

Yet, studying Deanne's beautiful expressive face, he knew she didn't trust him. She trusted no man after what that Darren had done to her.

And wouldn't this current course of action, make her trust him just as much?

Fingers on the handle, Sean winced. Did he dare?

Yes! He needed to know what power this Ex had over Deanne and opened the drawer.

With pen-light in his mouth, he peered into the deep wooden recess.

The light dropped from his gaping jaw.

'No. Bloody. Way.'

Sean screwed his nose up as he picked up his torch that only spotlighted the deep drawers' colourful clash of cardboard.

It'd been five months since the wedding and Sean remembered it well. It was the day Deanne walked into his life as the fallen angel with the saddest oceanic eyes who'd awoken his soul.

Sean frowned as his gloved fingers reached into the massive pile of cardboard. The *I'm Sorry* cards, *I love you* cards, *I miss you* cards, and loads of garish sap-crap.

The man got busted. The woman dumped him. So, move on, mate.

Was the Ex too dumb to take no for an answer, hoping to regain his ruined reputation?

Whatever, the loser had lost his chance and Sean wasn't giving up Deanne without a fight. He certainly wouldn't be hanging out here at three in the morning if he didn't care about her.

So why was Deanne keeping these love letters? Were they a reminder to guard against being with anyone new? Did she still care for the ex?

No, Sean didn't believe that.

Yet, he still couldn't understand why she kept them. Was this ex hoping to wear her down? Well aware of Deanne's sensitive caring nature, would she cave in?

Sean closed the drawer and re-locked it. His focus was on catching the person setting up Deanne first, and then he'd deal with the ex-factor.

Ensuring everything was in its place, careful to leave no signs. It was the most desired skill of any decent cat burglar, and that was to never let anyone know they'd visited until they were long gone. And Sean had been one of the best in the business. He'd never been caught because he always played it safe, meticulously planning these trips to make sure he never left a trace.

So why was he risking so much for Deanne?

How was Deanne going to react when she found out?

If she asked him anything he'd tell her everything. He wanted no secrets or lies when it came to their relationship. He wanted to do this right, for her.

But he'd been there for a reason, just as Deanne had said—to catch a crook you had to think like one, and so the ex-thief snuck off into the night.

TWENTY

Nan wiped her hands on her apron as she stood by the kitchen sink, staring through the window that faced the backyard. The talk-back radio chattered in the background with the aroma of coffee lingering in the mid-morning air.

'Morning, Nan. Are you busy?' Deanne asked, heading for her travel mug of coffee waiting on the bench.

Nan was surprised her granddaughter had slept so late. 'Why?'

'Are you able to drop me off at Clare's office?' Deanne took a sip of her coffee and sighed. 'It's like heaven in a cup, just perrrrrfect.'

Nan grabbed a muffin wrapped up in napkins she'd kept warm in the microwave and passed it to Deanne. 'Eat, child, can't live on coffee alone.'

'Thanks Nan.' Deanne kissed her grandmother on the top of her head, and then took a bite of her muffin. 'Fantabuloussss.'

Nan wheeled around and narrowed her eyes at her granddaughter being all giggly-girlie. 'I suppose you'll want to go now in your typical running style?'

'Yes please, Nan.'

'Fine. Gimme a sec.' Nan slipped out of her house slippers and into her slip-on shoes, she grabbed her bag and keys and headed out the back door. 'What time did you get in last night?'

'After two?' Deanne shouldered her workbag, with travel-mug in one hand, muffin in the other, she followed. Kicking the flyscreen door shut, Deanne dashed down the back stairs in her Saturday casual-clobber of jeans, boots, and a t-shirt. No work uniform today, it was supposed to be the child's day off.

Beside her small sedan, Nan, held out her keys into the sunlight, squinting at the tiny image. She pressed the button, only to re-lock the car, again. 'Dang. I hate this newfangled button. Why'd they make the words so small for?' She re-pressed it to unlock. 'Go out with the girls, did ya?'

'I worked at Clare's to finish the proposal, undisturbed.' Deanne jumped into the passenger seat and clipped on her seat belt.

'My word.' Nan stood in front of her little white car with keys in hand, squinting at her granddaughter.

At the tender age of eighty-two, Nan was still licensed. But no one in her family ever volunteered to be her passenger, swearing Nan scared the absolute crap out of every passenger.

Except today.

Nan hobbled into the driver's seat. She sat far forward, peeked over the steering wheel, and after a few stabs she successfully inserted the key into the ignition and started the car with a roar. 'Why d'ya work at Clare's and not at your own office, child?'

'So I wouldn't be disturbed.' Deanne sipped her coffee, bit on her muffin, to chew in silence while staring out the window.

'Reg said you'd finished it or something. Him and your brother were bragging about you last night.' Peeking between the gaps in the steering wheel, Nan shifted the gearstick until the R lit up on the dash. She then planted her foot on the accelerator and reversed out the driveway, straight out onto the road, just missing the letterbox.

Nan smiled at her luck because she liked the new letterbox.

When Nan's two feet hit the brake pedal and the small car squealed to a halt. She leaned forwards, slammed the gear shift until the 'D' light came on the dash and planted her shoe on the accelerator. Nan sat up, just in time to avoid swiping the street pole, and with a slight wheel wobble, they headed for town.

'I met Jimmy's date last night, too skinny. But gawd, she reminds me of Fleur. Except this other girl has this mucky-muddy brown hair colour. It's just not natural.'

'Most women colour their hair, Nan.'

'Don't know, muddy hair shows a muddy mind. Talking bout mud, those flowers you put in the other week by the tree are looking good. I told that brother of yours to bring home some fertiliser. Remind him, will you?'

'I'll text him now.' Deanne thumbed away on her phone's touch screen. 'Nan, why do you water by hand when we sell irrigation?'

'It's my thing, child.'

'Your thing?' Deanne giggled.

'Yeah, I stand outside, hose in hand and stare at the sky, listening to the neighbours yakking, children playing, birds flying as the clouds pass. All while watching the garden do its thing. I stand still in the middle of all this action like I'm meditating. It's my thing.'

'Huh, simple. I like it.' Deanne slipped her phone away. 'Nan, can I ask a favour?'

'Must be the morning for favours.' Nan raised an eyebrow at her granddaughter. As Nan looked left so did the vehicle, veering towards a group of parked cars.

'Please don't tell Dad and Jimmy I worked at Clare's.' Deanne sipped her coffee, munched on her muffin, and gazed out the window.

'Why?' Nan's eyes bulged at the oncoming collision. She yanked the steering wheel to the right, over-correcting herself to then cross the double lines in the middle of the road.

Giving the steering wheel a hard left, the car wobbled to resume its place in the correct lane. Nan held her breath, lowering her neck into her shoulders and waited for Deanne to blast her.

But nothing was said.

'You all right, child?'

'It's…' Deanne sighed.

'For the privacy, that's why you're working at Clare's?'

'Um, yeah.' Deanne sipped her coffee, nibbled on her muffin, and again glanced out the passenger window.

'Clare's, huh?' Nan gave a sharp left of the steering wheel, crossed two lanes, cutting-off traffic where cars blasted horns to the chorus of screaming tyres. Both women ignored the noise outside their vehicular bubble as Nan's car finally found itself on the correct side of the road and eased into the flow of traffic.

Then Nan snuck a glance at her granddaughter's

oblivious nature. By right, Deanne should've been hollering loud enough to open hell's gate by now. Her granddaughter should've been clutching the seat in terror with one hand while pulling the handbrake, demanding she be the driver.

But it never happened.

Deanne just sat in the passenger seat, sipping on that fancy coffee of hers and gazed at the outside world. Calm and casual, and so abnormal.

'How did you get home last night, child?' Nan asked. 'And where is your work car?'

'At Clare's. I got a lift home.' Deanne suppressed her smile behind her coffee cup.

'Who brought you home?' Nan's car swayed like a drunk-driver in the left lane at the top speed of forty kilometres. Irate drivers overtook while tooting their car horns and holding up their rude finger's in passing-protest. 'What's their problem,' Nan mumbled.

'Sean brought me home last night.' Deanne nibbled her muffin while gawking out the passenger window. 'It's a pretty morning.'

'Well...' Nan sat taller and smiled wider. 'Sean's a smart lad. He's got them shadowy eyes that miss nothing. And he's a boy who cares for his mother and sisters, an' that shows a moral heart. Are you going to keep seeing him?'

'Early days,' replied Deanne, sipping on her coffee.

Nan drove straight through a zebra crossing, just missing a pedestrian halfway across the road. 'Oops, sorry. But you should've walked faster.' Nan stuck her chin higher, ignoring the shouting walker, as she waited for

Deanne's rebuttal.

Again, it never happened.

'I reckon you've been working too hard, child. You're distracted, but a good kind of distracted.' Nan grinned. She leaned down to scratch an itch on her calf.

The car started leering towards the centre of the road.

A panicked horn blast came from the oncoming traffic.

Deanne, with half eaten muffin in her mouth, reached over and corrected the car's steering to avert a head on collision.

Nan gaped at her granddaughter in wide-eyed awe. By now Deanne should've screamed blue-bloody-murder about Nan being a danger to society's roads, demanding Nan surrender her license.

Instead, Deanne ate her muffin and sipped her fancy coffee. Oblivious.

'You are distracted.' Nan smiled widener, snorting a laugh. 'Child, I reckon you're in love with this Sean fella.'

'Don't be ridiculous.' Deanne scowled before shoving the last of her muffin into her gob, brushing the crumbs off her shirt.

Nan grinned at Deanne.

In front of her was a pushbike heading along the row of parked cars.

'Where did he come from?' She corrected the car with a hard right, just missing the bike rider's rear tyre. The rider was forced towards the parked cars. Dropping his bike he jumped to the pavement for his own safety, shouting and waving his fists at their passing car.

Nan winced, while Deanne waved and smiled at the foul-mouthed cyclist, then sighed and sipped her coffee.

Nan's jaw dropped, speechless…

But only for a moment.

'Ya heads right up in them clouds, child, coz I've never seen you like this, not even with Darren. Ever. It's Sean you've got on your mind.'

Nan entered the busy main road towards town. Her knuckles whitened on the steering wheel, as her eyes darted at the flow of busy traffic. 'Why do people got to rush for? Work's still going to be there?'

'I'm not sure if I'm ready?'

'Huh?' Nan arched her eyebrow at Deanne staring out the window. 'Oh, dating men,' she mumbled, rolling her eyes. 'Is anytime the right bloody time. But no need to rush.' Like Nan who cruised at forty in a sixty zone with her nose just peeking over the top of her steering wheel. 'But your trust's been broken, child, that'll take time to heal. An' if a fella's aware of your baggage and still sticking with you, I reckon he's the one for you. I like Sean, and you do too. You're just scared after what you've been through.'

'Maybe I am.'

'And we're here.' Nan pulled the handbrake and slammed both of her shoes onto the foot brake. Her car skidded to a stop. The vehicles behind screeched as their burning tyres polluted the air with thick black smoke.

Nan peeked at her rear-view mirror, then hunkered low into her seat. She gave Deanne a fleeing side glance, bracing for her granddaughter's lecture.

'Thanks for the lift, Nan.' Deanne kissed her grandmother's cheek and hopped out of the car.

'Take care, child, and don't work too hard. Remember, it's the weekend.'

How the heck did Deanne miss the eight-car pileup

behind them?

Well, that was none of their business. They didn't see a thing.

Nan leaned towards the dash, checked she was in gear, then planted her foot on the accelerator and quickly pulled on the steering wheel to avoid oncoming traffic. Horns blasted, tyres screeched, as Nan peered over the steering wheel and smiled.

Her granddaughter was in love.

And Nan got to keep her license for another day.

TWENTY-ONE

An hour later Deanne stood inside her own office. Her proposal, spread across her desk, had been tampered with. Because Sean had shown her how to set sneaky tell-tale traps by spelling words in different rows on the displayed documents.

Her hand slightly trembled as she read the sender's report, confirming a fax had been sent only an hour ago, from her own fax machine that sat silently on the bench.

A shiver squirrelled along her spine.

The culprit had to still be here. Downstairs.

Deanne's mobile rang, it made her jump. 'H-h-hello?'

'Hey, it's me. What's wrong?' Sean asked on the other end of the phone.

'They've faxed it.' Scrunching up the report in her hand, Deanne peeked through the slats of her window's blinds. The warehouse floor below was busy with customers and staff.

'I'm presuming you're at the office?'

'I had to, and I'm adding some changes. Besides, I normally do this, and it would've looked suspicious if I didn't show.' It was weird scrutinising all her routines and habits. Whatever happened to her safe and cosy cocoon of ignorant bliss?

'Knew you would. Hey, while you're there, can you get

a copy of today's staff roster and I'll meet you at Clare's around eleven?'

'Why eleven o'clock?'

'You don't stay all day, Saturday?'

'Okay, eleven it is. But take note, I'm beginning to despise your assumptions of being able to predict my time schedules.' She slept-walked through her days because it kept her going since the wedding. But Sean and this tender-stealing situation was forcing her to wake up.

'Sweetheart, you may be a creature of habit, but you're unpredictable in other areas. I can't wait to tap into that buried passion I got a glimpse of last night.'

Deanne dropped her head to hide her face in her hands. She'd never lunged at a man inside a car before. Nor had she ever made out like a teenager in her dad's front yard.

Oh, great! Had she unleashed another adolescent moment? Was it time to rebel, get body piercings and consider tattoos?

'Just keep performing your normal routine. Don't think, just do boring. See you soon, sweetheart.' Sean laughed.

'Prick,' she said to the silent phone.

How come Sean was making her revaluate her way of life? So what, if she worked in the same job since school and could do it with her eyes closed.

'This sucks!' Now she was talking to the roof.

Great, was it time she confirmed her booking for a padded-room-with-a-view.

Deanne slumped into her seat. Swinging her legs to gently rock her office chair. Was she in a rut?

And was everyone aware of her routine that when life surprised her, she was expected to collapse?

Hold on, she'd just suffered a major life change. Survived her thrilling escapade as the runaway bride at her own wedding. Became single and moved back home to live with her family. And now she had to deal with this threat against her professional reputation. Talk about a total overhaul!

Should she make herself available for chat shows and group therapy? Should she sell her story to some script writer to use as an added layer in some twisted daytime TV soap opera? Her life was already a much-publicised affair, why not milk it to pay for her hideaway on a tropical island?

No, Deanne couldn't leave her family. Besides, she was meant to be feeling better. *Um… yeah?*

She sat up and keenly worked on her documents, as planned. Then, as per her *not*-normal routine, she set her tell-tale traps, closed her office door, and went for her daily walk through the nursery.

This was a part of her normal routine and the last remnant of her smoking days when she used to duck outside for a smoke break. It was a habit Deanne didn't want to break because she enjoyed strolling through the nursery. It reminded her of Nan's hand watering, world watching, meditative moment.

Was this Deanne's thing? To stop and admire the texture, structure, and details on assorted healthy plants. Children's squeals of delight carried over from the store's small playground. Nearby, Beatrice and her off-siders worked in the café, where the aromas of home-baked cookies and freshly brewed coffee drifted amongst the heady floral aromas.

Nursery hands shared advice with customers on plant queries and selection. The customers' open excitement almost contagious with their plans for their homes. It was the same expression worn by those whose who walked the aisles, gathering the tools to start their next home project.

This hardware store wasn't just a store, it was a part of their home improvements.

It was a part of these peoples' quality of life.

Deanne frowned as she marched through the warehouse.

Which staff member set her up? She couldn't look at them without feeling sick, especially when she wanted to trust them.

Deanne jumped into her work-ute and gazed at the warehouse facade.

She grew up inside this shed, right beside her big brother Jimmy. After school, weekends and school holidays were spent at this shed. She'd twirled her skipping rope up and down the aisles when it rained. They'd spent hours riding pushbikes, skateboards, and roller skates in that shed. She even had her driving lessons within this carpark, now full of assorted vehicles.

The aroma of barbecued sausages and onions filled the air as part of another weekend fundraiser for one of the many local sporting groups they sponsored.

When she spied Jimmy at the nearby tradesmen's entrance waving at her. Deanne waved back.

As the sun shone, an epiphany hit as if the clouds were being cleared within her mind. She loved this place, and she loved her family. This wasn't about her anymore; this was for her family, for their employees, and for what they provided to this community.

Deanne had survived those bullying school-halls of hell. She'd grown up. And could hear Sean telling her that no one had the power to make her feel bad or squash her inner beliefs except herself.

Deanne straightened up, gripped the steering wheel, and stared at her reflection in the rear-view mirror. She repeated Lou's body-building mantra: *'I am not a victim. I am a survivor. A fighter who will fight for what I believe in, and I believe in me.'* She shifted the work-ute into gear and drove out the car park. She wasn't going to be beaten—not yet. Not now.

TWENTY-TWO

'*Knock. Knock,*' called out Clare from the other side of the office door.

Deanne smiled as she rolled up the last of her charts and dumped them into the box. The weight off her shoulders was amazing. 'Come in.'

Clare ducked her head around the door and tucked her midnight-black bob behind her ear. 'Hiya, honey, how's it going?'

'I've finished.' Deanne slipped her laptop into its bag and was ready to load her work-ute to go home and probably sleep for a week.

Hold on, she had other crap to tackle first. But at least this tender could now be crossed off her list. She'd given it her best and it was now up to fate to decide if it was worthy of winning.

'Good.' Clare opened the door wide to reveal the radiant Jane with her mop of white spring coiled curls and baby bump. Beside her stood Lou, clutching bottles of champagne like hand weights. 'We're way past due an office session, don't you think?'

'Aw if it isn't the Greatest-Girls-of-the-Galaxy.' Deanne hugged them all. It felt like a lifetime since she'd seen them.

Champagne opened and with glasses filled, they sat on

the rug, hidden within the reception area sharing pizza.

'How's the practising mother?' Deanne asked, tenderly rubbing Jane's well-formed baby bump.

'Countdown is four weeks, people. Bags are packed and waiting. But I still need you all there in case Petey faints.'

'I thought you were prepping him with birthing videos?'

'Petey can watch zombies eating brains, but we both can't stomach those birthing movies.'

'Ick.' Lou shuddered. 'I might faint in sympathy with Petey.'

Deanne giggled at the spikey-haired body builder. 'We'll all be there to prop the mother up.'

'Good. That's why as of now, all phones must be charged, and kept on you at all times,' said Jane.

'And during sex? I mean, do you know the baby's sex?' Clare asked.

'I hope not, it ruins the bloody surprise,' said Lou.

Jane shook her curls. 'We're keeping it a surprise. Petey reckons he'll get mileage from the betting pools from his workmates.'

Clare raised an immaculately groomed eyebrow that was the same colour as her perfectly sleeked hair. 'I just can't imagine tradesmen on a worksite betting on a baby.'

'They'd bet on anything,' said Deanne, smiling so wide her jaw ached. She felt normal. Better than normal. Was there a before-normal or was this a new-normal?

'So far, they're betting on the sex, weight, even the time, and birth date. Can't wait to meet the new member of our family.' Jane smiled at her tummy.

'How are your issues going, Lou?' Deanne asked. 'Has the vow of celibacy been tested? It's almost a year, Lou, since you made that vow.'

'Wow.' Clare's eyes widened. 'How can you do that?'

'I'm contemplating the nunnery myself,' mumbled Deanne, sipping on her champagne.

'At least you've dumped your bottled boyfriend,' said Jane.

Deanne's hand covered her heart and raised her glass in the air. 'To Black Johnny and our good times shared.' She sighed and smiled because this wasn't a Black Johnny moment.

'You're going to think I'm stupid,' Lou muttered, lowering her head.

'No, we wouldn't,' replied the other three.

'Well…' Lou inhaled deeply. 'I've agreed to go out on a date.' She then gave a shifty sideways glance at Deanne.

Deanne pointed at Lou with her pizza slice. 'No, you're finally going out with Chris?'

'Who?' Clare asked.

'Boy next door.' Deanne bit into her pizza and indulged in the flavours of food and champagne—*forget the calories, this was living.*

'What boy next door? They don't exist,' said Clare.

'Well, explain the Australian-Indian accountant, who plays the part as my loyal space-buddy, because he never leaves Dad's place,' said Deanne, as Clare's eyes widened with recognition.

'Chris told me his mother's arranging his marriage to these Bollywood brides,' said Jane.

Lou frowned. 'How did you know?'

'Email-brides is yesterday's news.' Clare shared a lazy half-shrug.

'Christopher promised he wouldn't blabber. That little bugger. I told him—'

'Calm down, Lou. I guessed because I know how much Chris adores you. I'm pleased for you both.' Deanne couldn't help herself and reached over and hugged Lou.

'Gawd, have I won the bloody triathlon?' Lou tried to suppress her smile.

'It's just a normal love-hug from Dee. You did the same when I agreed to date Petey, and our engagement,' said Jane, giggling.

'And the wedding. And the pregnancy. We remember how Dee was. Good to see it's back, babe.' Clare raised her glass at Deanne.

'I'm happy for the Greatest-Girls-of-the-Galaxy. You deserve the best.' Their glasses clinked together in a group salute. 'Chris will be a thorough gentleman, or I'll kick his arse. Are you going to wear a dress, Lou?'

'Hell no.'

'At your wedding you'll be the one wearing the suit and Chris will wear the dress.' Deanne smiled at the imagined scenario. It was so good to laugh again.

'So, what's happening with you, Dee?' Clare asked. 'How come you're working here and not at your own office?'

'You didn't tell Petey I was working here? Did you, Jane?'

'No. But why the secrecy? You're not doing anything wrong, are you?'

'As if Dee would.' Clare scoffed. 'Come on, we're

talking inner geek love child.'

'Am not.' Was she? 'Hey, am I boring?' There she'd voiced it. It was Sean's fault.

'Nooo.' Jane and Clare gushed in unison.

'You have been, lately.' Lou nodded, while the other two women glared at her. 'What? I'm not going to lie. Not to Dee. Truth is, you never used to be. But ever since the wedding you've been ducking us, always bloody working, and I get that.'

'We understand, Dee. Especially after what Darren did,' Clare said calmly, while she narrowed her eyes to glower at Lou.

'What I don't get is why Dee's working here?' Lou craned her thick muscular neck around the front reception area. 'You're not in trouble, are you?'

'I'm not doing anything illegal,' replied Deanne.

But the way her three friends looked at Deanne, she suddenly craved a cigarette.

'Are you avoiding Darren? Petey told me that Jimmy said Darren sent you flowers the other day.' Jane tried to reach for another piece of pizza, but her baby bump kept her grounded.

Lou lifted the box for the future-mother to grab a slice. 'The motherff— No offence with the mother word, Jane.' She smiled at Jane's wink.

'Trust my big brother and his big fat gob. Who else did Jimmy blab to?' Sean was right, Deanne's family were have-a-chats, *and* she was hanging out with tradesmen too much picking up their slang from the store. 'I hate being talked about.'

'You shouldn't bother about people gossiping, I don't.'

Lou pointed her slice of pizza like an extension of her finger. 'I only listen to and respect the three voices who happen to be in this room, and that's what matters to me. I've told you before Dee, you're not in high school anymore.'

'And you're not an army sergeant, Lou,' Clare said, faking a yawn.

'Jimmy's worried about you Dee, and so are we?' Jane glared at the duelling duo then turned back to Deanne. 'You can tell us what's going on.'

'Christopher told me the same thing that he'd heard from someone else,' muttered Lou as she bit into her pizza.

'Let me guess, Jimmy told Chris who told you.' Deanne rolled her eyes and emptied her entire champagne glass in one go. 'You do realise, Chris spends more time at home and only sleeps at his parent's house next door.'

Lou passed the champagne bottle to Deanne. 'Jimmy swears you were spotted sucking face with someone in the hardware store. So, who was it?'

'My bloody brother and his big mouth.' Deanne was annoyed at how Sean realised this. The man missed nothing. It was almost creepy, and annoying. And she missed him.

Oh no. She sat up straight and blinked as if ridding dust from her eyes. Deanne truly missed Sean.

'EEEEwww...' Lou grimaced, Jane's jaw dropped, while Clare bent over laughing, to slap at the carpet.

'NO. Gross, I wasn't kissing my brother.' Deanne hid her hot face inside her palms. 'I was complaining about Jimmy spreading gossip.'

'Don't change the subject. Tell them who kissed you.'

Clare nudged her elbow into Deanne's side. 'Explain the kiss.'

Deanne tried to act cool, even if her stomach was fluttering. 'It was...' She took a deep breath and whispered, 'Sean.' Now her biggest secret was out, she shirked her shoulders and waited for their reactions.

Jane sat as far forward as her baby bump would allow. 'Sean, from last weekend's barbecue, Sean?'

Deanne nodded.

Jane smiled. 'Sean was nice. Even your Nan likes him.'

'That's rare,' said Clare, cocking an eyebrow at Deanne.

'It's true, Nan likes Sean.' Now all Deanne had to do was make sense of how she felt about Sean. It'd be easier to dislike him. If she could.

'Who the hell is Sean?' Lou demanded.

'Tall, dark, and dreamy. He's got these intense dark eyes. And he wears his fringe long. It's sexy how he flicks it out of his eyes.' Clare gushed like a teenager.

Jane also copied the hair flick with her mop of curls. 'I know, I almost reached over to sweep it aside. It's so black and shiny too.'

Deanne giggled. 'I didn't know you had a thing for Sean's hair flick.'

Jane grinned behind her glass. 'Don't tell my husband or he'll want to grow his hair long.'

'Petey's beard is long enough to cover two mullet-heads, honey,' said Clare, patting Jane's curls.

'Who the hell are you talking about?' Snapped out Lou.

'Sean's the guy that was looking after Dee at the bar on the wedding night,' explained Clare. 'Remember? Sean's the guy who snogged Dee on the street before we put her into Nan's car. He's the guy that made Deanne speechless from that kiss, where you'd said she'd play drunk-dumb to not remember.'

'I do not play drunk-dumb.'

'Ah, hello, boyfriend-in-a-bottle's pretty dumb,' said Lou.

'Black Johnny was there when I needed him.'

'Do you still need him?' Jane asked.

'Um, no. Not for a while. Huh, Nan would be so proud to hear that.' The trio nodded in approval too. Had she really been that bad?

'Oi?' Lou faced Deanne. 'Are we talking about the bloke you kissed while wearing that puffy marshmallow dress months ago?'

'It was a pretty dress that complimented Dee's figure perfectly,' said Jane.

'It's nothing but ash now.' Pity Deanne's hurt feelings hadn't disappeared the same way.

'But did you see this guy again or not?' Lou asked.

'It's true.' Clare raised her glass to slice her way back into the conversation. 'Somehow, Sean tracked down Dee and within one minute of reuniting he kisses her in the middle of the hardware store.'

'Nooo.' Jane and Lou stared at Deanne with their eyes wide open.

'Swizzle-sticks.' Deanne felt the heat rise as she lowered her forehead to the floor to hide.

'Wow. You're in deep.' Jane tried to cover her smile with her fingertips.

'Am not.' Deanne's head whipped up, and she

somehow heard Nan telling her she was in love only this morning. 'Nope. Nooooooo. No. No. No. No.' She shook her head, always saying 'no' when it came to Sean. So, no. No, she was not in love with a man she'd technically just met.

Or was she?

'I hope you punched his bloody lights out for invading your body space.'

'What?' Deanne blinked up at Lou.

'Why?' Clare asked. 'Especially when you don't know him, Lou.'

'Sean's a nice guy,' said Jane.

'No one has the right to breach your personal body space. I teach that in my female self-defence classes. You're welcome to come along, anytime, you'll all get Mate's Rates.'

'We'll consider it, thank you, Lou.' Deanne winked at Lou who was all heart with lots of muscles to back-up her bite.

'Have you seen Sean since the barbecue last Saturday?' Jane asked, caressing her belly.

'And did he take you to dinner?' Clare asked.

'Dinner no. Lunch, coffee, brunch, meal deliveries and lots of conversations and many phone calls.' Quite the change from the guy shoving money down her shirt, threatening to sic her brother onto him. 'Is it too soon?'

'How do you mean, honey?' Clare sipped on her champagne.

Deanne felt her attraction to Sean, the skip of the heartbeat, the curl in her toes, the tingle in her hairline, all from just thinking of him. Yet, the man challenged her on so many levels whether she wanted it or not. 'Would Sean be a rebound? Like what Jimmy went through losing his childhood sweetheart Fleur, then rebounding to Casey with their quickie marriage and divorce?'

Lou sighed, playing with her shoelaces. 'I remember Jimmy's devastation. He's still devo. He reckons your mob's cursed.'

Clare screwed up her nose. 'They are not.'

'Lou's right,' said Deanne.

'What? You're cursed? Since when?' Clare asked.

'I'm saying Jimmy's never recovered from Fleur. And yes, my brother believes our household's cursed.' Hard to disagree with her family's bad luck when it came to love.

'But is it worth the risk putting myself back out there?' Was this the moment she started packing her bags to move into the nunnery?

Lou shrugged her beefy shoulders. 'You're the only one who can say you're ready. Hell, I'm still trying to work out my own sexual issues.'

'But it's so worth it when you find the right one.' Jane rubbed her baby bump like a genie's bottle.

'Take the risk, honey,' said Clare. 'You're always telling me, all those times we've consumed copious wine bottles, devouring boxes of chocolates, while I'm shedding tears, heartbroken from being dumped again. And you swore Mr Right's waiting for me.'

'Aw, come on, Clare, you never make it to the second date with these blokes,' blurted out Lou. 'Since when did you want a relationship? I thought men were your talking sex toys as a brief distraction from your art work?'

'We're not talking about me. And not all men are like

Darren,' said Clare.

'True.' Jane lay back on the cushions with her baby bump more pronounced against her petite frame. 'My Petey's adorable, and Chris is perfect for Lou. I like Sean and he may be the one for you, Dee. Then all we need is to find someone for Clare.'

'Fine. If you want to talk about me, let's talk about me.' Clare huffed dramatically, only to smile as she topped up her glass. 'I'm dating the new dentist down the road. We went to dinner, and he's intelligent, funny, and cute.'

'So, did you sleep with him on the first date?' Lou asked.

'Unlike Dee's dateless-tonsil-duel with Sean…' Clare wagged her tongue, Jane giggled, Lou rolled her eyes, as Deanne felt her cheeks heat from the champagne. '…I waited until after dinner when he'd escorted me to my front door to kiss me. And that's it. I'm meeting him again tomorrow night. He's so different to anyone I've dated before.'

'How so?' Deanne pursed her lips, well aware of Clare's man-eating habits as a self-proclaimed nymphomaniac.

'He's shorter than me.'

'Aren't most men shorter than you?' Lou smirked behind her pizza slice.

Jane shrugged. 'Everyone's taller than me.'

'I've only kissed the dentist, once. It was clean and nice.' Clare's swept her tongue across her teeth.

'How come, whenever we get together, we always end up talking about bloody men?' Lou asked, scratching at her cropped blonde hair. 'I thought we came here to find out about Dee's secret squirrel stuff.'

Deanne rolled her eyes. 'Thanks for reminding them, Lou.'

'Lou's right. So, what's going on, Dee?' Jane asked.

'Now, don't overreact, especially you, Lou.' Deanne nodded at the brash weightlifter. 'This doesn't leave the room. But I could do with your honest opinions.'

The three women huddled closer, and Deanne explained all about her Hardware Blues, except Sean's questionable, illegal activities.

How would her friends feel about Sean's retirement as a thief?

Clare would love it. Considering Clare was a known trinket kleptomaniac when drinking, having pinched Sean's lighter in the first place. Not to mention, she'd practically fitted-out Reg's Beer shed. Even the shot-glasses kept in Deanne's desk came from Clare's upmarket pub crawls.

But would Jane and Lou be okay about Sean's past life-skills?

'Bastard's stealing.' Lou's scowl was as ferocious as the fist she smacked into her open hand.

'How did they get a copy of your documents?' Jane asked.

'There's a spy in my camp, using my fax. In. My. Office.'

'Noooo,' the three women chorused.

Lou shook her head. 'You've got to trust your staff in a small business. You taught me that, Dee, when you helped me open my own gym.'

'There's a lot of staff at the hardware store,' said Jane.

'I'm lucky it's just me and Mum in the bookshop. Do you know who it is?'

'No idea. Someone's sussing it out.' What was Sean up to? Deanne had been too busy revising her proposal to ask him. Yet, if she did see him, did she dare ask? 'But I'm pleased to announce I'll make that deadline, which is midday Monday.'

'So, you've redesigned your whole document to not get caught plagiarising your own work,' said Clare, 'and finished it in less than forty-eight hours.'

'Yes' Now all she needed was to submit the tender and win. Easy—*not*.

'How long did it take you to do the first one?' Jane asked.

'Over four months of research. I'll admit it,' Deanne said, throwing her hands in the air, 'this project kept me going after everything went to dust.'

'You needed the distraction,' said Jane.

Lou shook her head. 'I'm not going to sit 'ere and lie to Dee. Look, this work-tender thingamajig was better than her drinking some bottled-boyfriend crap. Hey, in the beginning I was proud Dee had found a constructive way to get over the whole wedding thing. But it also became her excuse to hide too.'

'Well forget the tact and put it right out there, Lou,' said Clare.

'I'm right here ladies.' Deanne waved her hand between the pair.

'I've missed your interventions between this warring pair,' Jane said with a sigh.

'We don't war,' Lou said, grinning at Clare.

Clare winked back. 'We've just got strong personalities that clash. But we still love each other.'

'If this project's finished, what will you do with yourself? Will you go back to your normal routine?' Jane asked.

'Um…' Deanne inhaled heavily and verbalised what had somehow become normal. 'Am I in a rut, sleepwalking through my days.'

Her three friends all nodded in unison.

No way, Sean was right—again. 'What do I do?'

'Try another challenge?' Clare sipped on her glass.

'Come work for me.' Lou thumbed at her chest. 'I'll keep you busy.'

'Thanks, Lou. But I love the warehouse, even if I whinge about it, it's still my second home.' Deanne knew it, felt it, and believed it now.

'So, spice it up,' said Jane. 'Find a new goal outside the workplace. I've got lots of books in the self-help section to check out.'

'Let's pump a bit of energy into your life and we'll work out a new gym routine for you. And I'm just going to say it…' Lou raised her muscular arm. 'It's okay to not trust after what you've suffered. Trust is earned and shouldn't be so freely given to staff, friends, and new lovers, not until you're ready. Don't you think, now that this project's done, you're mourning period is over, too?' Lou toyed with the lace of her sports shoe and peeked at Deanne. 'So, I reckon you should go out with this Sean, and see what happens.'

'Lou,' whispered Deanne. 'That's so insightful.'

'Lou's right.' Jane grabbed Lou's hand and gave it a squeeze. Clare, on the other side, reached for Deanne's and their linked hands formed a circle.

'Thanks, ladies. Now that's why I call you the Greatest-Girls-of-the-Galaxy.' Deanne replicated their smiles and felt the unjudged love within the room. 'I'll think about it.'

But not tonight.

TWENTY-THREE

Deanne's ringing mobile vibrated across her bedside table. She snatched up the annoying contraption that dared to disturb her sleep. 'Hello.' It'd been forever since she'd slept-in, so this had better be good.

'Morning, sweetheart. Are you still in bed?'

'Hmm.' A soft smile spread across her lips at the sound of Sean's voice, making her sigh as her head sunk deeper into her soft pillows. Sean. *Yummy.* Now that was a man worth dreaming about.

'What time did you get in last night?'

'Late. I was drinking with the Greatest-Girls-of-the-Galaxy at Clare's office.'

'Good for you. Did you finish your work?'

'Aha.' Her eyes remained shut, keen for more sleep, but his voice sounded nice and dreamy. 'Where are you?'

'Downstairs. I believe you're home alone, and the front door's buzzer doesn't work.'

'Nan broke the doorbell ages ago, said it irritated her when there was this plague of people preaching to her, so everyone's trained to use the side gate.'

'Are you going to let me in?'

'Nope.' She smiled at his laugh, amused how she kept saying no to the man who refused to accept her rejections.

Good thing too because the man could kiss.

'Why not?'

'You're the thief. Break in.' She giggled, dumping the phone onto her bedside table. She then re-hugged her teddy bear and burrowed beneath the warm blankets in her childhood double bed. She wasn't getting out of bed for any man, no matter how sexy Sean was. She just wanted to wallow in bed and rest her brain for the day.

* * *

A few minutes later Sean's body weighed down Deanne's bed, crawling under the blankets he cuddled up to her back as his hand slid around her waist. 'So, this is the sacred domain of where you grew up as a kid, huh? It's pink.'

His brow crinkled at the pink patches scattered across the wall, along with outlines of missing posters. There was a cupboard painted with large faded purple flowers. Yellowed lace curtains shifted above assorted flower cushions and various stuffed toys covered the window seat. It was an outdated, awfully pink, child's room.

'Welcome to the Pink-walled-horror-titus, my pre-teenage phase. Hey, how'd you get in?'

'Picked the front door lock.'

Deanne giggled. 'We never lock the back door. You could've just walked in.'

'The security in this place is unbelievable.' Sean gently rolled Deanne onto her back. 'What have we here?' Pointing to her cuddled teddy bear. 'What's his name?'

'Why do you assume it's a male?'

'Most teddies are male.' The ragged brown fur was well-worn, with only one eye remaining, and the stuffing was stuffed.

'His name's Teddy.'

'Original.' Sean gazed at her curled locks that spilled across her pillow like silk spread over washed sand. Her sleepy aquamarine blue eyes, scattered with teal crystals, were like sea-glass windows to her inner soul. She was his Siren of the sea and he wanted to drown. 'There's room for only one male in this bed.' *Damn straight.* And he threw the teddy over his shoulder and leaned down to feather his lips across hers.

Her chest rose and her breath stalled. 'Are you going to do a kiss and run on me?'

'Not while I have you in bed and on your back, babe.' His lips traced her delicate throat. 'Especially when you're home alone. In your dad's house. And what's this?' He tugged on her flannelette pyjamas. 'It's got bunny rabbits on it. I think I'm living every teenage boy's fantasy here.' Sean grinned against her shoulder as the sound of her giggles vibrated from her gift-wrapped chest, and he wanted to open his present now.

'Your jammies are a total turn-on.' His lips caressed her jawbone, unbuttoning her top, one by one. His fingers followed his lips down her delectable chest.

'Don't mock my pyjamas.'

'Gimme flannelette any day.' The sides of his face rubbed on the warm soft material. His nose and lips against her skin, her scent, taste, touch, were a wondrous assault upon his senses as he immersed himself within her aura.

'Could be satin and lace?'

'I don't care what it is, it's what's underneath that matters.' And he wanted to indulge in it all.

His lips stroked against hers as he undid the last button that allowed his hungry fingers to glide across her smooth skin, caressing every curve and dip, chasing the goosepimples that spread across her lush figure.

He kissed her deeper, searching for that switch to arouse her, to turn her sensuality into overdrive. Hands massaged plump breasts, he teased her hardening nipples between fingertips as he licked, suckled, and relished the taste of her skin he'd craved for so long. And he was going to make her sing, the way she made his soul sing for her.

* * *

Deanne had never felt more exposed as her body spun into a crazed spiral of desire. Delicious warm waves of lust swirled from her core as her heart's pace and pulse quickened.

Pyjama pants gone; she moaned under his touch as she writhed and wriggled, never more alive. She panted as the heat built inside her, almost terrified at the swiftness of the heated emotions he invoked, but she was powerless to stop them.

She didn't want him to stop.

Clasping onto her bedhead to hang on for the ride of his magic fingers, while his hot mouth lavished her aching nipples.

Her heart's beat flooded her ears, she gasped for air as her flesh quivered, her centre tightened, and her back arched.

Hips twisted and bucked, defenceless under his onslaught, her whole mind, body, and soul collided until she'd become a re-born star that spiralled weightless through the heavens. There, behind closed eyelids, she glided on waves of immeasurable indulgent pleasure that washed throughout her entirety.

Breathless, she looked up at the man in awe. She really needed that.

Sean's dark eyes shone down at her. 'I've got to see you do that again.'

Deanne gave a dreamy smile, while she swam in a sea of sensual-ecstasy. She was happy to float forever.

This might be heaven on earth and Sean… a demi-god.

But no way would she tell him that. Not yet. Because she was still speechless and happy to go again—hell yeah.

* * *

Sean shrugged off his clothes, fast. His hardened body a heat-seeker that wanted in on this pleasure-play. He lay on top of her warmth to admire her sex-glazed eyes, a bright sea-green, alive with pure passion.

A shiver swept through him when her soft palms caressed his upper arms, and the slight scrape of her nails crossed his back.

Hungry, he licked her sweet mouth, and his weeping erection entered her inner sanctum. He stopped. Shuddered. And hissed.

His whole body quivered in all-encompassing waves

of pleasure that radiated from the one region which began from the tightness, followed by her scorching inner heat and the softness of her shroud. Sean forgot to breathe as her body accepted him whole. 'This is… heaven.'

He pulled back. Pushed her legs up and re-filled her deeper. Their bodies joined where his lustful hunger propelled him, and he gave pleasure as he took pleasure.

Quickening in pace, clinging to each other, they peaked together.

And together they collapsed, still clinging to each other.

Their desired thirsts quenched with their satiated bodies smattered in sweat. They trembled as arms tightened around each other as their heartbeats returned to normal.

It had been so intense neither could speak. Just feel.

Did they just make love?

Were they in love?

Would Deanne dare allow herself to love someone like Sean?

TWENTY-FOUR

Deanne gazed out the passenger window of Sean's car, when she frowned at the familiar stretch of shops. She swallowed and examined her hands in her lap, wishing, they'd gone another way in the hunt for brunch.

'Hey, what's the frown for?' Sean asked, steering them through the traffic.

'My ex worked there.' Deanne pointed towards the two-storey complex where retail stores were on the ground floor with assorted business offices situated upstairs. It was yet another reminder shoved in her face.

With hands clasped in her lap, Deanne wanted to go home and hide.

Was it too soon to be with Sean after what she'd been through with Darren?

'Did Darren work at the dentists there? I have no idea about the guy, I'm only aware of what he'd done to you.' Sean stroked her hair, but she pulled away.

Her jovial mood shut down all from one name— Darren.

'I'm trained to listen if you want to talk. No pressure.'

Deanne peeked up at Sean, who'd backed up everything that Nan had said. But was Sean willing to handle her baggage? After all the man had laid out all his personal luggage on the stone table the other morning. Was it her turn to shed?

'Darren…' Wow, she spoke his name. It'd have to be the first time she'd said it since the wedding. It was progress.

'*He* worked in the architects' office upstairs and used to visit the dentist's downstairs, a lot. He had this weird obsession with his teeth, always getting them cleaned and polished for this mega-white movie-star smile. Darren was forever checking his teeth in mirrors, windows, on the back of spoons.' Sure, she was nit-picking, surprisingly it felt great.

'How hygienic of him,' said Sean. 'I hate dentists myself.'

'I'm not fond of them either. But Darren went all the time.' No way! She'd said his name three times now. This was huge improvement.

'Did he bleach them, and put sparkling blingy diamantes on them too?'

Deanne giggled; grateful to Sean for lifting the mood. 'Not the bling, but I know he spent a fortune on them because he didn't want to be like his mum.'

'What's wrong with his mum?' Sean asked with a slight frown.

The man was like a lion, proud and yet fierce when it came to his family, especially his protectiveness over his mother and sister's wellbeing. 'Darren's mother had false teeth. When she laughed, they'd pop out onto the table.'

'That'd be a shocker.'

'It was her party trick. I know she did it on purpose because it used to embarrass Darren. His mum was nice.'

Shame about the son.

And that's enough time wasted talking about the ex. 'My friend, Clare—'

'The lighter thief.'

'Clare's not a thief,' she said to the retired thief.

Sean toyed with her fingers as he gave her a sly side grin. 'They come in all shapes, sweetheart.'

And the man was in great shape. Athletic even.

'Clare just started dating a dentist and hasn't slept with him. I hope it works out for her.' Deanne realised she'd never technically done the dinner date with Sean yet. Okay, they'd done lunch. Family barbecue. Coffee. Hot sweaty sessions fooling around in the car, and they'd jumped beyond the earth's atmosphere only this morning.

The only reason they'd left her bedroom was for food and to fetch her car, otherwise they'd still be indulging. What would the Greatest-Girls-of-the-Galaxy say about that?

'Does Clare sleep with men straight away? I'm not judging, I just want an insight.'

'Why?' Deanne arched her eyebrow at him.

He kissed her fingers while keeping an eye on the minimal Sunday traffic. 'Remember, I was the token male in my household of three sisters. I can handle the girl-talk.'

'For real?' Was this wonderful man really volunteering to hear this?

'But I don't do the cross-dressing for hemline adjustments. They ruined my sinuses from years of inhaling nail polish fumes in confined spaces, so please, don't ever ask me to paint your toenails. And hey, do not put makeup on me when I'm asleep either, that's just cruel.'

'Did your sisters do that?'

'They woke me up and sent me out to fetch milk after those bitches had covered my face in glitter and light blue eyeshadow.'

'I've never done that to Jimmy. Should've. Did they take photos?' His sisters sounded like they were fun and scary at the same time.

'No. But in that neighbourhood the crazies came out at night, I would've fit right in. So, please continue. But be warned, I'll give my honest male feedback because that's how I've been trained.'

Was Sean real, or pulling her into a defenceless lull? 'Clare claims she's a nymphomaniac where her sexual appetite scares men because she's —'

'A man-eater.'

'Who told you that?'

'That's how you introduced me to Clare, when your girlfriends stole you away from me the first night we met.'

Her heart liquefied, along with a tummy twirling swoon that weakened her knees. Thank goodness she was seated. 'You remembered?'

'I remember everything you say.'

'Wow.' She'd never had someone's undivided attention, not like this. Was she ready?

First, she had to get through tomorrow, being the deadline for the tender, and hopefully discover her letter writing saboteur. But that was tomorrow, and she couldn't help but enjoy Sean's company today, and smiled. Today, she was going to forget her past, and just focus on the present. To enjoy a day out, with Sean.

TWENTY-FIVE

Deanne awoke to the familiarities of her childhood home. The toilet flushed, signalling her dad's departure from his reading session of the morning paper on the loo. Jimmy had stopped strangulating songs in the shower. Coffee aromas mingled with bacon cooked by Nan downstairs. Even as she glanced at her patchy pink bedroom, Deanne still smiled.

'*Knock. Knock.* You awake yet, Dee?' Jimmy rapped his knuckles against her bedroom door.

Deanne sat up, fast. 'Yeah.' *Thank goodness for the lock.*

'Nan wants to know if Sean has one or two eggs for brekkie.'

Deanne glanced over her shoulder where Sean lay beside her, grinning at her while his fingertips tickled her bare spine.

Oh no. She had a naked man. In her bed. Inside her dad's house. Busted by her brother. *I'm so dead.* 'You were meant to leave,' she whispered to Sean.

'*Two eggs thanks, Jimmy,*' Sean shouted as he smiled wider.

'No worries. Dad reckons the shower's free in five.'

Deanne hid under the covers. *Why is it so hot? Why is he still here?*

'Do you still want me to climb out the window?' Sean

laughed harder, pulling the blanket away from Deanne's face. 'Sweetheart, stop being a prude. It's obvious they know I'm here with my car parked out front.' Sean pinned her back to the bed as his hungry eyes caressed her nakedness. 'Mm… What I'm going to do to your inner prude.' His lips feathered against her throat that spread prickles across her skin.

She couldn't stop. Didn't want to stop. But could only surrender to his seduction and quietly made love, all while the rest of her family prepared for work. She'd never done this before, but what a way to start her Monday, where nothing else mattered except Sean and the now.

* * *

'No friggin' way.' Jimmy frowned, with his loaded fork hovering over his plate. He frowned at Sean, coming down the hallway.

'Now you be nice to our guest,' warned Nan, waving her tongs at Jimmy.

Dammit. Jimmy shovelled the food into his gob to stop speaking. He didn't dare go against Nan, or she'd lock the beer shed up again. *Now where did she hide that key?*

'Morning, Sean.' Nan smiled at Sean entering her kitchen and placed a plate of bacon and eggs on the wooden table. The sounds of talk-back radio rattled in the background, competing with the hiss and sizzle of food cooking on the stove. 'That's yours. Help yourself to the coffee pot.'

'Morning, Nan, thanks.' Sean took a seat opposite Deanne's brother. 'Morning, Jimmy.'

'Sean.' He glowered at the uninvited breakfast guest.

'Can you pass the sauce please, Jimmy?'

Jimmy snatched the tomato sauce and slammed it on the table top making the coffee ripple inside their mugs.

'Go on, say it.' Sean forked the bacon and eggs into his gob.

'Hurt my sister and I'll break ya bloody neck.' Jimmy sipped his coffee. Thankfully, Nan was pre-occupied over by the stove with her radio's rant to tell him off for abusing their houseguests.

But Sean wasn't invited. And he shouldn't be in his sister's bed. In Dad's house.

Since when did Deanne start dating again?

Sean smirked as he loaded up his fork with more food. 'I don't say it as straight forward as you do, but I like it.'

'What?'

'I've got three younger sisters and I've warned all their past boyfriends. Even their husbands.'

'Huh? I forgot you had sisters.' Like Sean had forgotten to leave his sister's room before dawn!

'You're lucky you've only got the one sister to worry about. Mind you, your sister's a handful.' Sean sighed and smiled.

Jimmy clenched his mug of coffee so tight it trembled. He didn't need to hear about his sister that way over the breakfast table. 'Rough-up any of their exes?' Or new boyfriends who hadn't left the block yet.

'I've threatened a few. You?'

'There's a certain ex who bolted before I had my chance. Damned curse.' Jimmy tore at his toast with his teeth, keeping a death grip on his cutlery.

When he stopped at the expression on his sister's face as she walked into the kitchen. It was the happiest Jimmy had ever seen her.

'Morning,' sang out Deanne as she reached for her travel mug and made her coffee.

'Well, look at you, child.' Nan grinned, with her grey eyes shining as she held out the wrapped muffin. 'I can see you're having a fine morning.'

'Nan, do you mind, I'm eating over here.' Jimmy didn't need to hear this. But glared at Sean perving on his sister who was blushing while unwrapping her muffin. *What the hell is going on around here?*

'Don't you sit and eat breakfast?' Sean asked Deanne.

Nan shook her head while waving her egg flip. 'Child's always running out the door with coffee in one hand, food in the other.'

Sean pinched Deanne's muffin, placed it on a plate, then led her by the hand to the table and pulled out a chair for her. 'Please join me. It's breakfast, sweetheart. It's a simple pleasure in life to sit and enjoy a meal shared in good company.'

Jimmy wanted to gag. No way would his sister fall for that crap, she'd run for the door like normal, which is where Sean should be—gone.

'If you put it that way, sure.' Deanne sat beside Sean, who rewarded her with a kiss on the cheek. She blushed and lowered her head to avoid Jimmy's open mouth.

'Well...' Nan and Jimmy gawked at each other, then checked out Deanne full of smiles, eating breakfast, seated beside Sean.

Reg soon joined them and sat at the head of the table

without a word about Sean.

Then Nan sat at the table with her plate and cup of tea. 'It's been too long time since the whole family shared breakfast together. And we also have Sean with us.'

'Humph.' Jimmy bit his tongue, daring to say something about the unwanted visitor, because Nan looked happy.

Nan was a woman who liked simple things and family time. Jimmy had learned a long time ago that if Nan was happy it made for a happy home. Even his sister looked happy. And so did his dad. Even Sean too—who wasn't meant to be here.

Maybe, just maybe, this curse was over, and his sister had found her happiness.

So, where were Jimmy's happy pills for this Monday morning?

TWENTY-SIX

Seated behind her office desk, Deanne stared at the tender proposal that had been faxed to Brinestones *again*. Disgusted, she shoved the contaminated worksheets aside.

Trust—it was her number one weakness. Her sore spot that just kept getting stabbed at. And everyone else knew it.

Sean claimed the duck-egg blue letters were not only testing the trust she had for her staff, but this whole scheming of faxing her work to the opposition—from her own office—was purely to ruin her work reputation. But why?

She cradled her head in her hands and stared at the piece of paper Sean had given her.

He'd been carrying it inside his wallet all day yesterday, at lunch, and all the way through their first dinner date and romantic beach stroll. Sean said he didn't want to ruin their day out yesterday.

But this morning he'd done another info-dump before running out the door to leave her with...

The list of suspects.

Five staff members were rostered on the warehouse premises at the time the faxes were sent.

One of them had a criminal background, proven by the

hardcopy criminal history report provided by Sean. Deanne didn't ask how he got the information. Even if Sean was willing to tell her, she refused because she'd been trained to never ask questions by Darren.

Huh, perhaps as part of her un-training of the ex's habits, she should've questioned Sean?

Maybe not, considering Sean's past-life.

Deanne, again, glanced over the five employee personnel files and tried to find the connection. Most of all why.

The first file belonged to Brian, their locksmith. His credentials and seven-year work history were impeccable.

The next file was all about Brian's son, Craig. Arrested for stealing a car at fifteen while under peer pressure. Deanne knew all about Craig's history, ever since Brian first asked if his son could become his apprentice. Craig was about to celebrate his eighteenth and she knew he was proud to finally be free of his juvenile history.

The third personnel file belonged to Tracey. The shy, check-out operator of three months, who'd just survived a date with her brother, which Deanne had yet to bug Jimmy about for the details. She also wanted to hear why her big brother threatened Sean over breakfast in front of Nan who tattled, with loads of relish, over Jimmy's bullying performance.

Deanne could feel the heat rising up her neck all over again. Darren had never slept over at her dad's house, and she'd expected the lecture for daring to have Sean sleep-over. But it never came. Not even from her father.

Then she looked at the fourth file that made Deanne's whole stature deflate. Andrew, their leading horticulturist.

His recent return from Brinestones had made him Sean's number one suspect, because Andrew had the contacts at Brinestones and the skills to cut keys.

According to Janice, Deanne had the last working fax in the warehouse. A minor detail Deanne had forgotten, yet Sean worked out after asking a few simple questions in passing conversation with staff. The man was like a super spy, only sexier.

But, in Andrew's defence, he'd sent all his faxes while in Deanne's presence, because they discussed stock options and future plant displays. Which would be *boring* with an accompanied eye roll she'd expect from Sean, if he was ever privy to that sort of conversation on vegetation. But this wasn't about Sean, even if he had presented his list of suspects with a clever dialogue as to his reasons why.

Damn him.

It couldn't be Andrew. He wasn't her enemy, even if all of the evidence was pointing his way. It'd shatter her total trust in people if it was Andrew.

She refused to accept it, because she'd known Andrew forever, who'd only moved workplaces because of his wife, money, and a change of scenery. All good excuses that most people would consider perfectly normal.

Except now Andrew was separated, paying a mortgage on a place he didn't live in, and forced to stay with his mother, Beatrice.

Deanne could relate and felt sorry for the guy. Maybe the neighbour's grass wasn't always greener—even for horticulturists. *Ha!*

Which brought her to face the last of the five suspects—Patricia. The young eighteen-year-old all-rounder, who'd been a team member for almost a year. Patricia also had the dual role as Deanne's cousin, Katrina's BFF and house-mate.

Deanne pursed her lips at Patricia's file. Patricia still ran away whenever she saw Deanne and they hadn't spoken since the wedding.

Was Patricia in cahoots with Katrina as part of their revenge plan?

Deanne leaned back in her chair; her legs swung beneath her seat as she stared at the five personnel files. Which one was her culprit? What proof did she have?

None.

This Sherlock gig sucked!

Deanne glanced at her watch; it was ten o'clock. Time for her usual morning tea break. Yes, she was a creature of habit, but she looked forward to this part of the day.

With keys in hand, she unlocked her bottom desk drawer to put the personnel files away. Instead, she frowned at the large assortment of Sorry-cards Darren had continuously sent her. It was almost full.

Damn him.

Was she some game to Darren who was trying to ruin her life even more?

She frowned so hard her eyes squinted at the sight of the mish-mashed cardboard reminders of what that arsehole had done to her.

He. Cheated. On. Her.

Yes, she publicly shamed him—and herself.

It was over. Done.

It was time to let go of her past.

Deanne picked up the massive pile of Sorry-cards and

dumped them inside her rubbish-bin. Cramming them all inside, she shoved the bin back under her desk. It was time to focus on her present, even if it was another drama.

When was her life going to stop being a soap opera?

Deanne dropped the five personnel files into her empty drawer, right beside the small stack of shot glasses and her silent, half full, Black Johnny. She was surprised she didn't even want a nip or feel the need to cradle the glass. Had she outgrown her boyfriend-in-a-bottle, too?

Nan would be so pleased.

So, did that make Sean the new boyfriend? The intelligent, cocky, yet confident, handsome Sean, who was truly magical in bed.

Did she dare fall into the fairy-tale happily-ever-after BS like she'd done with her ex?

Or was she destined to drag her damaged goods with her, while in permanent sleepwalker mode, for the rest of her life?

Would she trust again?

She slammed the drawer shut and went in search of her coffee, and hopefully she'd find some answers.

Deanne sipped her coffee while she walked around the nursery and admired nature's dazzling beauty in potted displays. It showcased differing shapes, sizes, colours, and textures of their plant stock as they reached for the filtered sunlight that warmed the area. She inhaled the heady exotic scents of jasmine and gingers and smiled. It was a beautiful, yet too brief a reprieve from her problems. Nan had her thing of hand-watering her plants, this was Deanne's thing.

She sipped her coffee and looked over the vast area's infrastructure. Perhaps, she could use some of this area within the nursery to expand and include her office plant hiring business as a future side venture, in case the tender did or didn't go through. They had the room to grow and the skilled manpower already on hand. It might test her comfort zone in managing the project, even if it was currently being pushed to the brink—big time. Could she manage it?

'Zacchary,' yelled out the female customer a few rows over.

Deanne glanced at the flustered mother chasing a small boy around the nursery, hiking up her backpack that carried a little girl. The girl's infectious laughter echoed, as her tiny hands reached out and brushed against the young tree saplings and exotic palms.

'Come here, Zach.' The mother grabbed the toddler resisting her clutches. 'We've got to go to the dentist. I'll shout you an ice cream after.'

The girl in the backpack waved at Deanne with a plucked leaf.

Deanne waved back. 'Aww, too cute.'

'Morning, Deanne. Great day isn't it,' said Andrew, watering assorted pots of ferns.

'Ah, yeah, um, morning.' Andrew wasn't a suspect, Deanne's heart believed it, as her stomach twisted for even thinking bad of Andrew.

When her brain flashed like a lightning bolt, as whirled fragments clicked into place. 'Aww, frigging heck!?'

Deanne's eyes widened and her fingers let go of her coffee mug. It shattered across the cement floor, scattering porcelain and hot coffee everywhere. But she'd turned and fled on her heels before the cup's chips had settled, sprinting along the warehouse, past the main entrance, and up the stairs towards her office.

Halfway up the staircase, the fire alarm went off. Deanne stopped for a second, unable to see or smell any smoke. Yet the alarm rang loudly in her ears as she continued her dash up the stairs. She rounded the corridor's corner when the sprinklers started to spray in the management area.

But Deanne didn't stop.

She ran down the windowed corridor and pushed open her office door. 'YOU.'

Tracey stood on Deanne's desk, holding a cigarette lighter under the fire sprinklers in the ceiling.

'It was you the whole time.' Deanne stepped forward with fists clenched, pulse pounding, with her anger climbing to a whole new level of pure unadulterated hatred.

'What are you talking about?' Tracey smiled as she jumped off the desk.

'Don't play coy with me. I know you used to work in the dentist's downstairs from Darren's architect office. You were having an affair with Darren—along with everyone else! I know how often Darren visited because he was obsessed with his teeth.' Deanne pointed her finger, as the cold water soaked her to the bone, but she was too enraged to care.

'And you had no idea how long we were sleeping

together,' said Tracey, wiping the water from her eyebrows.

'You wrote those letters in duck-egg blue. It's Darren's favourite colour. Because yes, he was a man who was very specific with his colour preference.' Why did she still remember all those pathetic little details about the man? 'I remembered Beatrice in the café told me you were recovering from a broken heart. It was Darren who broke your heart, didn't he?'

They moved around the large desk. The shrilling fire alarm deafening. Deanne's anger almost overflowed, like the cold indoor rain that flooded everything. Her laptop, the books on the shelf, the electrical equipment, and all her work was destroyed. 'Why?'

'Because Darren should've married *me*. Instead, he had to marry you. He didn't love you, he loved ME.' Tracey stabbed her thumb at her drenched chest.

'Darren's a liar. Look at what he did to me—to you, and to Katrina. Darren deserted Katrina when she was pregnant with his baby. Hey, what did I ever do to you, when I gave you a JOB!'

'Darren swore Katrina preyed on him, and he was only using you for personal gain.'

'What personal gain, when I'm still living at home with my family.'

'Darren was going to talk you into extending this hardware business into building, where he would be the head architect and wanted to marry you for the connections.'

'Connections? We're not the Mafia with connections— it's a hardware store. Tell me you did not fall for his lies.'

Ugh, just like she'd done for years. *Damn him.*

'Darren was going to stay married to you for two years, then leave you to be with me. He promised me we'd be together.'

'Darren's gift is telling women all the lies they want to hear. I fell for it too. Trust me, it's all lies.' How could she expect Tracey to trust her when Deanne had trouble trusting others, including herself?

'When you dumped Darren in front of everyone at the wedding, you ruined it.'

'Are you for real? I RUINED MY OWN WEDDING.'

'It's your fault,' screamed out Tracey above the shrilling alarm.

'How? When you and Katrina were both sleeping with the guy.'

'When Darren moved to Queensland, I followed.' Tracey wiped at her tears that mixed with the overhead shower of water. 'Instead of saying he loved me, Darren says you're the one he loves. His dependable, loyal, golden girl.'

'Gee thanks, I sound like a golden retriever.'

'Darren said you did everything he wanted. He said you doted over him, ran-round after him and did everything he asked. Never saying no, and never questioning him, like he was a god.'

'Ugh, lesson learned to never do that again.'

'All he ever talks about is getting you back.'

'Not happening. EVER.'

'So, I wanted to find out what made you so special and came to this place.' Tracey raised her arms as if performing an indoor rain-dance. 'Here, all they talk about is the hardworking Deanne, poor little Deanne. When the worst part is how everyone blames Darren for hurting their precious Deanne. When I *hate* you for what you've done to Darren. It's because of you he dumped me, so it's all your fault.'

'HE CHEATED ON ME.'

'I lost my job chasing Darren.'

'Consider yourself fired as part of your new career pattern.'

'I lost Darren because of you.'

'Have him. I will never ever touch him again.'

'You're lying.'

'Come on, it's almost been six months since the wedding. It's time to get over it and move on.' But would Deanne remember this epiphany if she survived this moment?

'I can't.' Tracey's shoulders slumped as the water dripped from her lowered chin. 'It's not that easy.'

'I can relate… Maybe you should go find someone new.' Huh, was that what she'd done with Sean?

Oh no, Jimmy's date. '*Hey!*' Deanne whipped her finger up like a pointed dagger. '*As for my brother, stay away from him.*'

Tracey's thin lips curled into a snarl. 'You know, I sat in your father's backyard, inside a stupid garden shed, beside your pathetic brother, where they talked about their poor, hardworking, little Dee. Your family are dumber than fish jumping onto unbaited hooks.'

'*Leave my family out of this.*' Deanne's white-knuckled fists shook with rage, ignoring the nails that pierced her skin because no one disrespected her family.

'Guess what? I've been selling your stupid *shed-saving* proposal that your brother bragged about to your opposition. Too bad, you won't be able to send it in now, because your work and all of your equipment is ruined. And to think I was going to put out for your moronic brother.' Tracey clutched her throat and gagged.

'You have no right to talk about my brother like that.' Deanne snatched the pot plant from her desk and threw it. Tracey ducked, and the African violet flew through the open doorway, smashing into the corridor's windows and fell for the warehouse floor below.

'I can do what I want to you because you ruined my life.' Tracey snatched up the letter opener, her makeup smudged around her eyes, she squinted through the rain as the fire alarm screamed. Her heaving chest slowed, as Tracey's head tilted sideways, and she smiled pointing the weapon at Deanne. 'Now consider yourself ruined too.'

Deanne stepped back. This is what she'd feared the most from those letters. The one question that scared her...

Was the writer of those blue letters capable of hurting her?

Deanne had her answer.

TWENTY-SEVEN

The staff and customers had gathered in the warehouse carpark while the fire alarm competed with incoming sirens.

'*Jimmy?*' Sean weaved his way through the crowd. 'Where's Deanne?'

'She should be here. *Has anyone seen Deanne?*' Jimmy called out to the staff that milled around like sheep in a shearing yard.

'I spotted Dee running like a possessed Olympic sprinter in them heels of hers, all the way to her office. That was just before the fire alarm went off.' Beatrice adjusted her glasses. Their string of purple beads jiggled along their frame as she turned to her son beside her. 'Didn't you see Dee's dash, Andrew? She came from your section?'

'Dee dropped her coffee cup in the nursery just before that. She looked like she'd seen a ghost and bolted.'

'Oh no.' Sean felt his heart plummet and pushed through the crowd in a mad dash for the main entrance. Nothing mattered except Deanne's safety.

'OI. You can't go in there,' shouted Jimmy. 'We have to wait for the fire brigade.'

'*Your sister's in trouble.*'

'Where? Who?' Jimmy instantly gave chase.

They entered the warehouse, jumped the barricaded

check-outs, and tore a right towards the management offices. When the potted plant flew through the window, scattering shards of glass in a spectacular explosion.

'*Look out.*' Sean pulled Jimmy back and they skidded across the floor, their arms up to shield themselves from the shattering glass that rained over them, as the pot plant disintegrated into a mass of scattered pottery and dirt.

'DEANNE!' Sean shouted over the fire alarm.

But there was no reply.

TWENTY-EIGHT

Tracey pointed the knife-like letter opener at Deanne on the other side of her desk. Water streamed from the ceiling's sprinklers as the carpet squelched under her feet, and the relentless siren assaulted her ears.

Deanne was over playing the school bully's victim. This was her office. Her family business. Her turf. And she needed a plan. 'Let's bring Darren back and teach him a lesson for what he's done to us.'

But then in a moment of crystal clarity, she knew right then and there that she didn't love Darren. She had never truly loved Darren. Nor had she ever known what love was. What she had with Darren wasn't even close to what love should be. But it wasn't the time to think about that, except survive.

When Deanne spied her rubbish-bin shielded beneath her desk, that was full of her sorry cards. 'Why don't we use Darren's own words against him and trick him to return.'

'How?'

'Darren wrote me letters and Sorry-cards. I've kept them all.'

'Where?'

Deanne reached under her desk and picked up the

rubbish bin containing everything Darren had sent her. She was sick at the sight of those stupid Sorry-cards.

'See.' She held out a handful, noticing her trembling hands, not from the cold water that trickled down her spine, but from a mix of adrenalin-fuelled fear and hatred towards Darren. Because Darren's infidelity had caused all of this.

Tracey snatched an envelope from the many and opened the card. She squinted through falling water, her hand holding the letter opener wiped at her dripping fringe.

'And here's the rest, *you psycho*.' Deanne threw the cards, showering them over Tracey.

She knocked Tracey to the ground and used all her weight to pin the she-devil beneath her.

'*Deanne*.' Sean rushed through the door. Instantly he reacted, stepping on Tracey's wrist, to then toss the letter opener to the floor.

Jimmy kicked the lethal weapon further into the far corner of the raining office.

'Get off me,' cried out Tracey, struggling beneath Deanne.

Deanne clenched her right fist and punched Tracey — hard. Water splashed from the carpet where Tracey's head bounced against the floor.

Deanne swung her fist, except Sean captured it, pulling Deanne back from Tracey.

'Deanne, stop!' Sean spun her around to face him. 'Did she hurt you?'

The adrenalin fuelled her erratic pulse, she tried to break free from his grip, until she saw Sean's fear and worry for her. 'No. I'm okay. Just pumped.'

Jimmy's hand clutched his wet hair. *'What the hell is going on?'*

The sprinklers and the fire alarm suddenly stopped, the silence and dry air a blessing.

'There you are, Sean,' said a familiar voice. 'Are you all right, Deanne?' Mickey asked as he stepped into the office.

'Mickey?' Deanne wiped the water from her eyes to focus on Mickey, in the doorway, accompanied by two uniformed police officers. 'Mickey, what are you doing here? You're a barman?' He was the only barman she knew by name.

'Superintendent.' Mickey grinned as he showed her his badge. 'Young Sean told me what's been going on and we've reviewed your office surveillance tapes recording Tracey's actions. Sean, are your cameras waterproof and still taping all of this?'

'Yep.' Sean winced at Deanne.

Deanne looked between Mickey and Sean. 'What cameras? Oh no, you didn't?'

'I told you to ask and I'd tell.' Sean slipped his arm around Deanne's shoulders. 'I don't want there to be any secrets between us.'

Did Deanne want to know? Yes. Yes, she did. 'So speak.'

'Finally, she asks.' He chuckled at her frown. Sean then whispered to her, 'Mickey's the cop I told you about. I've known Mickey for over fifteen years and he's the one who made me retire.'

That's just great, when she still didn't know how to explain Sean's past life skills to her family. 'And the surveillance cameras?' Deanne hated being on any camera.

'I put hidden cameras in your office. I tried to tell you, but you didn't want to hear it.'

Okay that part was true. 'Why?' *Cameras, where?* She froze in her soaked clothes, suffering with a sudden bout of stage fright.

'We needed proof, so I gave Mickey those letters. After he'd reviewed a few of those tapes, Mickey raised a search warrant on Tracey's place. That's where we've been this morning with her landlord, where we found more threatening notes, and the same paper in the printer. We also found on her laptop, a journal detailing her affair with Darren and her plan for you.' A flash of fear passed over his face, he pulled her close, tightening his arms protectively around her. 'Are you sure you're okay?'

'I'm okay.' Kind of. Maybe? 'What else did they find?'

'From the evidence we'd gathered, they were coming here to arrest Tracey.' Sean placed both hands on her upper arms, then looked her in the eyes. 'I've been honest with you the whole time. If you'd asked me, I would've told you everything, but you never did. So please, question away.'

'What about Brinestones?' Deanne trembled from the cold, or was that the adrenalin rush?

'I diverted your fax; you saw me do it.'

'Did I?'

'Yes. Remember I asked you for the manual.'

'I thought that was to print out the log?'

'I did. But I also diverted the number Tracey used for Brinestones.'

'To where?'

'As of Friday, all of your faxes were being sent to my

bar,' said Mickey. 'Don't worry, we forwarded the others to their rightful places.' Mickey towered over Tracey that was still on the floor, being searched by two uniformed officers.

'I'd assumed your occupation was a barman, Mickey,' said Deanne.

'I told you I was moonlighting on the job, and that I own the place as part of my retirement plan. Are you sure you're okay, luv? I'll shout you a scotch at my bar later?'

Deanne could almost taste Black Johnny. Instead, she turned to Sean and Mickey, she was done with dwelling in her bubble of denial. 'Tell me everything.'

'About time.' Sean smiled at her. 'We needed to set Tracey up using your false proposal and fax diversion for proof. So, when Brinestones didn't receive their faxes, they didn't pay Tracey, who only had today to finish it. I didn't think she'd do it while you were on your predictable morning break.' His fingers gently brushed away the wet hair from her face.

'Will someone explain what the hell's going on here?' Reg stood in the doorway, pushing his glasses up his nose.

'I'm still trying to work it out myself, Dad,' Jimmy said, wringing water from the bottom his shirt.

Deanne approached her father and brother. 'Tracey's been sending my proposal for the new shopping centre directly to Brinestones.'

'*What*?' Jimmy and Reg glared at Tracey, who shirked as far as she could on the soaked floor while being handcuffed by the police.

'Tracey also sent Deanne threatening letters.' Sean caught Deanne's frown and grabbed her hand to give it a gentle squeeze. 'They deserve to know, and I'm glad you put Darren's mail to good use.'

Deanne watched Tracey being dragged to her feet, handcuffed, and marched out the door by the police, leaving a trail of soggy Sorry-cards behind her. How did Sean know about Darren's correspondence? Had Sean snooped through her office?

Deanne rubbed her arms as the chill caused her teeth to chatter.

Reg placed his hands on his daughters' upper arms. 'Why was Tracey threatening you?'

'Tracey was having an affair with Darren.' She prayed there were no more scorned women to come out of Darren's ditched-mistress closet to seek their revenge against her.

'You're kidding me? This is all to do with Darren?' Jimmy asked.

Deanne nodded. 'Tracey chased Darren to Queensland, assuming they'd be together. Instead, she got dumped, lost her job, and decided to ruin me for it.' It was all Darren's fault. Why couldn't he just leave her alone?

Reg scratched the back of his head. 'But, what about Brinestones?'

'We've contacted Brinestones and they're dealing with their staff member who was paying Tracey for Deanne's work,' said Mickey. 'We'll be charging Tracey for the damage, threats, and assault, and I'm sure there'll be more charges to add to the long list.'

Deanne sighed in relief that it was over. Yet her dad didn't look happy, and she grabbed Reg's large hand with her two small cold ones. 'Sorry, Dad.'

'The proposal? Your work's ruined, Dee.' Reg pushed up his glasses and shook his head at the room where drips fell from the ceiling. 'Your office?'

'It's okay, Dad. I worked from Clare's office and let Brinestones have the fake document. It was all Sean's idea. He helped me.' She couldn't be angry with the guy who winked at her. 'Clare hand-delivered my proposal on her way to work this morning.'

'Tracey didn't hurt you?' Reg took off his jacket and slipped it across her shoulders.

'No. She scared me, but I'm okay.' With teeth chattering, she hugged her father.

'Why didn't you say anything?' Jimmy asked. 'We would've helped?'

'You're both dating staff and we weren't sure who the suspect was,' said Sean.

Jimmy held up his finger. 'I dated Tracey once.'

'Tracey said…' Deanne screwed her face up.

Jimmy shook his head. 'I never touched her. Ever since I divorced Casey, I've always trusted Nan's judgement. That's why I took her to meet Nan, who didn't like Tracey or her muddy hair, reckons it led to a muddy brain.'

Deanne was grateful for the lift in mood. 'It's boyfriend time.'

'What boyfriend?' Sean frowned.

'Oh yeah, bring it on, Sis.' Jimmy grinned. 'Don't stress, Sean, it's just her boyfriend-in-a-bottle.'

'Her what?'

'Hello lover.' Deanne pulled out the bottle from the desk drawer. She grabbed her mismatched stack of shot glasses that Clare had pinched, that she was now sharing with a superintendent who owned his own bar—how surreal.

'So, this is black Johnny, eh,' said the superintendent with a wry grin.

'How do you know, Mickey?' Sean asked.

'We were introduced when I tried to warn the girl about you.'

'And look how that turned out.' Sean smiled at his lady.

'Err, hello.' Deanne waved at her saturated office full of ruined electrical equipment.

'Insurance, sweetheart.'

'That's true.' Deanne filled the nip glasses and passed them around. 'Mickey, it's my shout, I think I owe you a couple.'

'Can't say no to the lady,' said Mickey with a nod as he grabbed his glass.

'I know I can't. But I'll check-out this Black Johnny.' Sean took his shot glass and raised an eyebrow at her as he raised the glass to his lips. 'Your boyfriend-in-a-bottle, huh?'

'Oh yeah, Black Johnny never backchats, he's the perfect listener who doesn't need much space.' Deanne took a gulp of the scotch and sighed heavily. 'And he oh so warms my heart.'

Sean pulled Deanne close to his side and nuzzled into her ear. 'I'll do all that for you, and more. Any day. All day. Every day.'

Deanne pointed at him. 'Ah huh, only after you've finished explaining everything.'

'You ask the questions, I'll answer. I won't keep any secrets from you.' He clutched her raised finger gently and rested his forehead against hers, staring deep into her soul. 'I just want to keep you safe, sweetheart.'

'I am.' Even if she was saturated and her office ruined, she'd taken on her bully and won.

TWENTY-NINE

'Dee these came for you,' said Janice, carrying a bunch of white roses into Deanne's office.

'Wow.' Deanne smiled at the floral display placed on her desk.

'Nice smile, honey. Well, I'm off to collect your dad from non-golfing. Have a good weekend and no working, young lady?'

'No worries, Janice, I hope Dad's handicap's improved.' Deanne laughed; it was all back to blissful normality. Almost sleep-walking normality. But not. Because it had many wonderful surprises like the Sean-factor, and these flowers.

Deanne tugged the small envelope free from the flowers. The delicate aroma was as inviting and as soft as the white petals. Still smiling wide, she opened the card and read:

> *'Dee, sorry to hear what happened with Tracey. I had*
> *nothing to do with it.*
> *It's you I love. Please forgive me.*
> *I haven't stopped loving you and I will always love you.*
> *Darren.'*

'*Bastard.*' Deanne flung the card onto her desk.

Clutching fingers through her hair, she rested her elbows on her desk.

Why couldn't Darren just stop sending her letters?

It'd been six months since their failed wedding ceremony. It was also his fault her office equipment had to be replaced. Her career almost ruined. The hardware store's livelihood threatened, forcing her to look at her staff like they were the enemy.

But most of all, Darren caused her unwillingness to trust Sean, who'd remained by her side and had taken care of her this past week ever since Tracey's arrest.

In fact, Sean had looked after her, like the first time they'd met when she was wearing her bridal gown.

She'd come a long way since that day.

Yet too many questions lingered that she hadn't dared to ask Sean. All because of the ex.

'Are those roses from Darren? I prefer red roses for romance and passion, so they're not from me.' Sean wore a solemn expression, leaning against the open doorway holding a single red rose. 'White reminds me of purity, honesty, and eternity. Ironic if they're from your deceitful ex.' Sean placed his red rose on the desk in front of her. With a fingertip, he spun the card around, then frowned. 'Are you going to keep this card like the others?'

'How did you know about the Sorry-cards? No one knew about them.' Deanne hesitated, because Jimmy did. It was Jimmy who told Dad, and Petey, and probably half the tradesmen who visited the shed! 'They were locked away. You went through my desk, didn't you!' Her voice elevated as she stood, glaring at him. 'What else did you help yourself to?'

'Your brother told me about the Sorry-cards, and when I set up the cameras, I couldn't help myself. Which is a first for me, because I've never bothered before.'

'Why do it?'

'I had to know if it was true. Because every time I think you're getting over Darren, you'd see something on the street, or he'd send you another reminder where you'd shut me out—just like this. Just like you did the other day in the car, when we drove past his work when you dropped your smile and lost the shine in your eyes, when we'd been having the best morning. I had to pry it out of you to find out what was wrong and why you'd had this sudden change.'

'How can I trust you when you broke in? Don't you have any personal boundaries as to what is considered private space?'

'I'm sorry, but I said I'd tell you everything. I'm still waiting, hoping you'll ask. But you kept saying you didn't want to know. You'd rather walk around with blinkers on and not stick your nose out in case you got hurt.'

'*Screw you.*' Lips pursed. Arms crossed. Brow furrowed. Their heated words gripped tightly around her heart, making it harder for her to breathe.

'I've never lied or kept secrets from you. So, here's me, telling you more truths. I did it once and I'm sorry I did it. It's the only thing I checked; I swear it.'

'Why?'

'Because I couldn't understand why you kept pulling away from me. Why you never gave me a chance? It's because that bastard won't let you forget.' He pointed at the flowers. 'How can you be expected to move on when he won't let you go? I bet Darren's hoping his reminders will wear you down, so you'd run back to him. But forget him. He's had his shot. Let me have a turn.' Sean swept his fingers through his thick hair. 'I told you I'd never want to hurt you—'

'You can have any woman you want. Why me? I'm no one. I'm not good looking or smart. I'm just a kid from the burbs who has only ever worked in a family hardware store, who's still living at home.'

'You don't see it, do you?' Sean's eyes widened. 'You're the most beautiful, caring, sensitive woman I've ever met.' He reached out, but she backed away from him. He dropped his hand as his shoulders sagged in defeat. 'I fell in love with you, Deanne.'

'What? You can't.' Furiously blinking, as if trying to rid some imaginary dirt from her eyes.

'I can. I do. And I'm not afraid to say it. I love you, Deanne.' He stepped forward and wrapped her up in his arms.

'How? It's only been a few weeks.' She pushed herself free from his embrace.

'Well, this is not how I'd planned to tell you.' Sean pressed the heel of his palm against his forehead. 'It's true. It's also the first time I've said that to anyone, because I've never felt like this with anyone, but you.'

Deanne clutched her fingers so hard they were white. Was it true? Did Sean love her?

'I know you feel it too, but you've been mistreated so badly by that wanker you won't dare trust me, or trust in us.' His sad eyes peered through his long fringe. 'I guess we'll never have a chance while this arsehole keeps sending you this crap.' His hand flicked over the white roses scattering petals across her desk as he backed away from her. 'Whenever you receive anything from him, you put that damned wall up, shutting me out, believing I'll do the same to you too. Well, I won't. Remember, I've been there too, sweetheart. I know how it feels to be betrayed.' He walked out slamming the door behind him.

Deanne stared at the white petals covering Sean's red rose. She snatched up the remaining white rose bouquet and card, ripped open her door, stormed into the corridor, and slammed them into the rubbish bin.

'You all right, sis?' Jimmy asked from his office doorway next to hers.

'*Fine*,' she said through clenched teeth and fisted hands. 'Bloody men.' She stomped past Jimmy, back into her office and kicked the door shut behind her.

Yes, she adored Sean, she couldn't deny that. But she was angry he'd gone through her desk.

She dropped into her seat and stared at the scattered white petals and Sean's red rose.

Sean was right. Darren wasn't letting her move forward.

Sean had said he loved her.

Eyebrows raised and her breath caught in her throat, her chest ached, and it was hard to swallow. Did she dare believe him?

Her fingertips surrounded the green thornless stem of Sean's red rose, twirling it slowly to examine its beauty. The vivid enflamed red of the petals with its delicate depth of fine spider veins spread from its core. Its outer shield a sensual, soft, fine velvet was beautiful and flawless.

She plucked free one it red petals. 'Does he love me?' From raised fingertips, Deanne watched it float and land like a drop of blood amidst a field of powdery-white snow. It was a stark contrast amongst the white rose petals scattered across her desk.

She plucked another petal. 'Does he love me not?' She let it go—but did she want to let go of Sean?

Clutching her heart as the tears formed and her throat ached, it hurt to argue with Sean.

Unlike her relationship with Darren, Deanne had never exposed her true self when in her ex's company, or with any other male she had dated.

Until she'd met Sean.

He'd met her when she'd been at her worst, challenging Deanne to be more than what she was.

He'd made her wake up not only in mind and body, it scared her.

This emotional vacuum of these newly opened feelings, sucked so badly, how was her damaged soul supposed to cope?

Where was her hardened unemotional one-woman-show now?

Tears burst as she clutched Sean's rose. She cradled her head in her arms and wept.

What had she done?

* * *

Jimmy stood at Deanne's office doorway. His shoulders drooped as his heart gripped, watching his baby sister crying through the glass door. He frowned, releasing her door handle he stepped back into his office.

Just when he thought Deanne had been happy, now this.

He snatched up his car keys and headed out of the warehouse.

That damned curse was buggering up everything.

His dad's, Nan's, his own, and now Deanne's relationship with Sean, all ruined.

What the hell did he have to do to break it, so they'd all find their happily-ever-afters?

THIRTY

'Why are we bothering to visit the pub now?' Complained Chris as he rolled out of the taxi, with Petey and Jimmy scrambling from the back seat.

Still fuming at his inadequacies in not being able to help his sister, Jimmy straightened up his shirt and combed fingers through his hair. 'Because we ran out of beer at home.'

'Bloody pub shuts in less than an hour. It's a bugger the takeaway's shut,' said Petey, stroking his long beard as his shaved head glinted under the street lights.

The three men stood in a shambled line and tried to walk as straight as possible into their local pub. They strolled up to the bar, ordered their drinks and glanced at the few customers that remained.

'The bastard.' Jimmy stormed towards the man who'd upset his sister. Sean.

'Jimmy,' Sean mumbled, sipping his beer.

'You, arsehole, I want to talk to you, outside,' bellowed Jimmy.

Sean cocked an eyebrow from beneath his fringe. 'For a chat, huh?'

Jimmy shrugged Petey's hand off his shoulder as he leaned in closer to Sean and snarled. 'Outside, or I'll bloody drag you out.'

'Fine, after you.' Sean followed Jimmy, with Petey and Chris in pursuit. They gathered under the glow of the street lights of the pub's near-empty carpark.

'I'm here, so what did you want to chat about, Jimmy?' Sean asked, facing Deanne's brother.

Jimmy's finger stabbed the air between them. 'I warned you that if you ever hurt my sister, I'd break your bloody neck.'

'So, you're playing big brother, huh? Why? What did Deanne tell you?'

'Nothing. I overheard you two arguing, and I saw how upset she is, and I'm not letting another wanker upset her. Not when Deanne's already suffered enough.'

The two men circled each other. Chris jumped and twitched like a timid mouse, hiding behind Petey who'd leaned his stocky shoulder against the light pole, casually sipping from his beer glass as if watching a game of footy on the tellie.

'And what about how I feel?' Sean jabbed his thumb into his chest.

'It's my sister I care about.' All Jimmy had was his family.

'Me too.'

'Then why is she so upset?'

'Because I told Deanne I loved her. But she won't believe me, not when Darren keeps sending flowers and love letters, like he did this afternoon. He won't let her go. It's Darren who keeps upsetting Deanne, always reminding her of what he'd done. So, if you want to hurt me you can try, but you'll never hurt me as much as

Deanne has.' Sean stepped up and stood mere centimetres from Jimmy's face, lifting his chin. 'Go on, give it ya best shot, mate.'

Jimmy didn't need to be told twice. Carrying all that frustration he took a swing.

Sean ducked.

Both drunken men grappled each other. They wrestled and rolled across the car park's asphalt where punches were thrown in wild swings. Until Petey pulled them apart, while Chris stood well clear and stole tiny sips from Petey's beer glass.

'Stop it, you two,' said the strong and stocky, Petey, standing between the warring men. 'Oi, enough. We'll get banned from the pub if you keep this up.'

They stopped to stare at the hallowed inn.

Chris stepped forward, cradling Petey's half-drunk beer and said, 'Sean, did you mean it when you said you loved Deanne?'

'Bloody oath, I meant it.' Sean wiped at his mouth, straightening his shirt.

'Jimmy, are you listening?' Called out Chris, raising his beer glass to his lips.

Petey frowned as he snatched his near empty glass from Chris who just shrugged. 'Jimmy, there's no women round to play selective hearing, mate,' said Petey, 'and if I heard Sean say it, I know you did too.'

'Dammit.' Jimmy massaged his jaw and licked his fattening lip. 'Did you really tell Dee you loved her?'

'Yes, I did. But she didn't believe me and tossed it back in my face.'

'That's rough.' Jimmy gave Sean a sideways glance.

His will to fight gone in one slow shake of his head.

'The thing is, I know she loves me. I can see it. But she just won't go there.'

Jimmy had seen it too in his sister, it was hard to miss in his household. But so too was the misery he'd seen in Deanne this afternoon.

'Come on,' Jimmy said, patting Sean's shoulder. 'I'll buy you a beer.'

'I might even shout you one back. By the way, nice left hook.' Sean rubbed his jaw as they headed for the door.

'Not a bad right jab yourself.' Jimmy mirrored Sean's grin as they tidied themselves up, and re-entered the pub, followed by the open-mouthed Chris, with Petey laughing at the rear.

* * *

Sean rubbed his jaw as he sat beside Jimmy. To think, just a few days ago they'd joked like friends, to becoming instant sparring buddies in the carpark.

It couldn't make him feel any worse. In fact, it improved the frustration he'd felt since his argument earlier with Deanne. Still, how could he make it right with Deanne?

The bartender served a round of beers at the workman's bar and he sipped the amber liquid searching for an answer like he'd done all afternoon.

'So, you told my sister you loved her,' said Jimmy, 'and she threw it back in your face?'

'Yep.' Sean sighed, wiping the condensation off his

beer glass.

Jimmy gave a slight nod raising his own beer glass to his lips. 'I've had that happen to me, too. Sucks, huh?'

'Really? With who?'

Jimmy rested elbows on the bar. 'Fleur.'

Petey, standing beside Jimmy, raised a bushy eyebrow at them. 'Fleur? Wow, talk about a blast from the past.'

'Who's Fleur?' Sean asked.

Chris leaned forwards, being furthest away, and said, 'Fleur was from the far side of town, where every school holiday she'd stayed at her grandparents' place at the end of our street.'

'I fell in love the day I met Fleur. I think she was six and me, nine,' said Jimmy.

'Bit young, don't you think?' Sean laughed with Petey, while Chris grinned and nodded.

'I didn't realise it at the time, and nothing happened until she was a teenager. Fleur's the first girl I ever kissed.'

'What happened?' Sean asked.

'Fleur's grandfather died, and her grandmother moved across town to this retirement village. But we kept seeing each other, until Fleur's father moved his family to Queensland.'

'Did you follow, or let her go?' Sean doubted he'd be able to let Deanne go.

'We wrote,' replied Jimmy. 'I'd send flowers and we'd ring each other all the time. Even when her father told me to stop, we didn't. He didn't approve of me because he's some hotshot pilot and I'm just a warehouse manager.'

'Bloody white-collar nobs,' mumbled Petey from behind his glass.

'Oi, I'm a white-collar nob,' said Chris.

'You said it, not me, and I'll remember that, bean-counterer.' Jimmy playfully winked at the neighbour, Chris, who grinned. But then Jimmy's shoulders sunk, and his hand cradled his beer. 'When I could, I'd fly up to see Fleur. But I had to make sure I wasn't on any of her dad's planes because he'd chuck me off. He was a cranky prick.'

'How long did this go on for?' Sean asked.

'Two years. Then one day Fleur tells me to stop calling, and six months later she marries this pilot.' Jimmy drank his beer dry, plonked it on the bar and nodded to the barmaid for a refill.

'That's rough.'

'Yep, Fleur told me she couldn't love me and married another guy. A week later I met Casey, got married at the registry office as soon as we could—the whole time we were together we were drunk… It was pure rebound and never destined to last.'

Jimmy scooped a deep mouthful from his fresh beer. Wiping the froth from his lips, he eyed Sean seated beside him. 'I reckon that's why Dee's holding back with you. Dee warned me about Casey and told me I was in a rebound relationship. My sister saw what happened to me and held my hand the whole way through. She took care of me.' Jimmy shook his head as he stared at the wood grains that made up the bar. 'I feel like I've let Dee down letting her get hurt by our own cousin. What a whacked-out family we've got.'

'Not as bad as mine. Remember my mother wants me to marry some distant cousin I've never met.' Chris shuddered on his stool.

Petey stroked his long beard. 'All families are whacked. I've got family I don't even acknowledge. But now that I've got my own family growing, I hope we don't end up whacked too.'

'You won't,' said Jimmy. 'I'm talking about extended family. You know, my sister did heaps for our cousin. Dee's always helping people.'

'Dee's always helping out Jane, especially with the baby coming,' said Petey. 'Hey, get this, Jane reckons I'm going to faint at the birth?' And the three men gawked at the bearded, bald, tattooed tradesman. 'I know, right.'

'Dee has helped me all my life. We're smoking space buddies,' said Chris with a cheesy grin.

'What?' Sean asked.

'It's a Dee boyfriend-in-a-bottle bender moment,' Jimmy replied with a wave of his hand. 'Before your time.'

'We created our own alien dialect. Good times,' said Chris.

'Dude, that good time was when my sister had just outed her cheating ex in front of everyone at the wedding. To then bolt in her bridal gown as the start of her week-long honeymoon binge with Black Johnny, which led to our beer shed lockout.'

'That was a bad time.' Petey shook his head slowly.

'Sounds like it.' Sean could only imagine what Deanne had gone through in the days after their first meeting. A woman who'd only just found out her fiancé cheated on her, minutes before marrying the guy. Close call if ever there was one. 'Deanne says she's not good enough for me, and she doesn't see herself for who she is.'

'Dee's always been that way,' replied Jimmy.

'Can't she see how amazing she is?' He saw it in her smile, her eyes, everything about her.

Jimmy rested his elbows on the bar. 'Our mother died in a car accident and Dee blamed herself for it. She reckoned it was all her fault.'

'How?' Asked Sean.

'Because my sister begged Mum to take her to ballet classes. Dee believed if she hadn't hassled Mum, she'd still be alive. But it was a stupid drunk driver who caused the crash.'

'Deanne's sensitive nature would've taken it hard.'

'She put on stacks of weight, bingeing on what Nan called *comfort food*.'

'Dee was huge,' Chris said.

'My sister got bullied at school about her weight. Never in front of me,' said Jimmy. 'But I know when I left school, they hammered her hard those final years, calling her thunder-tree-thighs. It was Lou who helped Dee lose the weight when they met at Uni.'

'Lou…' Chris sighed, resting his chin on his palm, wearing a dreamy smile. 'Dee met Lou at the Uni gym, where she took on Dee as a project for her qualification's thingy as a personal trainer.'

'Dee got with the programme and realised our mum's death was an accident and got her act together,' said Jimmy.

'Dee got hot,' blurted out Petey. The other three men gawked at him. 'Hey fellas, don't worry about me, I'm a happily married man.'

'Anyway, my sister started dating Darren and right from the start, she ran around after that prick.' Jimmy gave a slow shake of his head. 'It was painful watching her do everything for the guy, like she was his slave. And I was stupid enough to let her do it.'

'Did you say anything to make her stop?' Sean asked.

'Hell, yeah. But I should've kept warning her. Dee's excuse was if she kept doting over Darren, making him think he was special; he wouldn't see her faults and dump her. The truth is, Deanne was always too good for him.'

'Lou told me Dee has trust issues,' said Chris. 'Dee adores Sean, but she's too scared she'll get hurt again.'

'When did you talk to Lou?' Jimmy asked Chris.

Chris's posture shrunk onto his barstool. 'Ah, um, last night.'

'What were you doing with Lou last night?' Petey asked, nudging Chris with his elbow.

'Um, err...' Chris smiled and studied the floor, pressing hand together in his lap as if in prayer, but smiling.

'Bloody hell, if you weren't a half Indian, mate, I'd swear you were blushing.' Jimmy leaned down for a closer look at Chris.

'You and body-building Lou?' Sean grinned at Chris blushing like a schoolgirl.

'Chris has been infatuated with Lou since forever, but he's never had the guts to ask her out.' Petey laughed, patting Chris's back.

'You mean bodybuilding, lesbian Lou?' Sean raised an eyebrow. 'Who's taken a vow of celibacy?'

'She used to.' Chris sat up, puffing out his skinny chest. 'I think she has?' He then winced. 'Lou won't return any of my calls.'

'Maybe Lou's busy or shy? Nah, Lou's not shy.' Petey patted Chris's back. 'Don't give in mate, you've been patient this long.'

'We all can't have the perfect relationship like you've got with Jane,' Jimmy said to Petey.

'I've suffered through many camouflaged cane toads to find my princess. Even if she's all hormonal being pregnant, demanding ice cream and pickles for dinner. The burps in her sleep are toxic.' But Petey grinned wide. 'Women, you've got to luv 'em.'

'Try bloody sisters,' mumbled Jimmy.

'I can relate,' said Sean.

'Do you reckon the problem with you and Dee is Darren?'

Sean nodded. 'The ex keeps sending letters and cards a few times a week. Not sure about the amounts?'

'Twice a week on the notes or cards. Flowers once a week.' Petey shrugged. 'Jane told me.'

'The guy won't leave her alone.' Sean frowned under his fringe.

'LAST DRINKS,' shouted the bar manager.

Jimmy clutched his glass. 'Bugger it. No beer? I want another drink to keep this conversation. Because I reckon, we can work out a way to break this damn curse.'

'What curse?' Sean asked Jimmy.

'My family's cursed when it comes to our love life and partners.'

'You're not cursed,' said Petey.

'Yes, we are, and I'm not continuing this debate while I'm still thirsty.' Jimmy held up his empty beer glass.

'There's a bar in town we can visit,' said Sean. This

could be a good way to find the answers he'd been searching for. Who better to ask than Deanne's big brother?

THIRTY-ONE

Dim fairy lights wrapped around the jacaranda tree that highlighted the flowerbed that stood in the corner of the backyard. From the house, the open backdoor's light spread grey shadows across the clipped lawn.

Inside the beer shed, the music played in the background, while the television was in a rare moment of silence. Deanne happily played bartender, pouring drinks from behind the bar for the Greatest-Girls-of-the-Galaxy.

'Where is everyone?' Clare asked, resting her elbows on the counter.

'Dad's at Janice's and Nan wanted a weekend away and went to visit her other grandchildren. They won't visit here because they're ashamed of what Katrina's done, even though I've told them it's not their fault.' But could Deanne ever forgive Katrina?

'So, where's Jimmy? At the pub?' Clare asked as she swivelled on the barstool, while Jane and Lou glanced at each other.

'You won't believe this, but Jimmy's gone hunting.'

'Hunting?' Lou said with her face all screwed up.

'That's exactly how I reacted.' Deanne nodded at Lou's expression. 'And yep, my big bro's having a few days off to go hunting. We're talking Jimmy, the stay-at-home hang-out-in-the-beer-shed kinda guy. The hang-out-in-the-work-shed kinda guy. Jimmy's a shed dweller, not a hunter.' Was her brother going through some early mid-life crisis?

'Why'd Jimmy tell you that for?' Jane asked.

'Jimmy didn't. Dad did.'

'Where did he go?' Clare asked.

'I've got no idea, and I haven't seen Dad to find out because he's at Janice's. Do you know how rare it is to be alone in this house?' Deanne gazed at her childhood home and smiled. 'I'm loving it.' Was she ready to move out again?

Clare stirred her wine with a painted nail. 'I didn't think Jimmy was into blood sports?'

Deanne shrugged. 'Hey, I'm proud Jimmy's willing to try something new. I'm working on new ventures to keep out of the rut too.' To try and live her days awake. Sean would be proud to hear that.

But Sean was a different matter she didn't want to think about, not tonight, not while the Greatest-Girls-of-the-Galaxy were here to keep her occupied. 'So, talking about blood sports... Lou, how did your date go with Chris?'

'Yeah, spill sister.' Clare swivelled around so fast on the stool her black hair whipped across her face.

'Where did Chris take you on your date?' Jane wriggled in her seat, her corkscrew curls bouncing.

Lou lowered her head and mumbled, 'Nowhere.'

'Wasn't Chris meant to take you out for dinner?' Clare frowned, stopping her chair twirling to face Lou.

'It, um, never happened.' Lou stared at her fingers in

her lap.

Deanne tenderly patted Lou's arm. 'What happened, Lou? Tell me. Or I'll walk next door and find out from Chris.'

'Well…' Lou scrubbed her hands across her face. 'Christopher came to pick me up from work while I was having a beer, locking up, and it just happened.' She nibbled her lower lip and turned away. 'And… and… next thing we're at it like rampant rabbits.'

The three women laughed as Lou smiled wider.

'I want details,' demanded Clare, raising her glass.

Deanne cringed. 'Not too much information please, Chris is like a little brother to me. I just want to know how?'

'When Christopher arrived, he gave me these native flower arrangements.'

'Aww,' said the trio with a collective sigh.

'One minute we're having a beer, and the next thing I'm tearing off his clothes and we're doing it all over my gym.'

'I hope you cleaned your equipment afterwards?' Jane clamped her hands over her mouth to suppress her giggle.

'So, you're straight, not gay?' Deanne asked. 'You know, we wouldn't care as long as you're happy.'

'I'm Christopher-straight,' announced Lou with a wide smile.

'Chris is a bigger girl than me and straighter than any metric ruler.' Deanne believed Chris and Lou were meant for each other.

'Here's to the end of Lou's sexual issues.' Clare held up her glass and they toasted Lou's decision.

'When are you seeing Chris again?' Deanne asked.

'Christopher's left dozens of messages at work and… I'm embarrassed how I acted. I've never done that to anyone, man, or woman.' Lou snatched up her wineglass and drank it dry.

'Sounds like he's keen for more,' said Jane, rubbing her baby bump.

'Chris has pined for you for years.' Deanne had heard all about Chris's infatuation many a night within this small suburban shed. 'You're the reason Chris kept saying no to his mother's email-order brides. You two are meant for each other. Chris will call again.' If not, Deanne would visit her neighbour and make him dial Lou in front of her.

And if Lou decided to dodge Chris's calls, being the sensitive woman underneath all that muscle, Deanne would let Chris use her own mobile to call her friend and she'd deal with Lou later.

Now, all she had to do was find someone special for her brother to show him that his silly curse didn't exist.

Deanne smiled so wide her cheeks ached as she topped up their glasses and returned the wine bottle into the near-empty beer fridge. It was a rare moment to be inside the shed without the men. She missed them. 'So, like randy rabbits, huh?'

Lou screwed up her nose. Then she went for the classic deflect. 'Talking about sex, Clare, have you had your dental check-up yet?'

Clare smiled like a Cheshire cat and spun around in her chair. 'Oh, hell yeah, baby.'

'Wow, when?' Deanne giggled at Clare's giddy schoolgirl routine.

'Don't tell me the how,' Jane said with a wince. 'Clare

gives way too much detail on her sex life.'

'Weeeell. There's no way to describe how good he is.' Clare placed her hand over her heart and sighed with a smile. 'Except to tell you that I'm in love.'

'You're always in love.' Lou rolled her eyes.

'Are you sure you're not confusing lust with love, Clare?' Because Clare had dated the dentist in a shorter time span than Deanne had been with Sean. Was she still with Sean? 'Can you fall in love that fast?'

'It's love, all right.' Clare threw her arms high above her head. 'I'm in love and I'm happy. Look, I know I promised myself to take it one step at a time, but once we started, we can't get enough of each other.' Clare then glanced at her watch. 'Oh, I'm meeting him in an hour. Is it still okay to drop me off, Jane?'

'Yep. Lou, do you want a lift or are you going to visit Chris?'

'I'll get a lift. Christopher's working tomorrow.' Lou winced. 'I'm not ready to meet the parents yet.'

'You've met Chris's parents when they've visited here,' said Deanne. 'They're the best neighbours.'

'How come Chris is working, when tomorrow is a public holiday?' Clare asked.

Lou shrugged. 'Christopher told me he's got some big audit happening.'

'Did you two actually hold a conversation in-between sexual positions?' Clare pointed at the body builder. 'Imagine the tag team wrestling positions Lou would enjoy in her smack down? Half time. Swap sides.' Clare shouted like an umpire at a football match and almost fell off the bar stool in hysterics as happy tears trickled down her cheeks.

Sean stepped out from the shadows and into the well-lit beer shed where it echoed with laughter. 'Sounds like you girls are having fun.'

The four women stopped and stared.

Just at the sight of Sean, Deanne's heart expanded as her stomach dropped like an uncontrolled amusement ride. Admittedly she'd missed him these past few days, but she'd never fully grasped the magnitude at how much she could miss a person—until now.

But he kind of killed the mood, considering their last encounter.

'Hi Sean, been here long?' Clare asked.

'Let's go, Clare, you've got a date.' Holding onto her baby bump, Jane jumped off her stool and grabbed Clare's arm, while Lou assisted on Clare's other side.

Deanne remained, unsure what to do or say to Sean, but blinked in amazement at Jane and Lou swiftly dragging Clare away.

'Leaving so soon, ladies?' Sean grinned, flicking the fringe away from his shiny eyes.

'We were meant to leave half an hour ago,' replied Lou as they headed up the pathway.

'Shut it, Lou,' said Jane behind Clare's back. 'Bye, Dee. Remember, I finally agreed to have a baby shower that's on next week. Also, keep your phone handy for my labour call to be my backup team. I swear Petey's going to faint.'

'I'll faint,' said Lou, leading the way along the dimly lit concrete path.

'I'll hold you up,' Clare said, resting her head on Lou's shoulder.

Deanne wiped at her happy tears, calling out to her friends. 'You can't go. I wanted to talk to you guys about my ideas for the plant watering business using the hardware's nursery area.'

'Call me later, and tell me which sign design you've chosen for the *Gossipers Cafe* to send it to the printers? Bye, Dee. Bye, Sean.' Clare swivelled between Jane and Lou, both pulling on Clare's arms toward the side gate. 'What's the rush?'

'We'll tell you in the car,' said Jane, waddling quickly as she clasped the gate shut behind them.

That left Deanne alone with Sean.

'How did you get in?' Waves of conflicted emotions rushed over her, happy to see him, miserable without him, and she scuttled her butt behind the bar to separate them.

'Through the side gate,' said Sean. 'I remembered you don't lock the back door. If you're home alone, would you have left it unlocked?'

'Don't know? It's rare to be home alone.' Yet, having hung around the security-conscious Sean, she'd become aware of household protection.

Hey, how did Sean know she was home alone?

Yet she wasn't game enough to ask—but she could talk work. 'I heard your company was awarded the security contract for the new shopping centre.'

'My sisters did that. When they'd spotted me with a copy of those plans you gave me, and after I survived their third-degree shakedown all about you, they'd discovered the security tender was open. All I did was tell them what the centre needed, and they worked out the figures and paperwork, that's their job. You'll get on well with them.

They can't wait to meet you. Mum, too.'

'Huh?' She raised her eyebrows. Great, now she knew how Lou felt about meeting the family.

'Congratulations on your tender's acceptance for the new supermarket,' he said.

'It was no contest when Brinestones withdrew.' Which was kind of a letdown considering what she'd gone through.

But Deanne was happy that the weight of the family business's future had shifted off her shoulders. Her dad had been ecstatic on the win, with Jimmy yet to be informed when he returned from his hunting expedition.

'Where have you been?' *Oops*—her hand flew to her mouth.

Sean chuckled. 'Went to see someone. Needed to fix something by talking to somebody.'

'Riddles?' Deanne sipped her wine, looking anywhere and everywhere but at Sean, who'd filled the room with his presence. 'Have you seen my brother?'

'Yep. Dropped him off at the pub on my way here.'

'Jimmy's been with you?'

'Yes. And I dare you to ask me why.' Sean stepped closer, flicking his fringe.

'Not my business.' She cursed at her well-trained leash that controlled her curiosity.

'But it is your business, and if you won't ask, I'll still tell you. I will not keep secrets from you, because the secrets we keep from those we care about are the ones that can cause the most trouble. I won't do that with you.'

Did she forget to breathe?

'So, after our argument I went to the pub waiting to see

if you'd call, which you didn't.'

Deanne pursed her lips together. Should she say sorry? For what?

'But by pure coincidence, I met up with Jimmy, and we had a scrap out the back of the pub.' Sean chuckled, shaking his head at the memory.

'What? Why?'

'Thank you, for asking, sweetheart. We have progress.' He took another step closer.

'Don't be a smart arse.' Even if he did have a great arse, along with his all over sexiness. *Damn.*

'We fought over you.'

'Me? Why?' She rolled her eyes. 'Yes, I'm asking.' With work she could ask questions, but when it came to her personal life, meh.

'I'm forever imprinting this moment in my memory.'

'To whine about it later?'

'Never.' Again, Sean took a step closer. 'Jimmy reckoned I'd hurt you, until I'd explained that it was Darren who was causing the wedge between us.'

'You didn't?'

'I'm not ashamed of you, Deanne. I want to be with you. So I spoke to Jimmy about it because he cares about you and only wants to see you happy.'

Men didn't do heart-to-hearts, especially not with her brother. 'You talked about what?'

'How we'd be cruising along fine until you'd get another card or a bunch of flowers from the ex and you'd slam your defensive walls back up. I told Jimmy how you can't begin to trust me or anyone else, even yourself, that you're unable to move on with your life because of Darren and his constant reminders. Jimmy agreed.'

'No way.' That turncoat sibling was going to cop-it when she saw him next. Or was Jimmy going to tease her forever?

'So, we stayed until the pub closed, then cabbed it to Mickey's bar. He says g'day.'

'I like Mickey. He's the only barman I know by name, and the only Police Superintendent I know too.' Pride filled her that her networking circle had increased to new areas.

'So, we drank until morning and hatched a plan.'

'Whoa, back up,' said Deanne, holding her palm up like a stop sign. 'You brawled with my brother?'

'Yes. Man to man. Big brother to big brother, we had a blue. Besides you, Jimmy and I'd worked out we had more in common than we'd realised.'

'Who won?'

'What?' Sean cocked an eyebrow at her.

'Did my brother kick your arse?'

'Did you want him to?'

'No. You didn't hurt Jimmy?'

'No. It was pathetic.' Sean chuckled at Deanne's confusion. 'I'd call it an even stoush considering how drunk we were. Weirdly, we both fought for the same woman. Jimmy, fought for his sister to protect you from getting hurt, again. And I did it because…' Sean stepped in front of her where the bar's timber separated them and said, 'I love you.'

Deanne gasped and stepped back against the fridge.

'You're the first woman I've ever said that to — but you won't dare love anyone else, not while Darren keeps interfering. So, your brother and I decided to do something.'

Deanne gulped, not realising she'd been holding her breath. 'Where have you two been?'

'In Queensland. We went hunting,' Sean said with a sly grin.

'Jimmy doesn't hunt.'

Sean grinned wider.

Deanne walked around the bar to stand in front of him. '*Who* were you hunting?'

'Darren.'

'You didn't?' Deanne sat hard on the nearest barstool, taking a big gulp from her wine glass.

Sean poured himself a drink and glanced at Deanne as he sipped his wine.

Was he waiting for her to respond?

No, she couldn't. Could she?

The seconds ticked by.

A neighbourhood dog barked. A car drove along the street and tooted a horn. The beer fridge motor clicked on as part of its cooling cycle.

This uncomfortable silence was loud.

Damn him. She gripped her drink in two hands, swallowing her pride and fear, she asked, 'Did you find him?'

'Yes, we did.'

'And?' She spun around in the bar stool and winced in preparation of his answer.

'We both did what we wanted to do.'

'Which was?'

'Jimmy punched Darren and told him to leave you

alone,' said Sean. 'I heard you punched the guy yourself?'

'In the heat of the moment during the wedding ceremony. I didn't travel across country to punch the guy. So, what did you do?'

'I shook his hand.' Sean smiled as she jerked her head up to give him her full attention.

'Why?'

'I've never met the guy. Jimmy had the beef with him, not me. It was your brother's idea because he was looking for a way to break his curse. I only planned to tell Darren to leave you alone and stop writing to you. Oh, and to say thanks.'

'Did Dad know?'

'Reg took us to the airport and picked us up. And before you ask, your Nan knew all about it because she packed Jimmy's bag and supplied Darren's address.'

'You mean my whole family were in on it?'

'Yep. Petey and Chris were sworn to secrecy until we returned, because they'd been drinking with us when Jimmy and I concocted the plan. Jane and Lou found out about it when they picked up Petey and Chris. Hey, you should've seen Lou pick up Chris like a sack of snoring spuds.'

Deanne shook her head. 'Everyone knew… Is that why my whole family has been avoiding me?'

'They didn't want to lie to you.'

Huh. She'd done the same to them, not even a week ago. 'It seems my friends and family like you?'

'I like them too,' said Sean, 'when normally I can't be bothered with people, but they're good people.'

'So, you two cowboys flew to Queensland, found

Darren, and did what? Bash his door down to terrorise him at midnight?'

'See, it's not that hard to ask the questions, sweetheart.' Sean winked at her.

'Ah huh.' She rolled her eyes at him. How could he be so cocky and cute at the same time? 'Can you please answer the question, or I'll go hunt down my bigmouth bully of a brother.'

'We knocked on Darren's door in the afternoon and he let us in. He even offered us a beer and it was all quite civil. But when Jimmy told Darren to leave you alone it became heated. Darren took a swing at Jimmy who let rip a good couple of punches, which knocked your ex on his arse. Darren's sporting a black eye, apparently, it's not as good as the shiner you gave him at the church.' Sean chuckled as Deanne winced. 'We called it self-defence because Darren swung first. I only shook Darren's hand when he was on his back and thanked him, while Jimmy was rummaging around in the freezer for some frozen peas to cover Darren's eye. We helped Darren to the couch and made sure we hadn't killed the guy. We even fetched him another beer. We were supposed to catch our return flight last night but decided to stay another night.'

'Why?' The questions now rolling off her tongue.

'Because your grandmother rang and gave Jimmy another address to visit while we were in the area.'

'Who?'

'Fleur.'

Deanne jumped to her feet. 'Not Jimmy's childhood sweetheart, Fleur?'

'Yep.'

'So, what happened? Is Jimmy okay? How is Fleur?'

'She's divorced. Her father's dying wish made her marry this pilot and forget Jimmy. She tried to, but her marriage only lasted a year after her father died. Fleur had planned to contact Jimmy but discovered he was married. She didn't know about his divorce and thought she'd let it be,' said Sean, closing the gap between them. 'Fleur will be here in a few weeks and Jimmy's happy and hopeful for their future. Your brother promises to fill you in tomorrow, and swears after what he'd done with Darren, it was a curse-breaker. So, there's no more curse.'

'There never was a curse.' *Or was there?*

Deanne shook her head to get her focus back on the conversation that mattered. 'Why did you shake Darren's hand and say thanks? For what?'

'Because Darren wrecked the best thing in his life. And because he screwed up in his world, you walked into mine, and I thanked him for that.' Sean grabbed her hand to softly toy with her fingers.

Deanne shivered from the intensity of his dark eyes that turned her insides into a liquid heat.

'You've become my anchor. Not my ball and chain, an anchor. Not because of your sea-changing mermaid eyes, but because I believe we balance each other out.'

'Really?'

'Your sensitivity and conservative nature will keep me in line. Yet the pleasure I get from watching you break your own boundaries to release your amazing inner passion, it's beautiful. I want to watch you grow and not live in a sleepwalking rut because I know you want change and I'll help you. But what you don't realise is, you make me want to change, to pull back and reconsider my next move so I don't hurt you. I'm scared of living my life without you and I'd never jeopardise risking any time away from you. The biggest crime I could ever commit is to hurt you or lose you. Don't you get it? Without doing anything, you balance me out. Together we create this magnificent balance between us, that you know is true.'

Deanne's mind was reeling, but her heart… bloomed.

'I met you without any façade when you were raw and emotional, when you were completely vulnerable, but you were real. That's who I fell in love with. The real you.'

Deanne pressed her fingertips against her lips.

'I love you, Deanne, and I intend to take care of you, and live the rest of my days with you, where we'll take care of each other. You are the one thing I want in this universe and that is to love you and be with you, for me to be beside you as you explore this world. I vote we go do a Caribbean cruise first to compare the seas to the colour of your eyes.'

'What?'

'All I'm saying is, when you want to take any risks, I'll be there to support you. I know you love me too and that you're scared to admit it. You're scared to trust in love in case you get hurt again. I understand that because I feel the same way.'

'You do?'

'Hell, yeah. This,' he said, pointing between them, 'us, and what I'm feeling for you, scares me too. I've never been like this before, and I only feel this with you. You have to stop thinking you're not good enough for me because its untrue, when I'm the one trying to meet your expectations. All I'm asking is for you to trust me because I love you.'

The sincerity of Sean's words crumbled all those barriers around her heart and there she found her truth. 'I love you too.'

Sean's smile shone as his hands cradled her face. 'Can I say I told you so?'

'Don't push it.' She stood on tiptoes, wrapping her arms around his strong shoulders. With fingertips, she brushed the hair away from his eyes that saw through to her soul, realising she wasn't scared to let him see.

'Let me love you the way you deserve to be loved.'

'I'll hold you to that—just don't let go.'

'Not in this lifetime.' Sean leaned in and kissed her, and it was better than their first perfect kiss. It was a promising taste of their many tomorrows, knowing they were destined to be together forever.

.

Did you like the story?

If so, your opinion matters to me!

It's true. A good reader's review is worth
a lot to this author.

So, if you enjoyed this book, please leave
a review & recommend it to your friends.

I'd appreciate it.

With much gratitude,

A. ROWE

ACKNOWLEDGEMENTS

Thank you for reading this story.

Thank you to the Handbrake for not disowning me.

Thank you to my writer friend, Renee Conoulty, for giving me the virtual kick I needed in her fur-lined hot pink crocs – the shoes, and not the four-legged kind that creeps around scaring the wildlife beyond my backyard.

Thank you to Anna Campbell, who was the author who'd dared to trek to the other side of the country and took the time to talk with me.

Thank you to my fabulously patient critique partner, Susan Frewin, for her amazing honesty and support.

Lastly, to you, dear reader, thank you for taking the time to read this story, where I look forward to sharing more with you in that *'Escape to Happily Ever After'*.

Until next time,

A. ROWE

ABOUT THE AUTHOR

Australian bestselling author, Mel A ROWE, creates escapes for today's busy women to enjoy from the comfort of their home.

Delivered with a dash of drama, witty humour and quirky family units, Mel is known for reinventing romantic versions of home, taking her common characters on uncommon journeys that lead from boardrooms to billabongs as they try to find their own HAPPILY EVER AFTER.

Living in Australia's Northern Territory, Mel enjoys random outback road trips, fumbling with her camera, annoying her family with her bad singing, and making new friends in the middle of nowhere— except for water buffalos. She's been chased by a few.

Feel free to contact Mel, as her word journey continues, at

MelAROWE.com

Receive exclusive insights, and news
of upcoming releases by joining:
https://melarowe.com/newsletter/

Also by MEL A ROWE

Australian Bestselling ELSIE CREEK SERIES

The ART of DUST

DIAMOND in the DUST

CAKED in DUST

XMAS DUST

MUSTER in the DUST

ROLLED in DUST

WRITTEN in DUST

Standalone Stories

Avoiding the Pity Party

Unplanned Party

The Football Whisperer

Winter's Walk

Run Beautiful Run

The Sister Trip

For story exclusives & more visit MelAROWE.com

www.ingramcontent.com/pod-product-compliance
Lightning Source LLC
Chambersburg PA
CBHW050145120726
47903CB00002B/502